Marianne C

Regret, cold and relentless sliced into Jack's gut. He wished Marianne were a girl once more. With an unexpected ferocity, he wanted to go back, to do it again, do it right this time. If they could return to another summer morning, nine years ago, they might....

Straightening his shoulders, he closed his mind to pointless might-have-beens. She was a woman, not the girl he had loved. They could never go back. Instead of wishing for the impossible, he should say something, wait for Marianne to turn and see him, wait for her smile to fade. But he allowed himself just a second more to look at her, to think how her unchanged freshness suited the unchanging charm of this front porch and this quiet, tree-draped street.

Finally, he tried to call out to her, but her name stuck in his throat....

Dear Reader,

Welcome to Silhouette **Special Edition** . . . welcome to romance.

Last year, I requested your opinions on the books that we publish. Thank you for the many thoughtful comments. For the next couple of months, I'd like to share quotes with you from those letters. This seems very appropriate while we are in the midst of the THAT SPECIAL WOMAN! promotion. Each one of our readers is a *special* woman, as heroic as the heroines in our books.

Our THAT SPECIAL WOMAN! title for this month is *Kate's Vow,* by Sherryl Woods. You may remember Kate from Sherryl's VOWS trilogy. Kate has taken on a new client—and the verdict is love!

July is full of heat with *The Rogue* by Lindsay McKenna. This book continues her new series, MORGAN'S MERCENARIES. Also in store is Laurie Paige's *Home for a Wild Heart*—the first book of her WILD RIVER TRILOGY. And wrapping up this month of fireworks are books from other favorite authors: Christine Flynn, Celeste Hamilton and Bay Matthews!

I hope you enjoy this book, and all of the stories to come!

Sincerely,

Tara Gavin
Senior Editor

Quote of the Month: "I enjoy a well-thought-out romance. I enjoy complex issues—dealing with several perceptions of one situation. When I was young, romances taught me how to ask to be treated—what type of goals I could set my sights on. They really were my model for healthy relationships. The concept of not being able to judge 'Mr. Right' by first impressions helped me to find my husband, and the image of a strong woman helped me to stay strong." —L. Montgomery, Connecticut

CELESTE HAMILTON

CHILD OF DREAMS

SPECIAL EDITION®

Published by Silhouette Books New York
America's Publisher of Contemporary Romance

For my brother,
Joe Hamilton,
who, like this book's hero,
made hometown his home.

SILHOUETTE BOOKS
300 East 42nd St., New York, N.Y. 10017

CHILD OF DREAMS

Copyright © 1993 by Jan Hamilton Powell

All rights reserved. Except for use in any review, the reproduction or utilization of this work in whole or in part in any form by any electronic, mechanical or other means, now known or hereafter invented, including xerography, photocopying and recording, or in any information storage or retrieval system, is forbidden without the permission of the publisher, Silhouette Books, 300 E. 42nd St., New York, N.Y. 10017

ISBN: 0-373-09827-8

First Silhouette Books printing July 1993

All the characters in this book have no existence outside the imagination of the author and have no relation whatsoever to anyone bearing the same name or names. They are not even distantly inspired by any individual known or unknown to the author, and all incidents are pure invention.

®: Trademark used under license and registered in the United States Patent and Trademark Office and in other countries.

Printed in the U.S.A.

Books by Celeste Hamilton

Silhouette Special Edition

Torn Asunder #418
Silent Partner #447
A Fine Spring Rain #503
Face Value #532
No Place To Hide #620
Don't Look Back #690
Baby, It's You #708
Single Father #738
Father Figure #779
Child of Dreams #827

Silhouette Desire

*The Diamond's Sparkle #537
*Ruby Fire #549
*The Hidden Pearl #561

*Aunt Eugenia's Treasures trilogy

CELESTE HAMILTON

has been writing since she was ten years old, with the encouragement of parents who told her she could do anything she set out to do and teachers who helped her refine her talents.

The broadcast media captured her interest in high school, and she graduated from the University of Tennessee with a B.S. in Communications. From there, she began writing and producing commercials at a Chattanooga, Tennessee, radio station.

Celeste began writing romances in 1985 and now works at her craft full-time. Married to a policeman, she likes nothing better than spending time at home with him and their two much-loved cats, although she and her husband also enjoy traveling when their busy schedules permit. Wherever they go, however, "It's always nice to come home to East Tennessee—one of the most beautiful corners of the world."

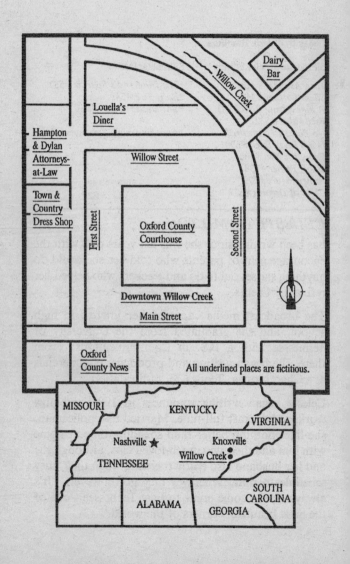

Dairy Bar

Willow Creek

Louella's Diner

Hampton & Dylan Attorneys-at-Law

Town & Country Dress Shop

Willow Street

First Street

Second Street

Oxford County Courthouse

Downtown Willow Creek

Main Street

N

Oxford County News

All underlined places are fictitious.

MISSOURI

KENTUCKY

VIRGINIA

Nashville ★

Knoxville

Willow Creek ●

TENNESSEE

SOUTH CAROLINA

ALABAMA

GEORGIA

Chapter One

Seven baskets hung on the front porch of the house at the corner of Willow and Douglas. Though Jack Dylan counted them as he drew his car to a stop across the street, he wondered why he bothered. Every spring he could remember, the same number of hanging ferns appeared on this porch. Each June, green fronds dripped from the baskets and swung in the breeze, as they were doing now. Come the first heavy frost of autumn, the ferns would be removed and Halloween pumpkins would line the railing. Christmas garland would materialize in early December and stay up until the New Year. Then, bare as a tree in winter, the porch would wait for spring, for another seven green ferns.

Sighing, Jack stepped from the car. The broad porch of this white Victorian home echoed the ceaseless rhythms of this town. He supposed switching from ferns to begonias or foregoing the pumpkins or garland would be tantamount to open rebellion.

"But maybe we could use a little rebellion," he muttered. Then he shook his head at his foolishness. For most of his life, he had engaged in rebellion, open and otherwise, but Willow Creek, Tennessee, just went on, its patterns smooth and set and steady, as it had been for more than a hundred years. Perhaps the town's ability to tolerate rebellion was what really kept him here.

Smiling, he inhaled the Saturday morning fragrance of damp, newly mown grass. Somewhere a lawn sprinkler sputtered, a screen door slammed. The scents and sounds were as familiar as the seven green ferns. As recognizable as the girl, no, the *woman* who now crossed the porch.

Jack's heart shifted into hyper speed at the sight of her. This was a wrinkle in Willow Creek's rhythm.

Marianne Cole was home.

Of course, he had known she was here. The town had been buzzing with news of her impending return for weeks. The minute her car crossed the county line two days ago, bulletins had flashed through the local gossip network. By listening to a few conversations yesterday at lunch in Louella's Diner, Jack had learned that Marianne drove a late-model Toyota, that her hair was blonder and her weight higher, that the recent tragedies of her life had aged her beyond her thirty years.

Jack didn't know about her car, but from where he stood now, the other reports appeared false. Without glancing his way, she busied herself on the right-hand side of the porch. She pulled a green garden hose around to the front and lifted it to the first hanging fern. Sunlight glinted off hair the same strawberry blond he remembered. The style was short and curly rather than the long spill of waves of her teenage years, but the change suited her. Denim shorts and a neatly tucked-in pink T-shirt clothed a firm and rounded figure. The curves were a bit more pronounced than he recalled, but the additional weight was both flattering and understandable given that nine years had passed since she had lived in Willow Creek. And despite the whispers of the regulars at Louella's, Marianne looked as happy and as free of tragedy as she had been as a girl.

Regret, cold and relentless, sliced into Jack's gut. He wished Marianne were a girl once more. With an unexpected ferocity, he wanted to go back, do it again, do it right this time. If they could return to another summer morning nine years ago, they might...

Straightening his shoulders, he closed his mind to pointless might-have-beens. Marianne was a woman, not the girl he had loved. They could never go back. Instead of wishing for the impossible, he knew he should say something, wait for Marianne to turn and see him, wait for her smile to fade. But before that inevitable moment of pain, he allowed himself just a second more to look at her, to think how her unchanged freshness suited the unchanging charm of this front porch and this quiet, tree-draped street. Finally, he tried to call out to her, but her name stuck in his throat.

When Marianne moved the hose to the second fern, Jack slammed his car door. She looked his way, lifting a hand to shade her eyes. He squared his shoulders and started up the brick sidewalk that bisected the front yard. He saw the recognition dawn in her face. The hose swung down. Water cascaded over the railing in a thin, silver stream and splashed on the boxwoods surrounding the porch. Marianne stared at the water and then at Jack, her mouth slightly open, rosy color staining her cheeks. He paused at the bottom of the steps, but neither of them spoke. He walked slowly onto the porch and faced her, and still couldn't find his voice.

Marianne found hers. "You look just the same." Contrary to the tension that vibrated between them, her tone was light and faintly teasing, the sound as familiar as the spray of coppery freckles across her small, tip-tilted nose.

Struggling to match her casual air, he touched a hand to his temple. "Not really. I'm going gray."

She cocked her head to the side. "Maybe just a bit."

"You're not."

Smiling, she looked him from head to toe. "Are those the same jeans you used to wear in college? The ones you only washed once a month?"

He glanced at the patched and worn light blue denim that covered his legs. "Those jeans wouldn't button nowadays."

"These are every bit as shabby. So's that holey T-shirt."

"Thank you."

"That wasn't a compliment."

"My clothes are comfortable, not shabby."

Smile spreading wider, Marianne clucked in disapproval. "Now, Jack, ripped knees and torn hems are just downright shabby."

A smile to echo hers tugged at his mouth. This argument about the state of his attire was as old as their friendship. "Not everyone is obsessed with superficial appearances, Miss La-di-da Cole." As soon as he spoke the last word, his smile slipped. "I mean, *Mrs. Wingate*."

Marianne grew somber. She glanced toward the still-running water, opened her mouth as if to speak, but didn't.

Angry thoughts crowded Jack's head, startling him with their intensity. Funny how one word, one name, could evoke the fury he thought he had long since conquered. He was a thirty-two-year-old adult, not the immature young man who had once stood on this porch and faced Marianne with a bruised heart and battered pride. He was well aware anger would serve no purpose. Nine years ago, he thought he would hurt forever, but the hurt had become a mostly forgotten throb. Until now.

He didn't know why the pain was suddenly so fresh. Damn it, he had learned to live with his mistakes. He had dealt with what had transpired between himself and Marianne, had reconciled himself to the consequences of the choices they each made. Even when he found out she was coming home to Willow Creek, he felt no stirring of outrage. This morning, he decided to come over, say hello, resume their acquaintance, if not their friendship. But one word reversed nine years of healing.

Wingate.

While the name burned inside him, Marianne glanced up, bit her lip, then looked toward the front yard. "One minute it seems like forever since I saw this street, and the next minute I feel as if I never left."

Jack struggled to answer her, to keep the anger out of his voice. "The street hasn't changed much, but nine years is a long time."

Marianne nodded. "It's been too long. I should have come home to see Aunt Delilah. And Uncle Jeb, too."

Jack was all too aware that in nine years, Marianne had come home only once. But he knew her relatives had seen her. "They've visited you in D.C."

"But it's not the same," Marianne insisted. "Delilah is the last of Dad's family, and Jeb is the last of Mom's, and I've neglected them by not coming home."

"They've had plenty to keep them busy."

"I know, I know—Delilah's dedicated to her newspaper and Jeb to his law practice. Those jobs have been their entire lives."

"You think so?" Jack said tightly. There was a lot Marianne didn't know about the people she had left behind.

She turned from her perusal of the front yard. "I know so. Just as I know it's time they both slowed down a bit."

"Neither of them are ready for the grave yet."

"But they are getting on in years. And since Delilah never married and neither she nor Jeb ever had a family, they have no one but me. I don't want them to be alone."

He made a dismissive sound. "Alone? Here? They're on every committee and in each civic club in the county. They each have more friends than any other ten people combined. And they have each other."

"I know they've always been friends—"

His short burst of laughter cut her off. "They're more than friends, Marianne. Together, they practically run this whole section of the state."

"Friends aren't family."

"Good friends are sometimes better than family." Jack couldn't help thinking that his friendship with her had once been deeper than blood.

Perhaps Marianne's thoughts were the same, for her gaze fell from his. "I guess I'm just worried for myself, worried about losing the little family I have left."

Remembering that she had incurred her share of losses recently, Jack's anger eased a bit. "Jeb wouldn't want anyone to know it, but he has cut back since his heart attack. I'm handling the lion's share of the practice these days."

She looked up at him again. "I guess after working with Uncle Jeb for seven years, you know more about him than I do."

"I'm sure I do," Jack said bluntly.

Marianne lifted her chin. "That's why I'm here."

"To get to know Jeb?"

"To be here for him and Delilah. I'm going to take her place at the newspaper."

"Is that her idea or yours?"

Marianne frowned at him. "You don't approve?"

No, he didn't. He wished she weren't here. He certainly didn't want her to stay. He wanted her to go back to Washington, D.C., back to the perfect life that had kept her away from Willow Creek all these years, back to the fulfillment of all her dreams. Marianne had gotten exactly what she wanted out of life, just what he wanted her to have. So why was she here? And, God help him, why was he still so angry?

He didn't want to feel this anger. He wanted to look into Marianne's bright blue eyes and feel nothing but nostalgia for the girl who once shared his youthful dreams. But there were too many years, and there was too much deceit between them. For a long time, he thought he didn't need to hear the truth from Marianne. But now he wanted to shake some honesty out of her. Hell, she owed him the truth.

Hands curling into fists at his sides, he fought the urge to grasp her shoulders, to demand answers to questions he had stopped asking himself long ago.

Some of his fury must have shown in his face, for Marianne took half a step backward. Water from the hose splashed from the railing to the porch. "Jack? What—"

His tenuous control ripped in two, giving way to an angry demand. "Why did you do it?"

She fell back another step, looking confused. "Do what?"

"Don't play games," he growled. "Why didn't you tell—"

Jack's furious question was cut off by a young voice. Clear and strong and full of impatience, the voice called, "Mom? What are you doing?"

Whirling around, Jack found a girl standing on the other side of the front screen door.

"Mom?" she said again, more tentatively this time, her gaze going to Jack, then skittering to Marianne.

He stared at the child. And felt the air leave his lungs.

When he was ten, he had fallen from the top of a tractor-drawn wagon piled high with bales of hay. When he hit the ground on his back, he could remember the loud, deadly *whoosh* of his breath leaving his body. For eons it seemed, he lay in the stubble of the newly mown pasture, fighting for air. The clear blue sky spun above him. The frantic shouts of his father and brother and the steady drone of the tractor's engine receded to the background. All he had known was that he had to breathe. His choices had been clear. He could force his lungs to work. Or he could die.

Right now, staring into the face of this child, *Marianne's* child, he felt the same suffocation, faced the same choice. And a part of him just wanted to die.

"Laura," Marianne said, her voice sounding faint and faraway. "Come out and meet a . . . an old friend."

As the girl pushed the screen door open, Jack somehow caught his breath. The world stopped spinning. Sounds became clear again. The child was incredibly like Marianne. Though he searched, there was no hint of anyone else. Mother and daughter had the same tiny nose, even the same freckles. Laura's hair was lighter and caught back from her face in a long braid, her lips were somewhat fuller, but to the casual observer, to someone who hadn't spent nearly half his life memorizing Marianne Cole's every feature, the child was simply an eight-year-old replica of her mother.

"Jack Dylan, this is my daughter, Laura," Marianne said unnecessarily. Tossing the hose over the porch railing, she put both hands on Laura's shoulders and beamed with pride.

He could only nod. Laura offered him a shy, rather unsure smile and ducked her head. In that respect, she seemed unlike Marianne, who had always been outgoing, the sort of child his mother used to say "never met a stranger." Even in grade school, when his rough-and-tumble friends dismissed her as a rich little brat, Jack could remember admiring Marianne's confidence when she stood up to read a poem in a clear, unwavering voice in front of the morning assembly. Later, as an upperclassman who taunted the freshman girls in the high school halls, he had been impressed with the way she met his gaze and smiled with self-possessed ease. She had always been open and friendly. Only once had Marianne ever been shy with him.

Painful memories pressed in, threatened his equilibrium as he managed a terse hello to the child. Laura looked up at her mother instead of at him while Marianne explained that she and Jack had known each other their whole lives.

Their whole lives. Except for the last nine years.

"Is Jeb over here?" he interrupted. Laura shot him a puzzled glance.

Marianne regarded him with the same confusion as her daughter. "Jeb's inside with Delilah. He came over for breakfast."

Jack knew he was being rude, but he simply couldn't look at them any longer. Without another word, he turned on his heel and went in the house.

Marianne bit her lip as the screen door swung shut behind him. She had expected her first meeting with Jack to be awkward, but she hadn't counted on him hurling angry questions at her. And why? What did he have to be angry about? The last time they saw each other, he had been cruel to her. She was the one who should be stalking away.

"Mom?"

She glanced at her daughter and forced herself to pick up the garden hose again. "Goodness, Laura, look at all the water I've wasted."

"Was he one of your boyfriends?"

Good question, Marianne said to herself. Just what had Jack been to her?

Laura giggled. "Yeah, he must have been one of those boyfriends Aunt Delilah told me about. Otherwise you wouldn't be all red."

Marianne lifted the hose to the next fern. "It's just hot out here."

"It doesn't feel hot to me."

"Well, it is," Marianne said. "And Jack was just a friend who happened to be a boy."

From the other side of the screen door came a throaty chuckle. "Jack Dylan wasn't just a friend or a boy. He was a hooligan."

Laura and Marianne turned as Delilah Cole pushed open the door. Marianne was struck anew by the woman's vitality. Delilah had a spring to her step, which had been absent the last time Marianne saw her. Since her Christmas visit to D.C., she had trimmed ten pounds from her petite frame. A honey-blond rinse now covered the gray in her short, curly hair. Her eyes, snapping with life and energy, were complemented by linen shorts and blouse in a matching shade of blue. All in all, she possessed the style and pizzazz of a woman much younger than her sixty-five years.

Delilah certainly didn't look ready for retirement, but Marianne wanted her to stop working now, while she was still young enough to enjoy herself. Marianne knew it wouldn't be easy for her aunt to turn over the reins of the newspaper. The *Oxford County News* had claimed most of the older woman's energy and attention for forty years. Though Marianne's father, Elliot Cole, had worked with Delilah before his death, he never had his sister's enthusiasm for the family owned biweekly.

"A hooligan," Delilah repeated, joining Laura and Marianne by the porch railing. "That's what Jack Dylan was. And he's still something of a rounder. Jeb says it serves him well in court."

Marianne looked toward the door, expecting Jack to appear at any moment. "I had forgotten you used to think he was wild. Since I moved away, you've spoken of him with such fondness."

"He grew up. Some of those rough, spiny edges of his softened, even if they haven't disappeared entirely."

"What's a hooligan?" Laura interrupted.

Grinning, Delilah straightened the black and white, polka-dotted bow in the girl's hair. "Something like a punk, I guess."

"Like a scuzzy redneck?"

"Where did you get that?" Marianne asked as she moved to water the fourth fern.

Shrugging away from Delilah, Laura flipped her braid over her shoulder. "Alissa Johns said everyone here in Tennessee would be scuzzy rednecks."

Marianne was heartily sick of hearing what Alissa Johns, who had been Laura's best friend in D.C., thought of everything, but she held her temper. "I think you'll discover there are lots of different kinds of people here in Willow Creek, just as there were different kinds of people at home."

Laura let out a glum sigh. "Sure. Lots of different scuzzy rednecks."

"Laura . . ." Marianne said in warning, while over her daughter's head, her gaze met Delilah's.

"Tell you what," the older woman said to Laura. "How about if you take over watering those ferns for your mother? This was always her chore when she was your age, but I don't remember her getting as much water on the porch as she's done today."

The girl pursed her lips, and in a precocious tone replied, "We didn't have ferns at home. And we had a maid, so Mom and I didn't have to bother with stuff like this."

Marianne exhaled in exasperation. "Laura Delilah Wingate, you sound like a little snob, and I won't have it."

Laura tossed her head in defiance. "Well, I don't want to water her dumb old ferns."

"Laura!" Dropping the hose again, Marianne started forward. But before she could take more than a step, Laura dashed down the front steps and around the corner of the house.

Gently taking Marianne's arm, Delilah said, "Let her be."

"I'm not going to tolerate that kind of rudeness to you."

"Think of what she's tolerating."

Marianne was surprised by the older woman's sharp tone.

Calmly, Delilah picked up the hose. "Allow me to take over. If I don't, I expect you'll drain the well dry without ever getting these properly watered." She lifted the hose to the fifth basket.

Plopping down in a yellow-cushioned glider, Marianne gave a heavy sigh. "Okay, Delilah, dispense some wisdom about my daughter."

"I have no wisdom," Delilah retorted. "But you can't expect her to adapt to a new environment overnight. As for her being rude to me, well, although I love her dearly, she barely knows me. We'll adjust in time. For now, it's just common sense to know that a child wouldn't want to leave the only home she's ever known, especially when it was a happy home."

"I don't know that it was so happy." Marianne felt rather than saw the glance her aunt sent her way.

Delilah cleared her throat before continuing in a quiet tone. "It was the only home Laura shared with her father,

Marianne. It's him she misses, not this Alissa Johns person, not Washington, D.C."

"I know. Believe me, I know." The glider squeaked as Marianne set it rocking. For the next few minutes, the only sounds were that squeak, the gurgle of water and the usual busy hum of a Saturday summer morning.

Delilah finished watering all seven of the ferns, put away the hose and came to sit beside her niece. She said nothing further about Laura or about Marianne's intimation that all had not been well in D.C. She asked instead what had passed between Marianne and Jack. "He came charging into the house looking mad as a hive of stirred-up hornets."

Marianne shrugged, once more glancing at the screen door. Since the demise of their friendship, Jack wasn't a subject she had explored in depth with anyone. Oh, through the years, she had heard about Jack's accomplishments from Jeb and Delilah, and she had occasionally asked about him. But she had never discussed their relationship. With him sitting just inside the house, she didn't think now was the time to begin.

"He's out back in the kitchen with Jeb," Delilah said, reading Marianne's thoughts. "He said he wanted to talk over some new case, but that sounded like a trumped-up excuse to me."

With another forceful kick, Marianne sent the glider in motion again. "Well, I don't think he came over here to see me."

Delilah raised an eyebrow. "You two used to be together all the time. I didn't understand why you liked him so much at first. Every time he pulled up here in that rattletrap car of his, I started worrying. He always drove too fast."

Getting to her feet, Marianne crossed the porch and studied the vintage red T-bird convertible parked in front of the house. "At least his rattletrap is gone. That's some car."

"Which he still drives entirely too fast. Although I must say the women's heads turn when he goes flying through town in it."

Marianne didn't doubt that Jack still liked speed. She could see him racing down some narrow country road in this car, one of the same roads they used to drive on Sunday afternoons when there was nothing to do in Willow Creek save dream about getting out. If she closed her eyes, she could smell the fumes from Jack's rusted old Mustang. She could hear Bruce Springsteen's tough-tender voice blasting from the tape deck. Like a million other teenagers, she and Jack were sure his songs of alienation and escape were written just for them.

God, the plans they made. Somehow, the two of them, who came from such different worlds, had been able to dream aloud together. In the confusion of her adolescence, Jack had been Marianne's one, true friend. Not a boyfriend. He was more to her than any of the boys who professed love and tried to relieve her of her innocence on countless Saturday nights. She never believed any of them. But she always believed in Jack. He was her confidante, her pal, her support. They had been unlikely comrades—smart Marianne Cole, offspring of the town's two most prominent families, and rebellious Jack Dylan, roughneck country boy. They were bound by dreams of finding something more, somewhere other than Willow Creek.

But in the end Jack stayed here.

And Marianne still didn't understand why.

"I never would have thought it back then," Delilah was saying, drawing Marianne back to the present.

She turned to her aunt. "Thought what?"

"That Jack would stick it out and become a lawyer."

I did, Marianne thought, once more looking over the front yard. She had always known Jack could be whatever he chose. The only surprise was that he had remained in a place he had professed to hate. The same place that had drawn her back. She had to smile at the irony of their situations. Here they were, each of them in the town they were once so eager to leave.

Delilah pushed herself out of the glider and came to lean against the railing beside Marianne. "Jeb thinks the world of Jack. Says he's the best lawyer in the state."

"No joke. Every letter Jeb wrote me in D.C. was full of Jack this and Jack that. You'd think he was the next Perry Mason."

"He reminds me of your father."

Startled, Marianne stared at her aunt for a moment. She had thought herself the only person capable of seeing the similarities, both good and bad, between Jack Dylan and Elliot Cole.

With a soft chuckle, Delilah said, "Your father was a hooligan, too, you know."

"Maybe once upon a time. Then he was just a drunk."

The blunt honesty of the statement made Delilah's smile disappear. "I hate remembering him that way."

Marianne crossed her arms and hugged them to her midriff. "He was the most unhappy person I've ever known. I wanted so much to make him happy, but I never could."

"You didn't cause his bitterness. You weren't part of Elliot's problems. He loved you so much."

"And I adored him. Despite the drinking."

"He knew that. I think it was for your sake that he even tried for sobriety."

Marianne was silent for a moment, studying the lacy shadows made by the morning sun and the front yard's canopy of trees. "Why didn't Dad and I leave here after Mother died?" It was an old question, but one she couldn't stop exploring.

"You were a baby," Delilah replied. "I think he was afraid he couldn't do right by you somewhere else."

"So he stayed here, grew bitter, drank too much."

"He didn't start out that way."

"But he hated the newspaper, hated this town, hated the narrowness of it all. He had all kinds of talent. All I have to do is read some of his old stories and editorials to know that. He could have gone anywhere. So why did he stay here?"

"I don't know." Delilah paused, her gaze capturing Marianne's. "Why have *you* come back?"

Marianne hesitated only a second. "I need to be here."

"I hope not for my sake."

"Delilah—"

"I mean it." Delilah straightened her shoulders. "I didn't ask you to come home. You seemed to have a good life in D.C. I missed you, but I was proud of your success as a reporter and columnist, proud of Laura, of your marriage."

"But I haven't been happy."

Delilah patted her arm. "It's only been a year and a half, Marianne. You can't expect to forget your life with Kyle so quickly."

"I've been unhappy for much longer than that."

Her aunt gave her a long, searching look.

Marianne turned away after a few moments. Just as she didn't want to talk about Jack, neither did she feel up to expounding on the disappointment her marriage had become.

Delilah had always respected Marianne's privacy, so it was no surprise that she didn't push for more answers now. Instead, she patted her arm again, said softly, "I'm glad you're here. But the most important thing to me is that you're happy. If your taking over the paper doesn't work out—"

"It will."

"But if it doesn't, I want you to know that I will never, ever try to hold you here."

Looking into the other woman's eyes again, Marianne squeezed her hand. "I know that."

The two of them swapped a pair of tremulous smiles, then Delilah glanced at her watch. "Goodness me, but look at the time. Jeb and I are due at the Civitan barbecue in twenty minutes, then I've got to hurry back here and finish up things for your welcome home party."

"I can finish things up here."

"Nonsense. Not for your own party." Delilah bustled toward the door. "Are you sure you and Laura won't come to the barbecue with Jeb and I?"

Marianne shook her head. "I wouldn't want to overwhelm her with too many scuzzy rednecks on her first Saturday in town. I'm sure she'll be suitably dazed by everyone she meets at the party tonight. I'd best go see if she decided to hitchhike back to D.C."

Delilah chuckled. "Most likely she's hiding out back in the tree house. I told her that's where you used to go after your father or I punished you."

"Me? Punished?" Marianne demanded with mock horror. "I thought I was a perfect child."

Her aunt's hearty laughter preceded and followed the slam of the screen door.

Grinning, Marianne pushed away from the porch railing. Her attention was caught once again by the shiny red convertible parked out front. How like Jack to choose such an unconventional mode of transportation. The car suited the man he had become, complimented his longer than stylish dark hair, fit in with his tight jeans and ripped T-shirt. He didn't comply with the usual buttoned-down lawyer stereotypes. Most of the attorneys of Marianne's acquaintance, including Uncle Jeb, cultivated a polished appearance, even during their leisure time. None of them would have looked right in Jack's jeans or his convertible. But none of them had Jack's raw sexuality, either. Marianne could understand why female heads turned when he spun through town in this red fireball of a car. The big but sleekly molded automobile was as sexy as its owner. She wondered how many conquests Jack had made in that broad, front seat.

Drawing in a quick breath, she reined in her imagination. Whether Jack Dylan was an attractive man or not didn't matter to her. She didn't care what might have transpired in his car. What she wanted, all she wanted, was to be his friend again. To do that, she had to figure out why he was so angry with her.

Before Laura interrupted, he had demanded, *"Why did you do it?"* Marianne didn't know what he meant. Do what? If he was criticizing any actions she had taken after their friendship ended, then he was out of line. She was the one who had been hurt by his cruelty. God knows, she had tried to hate him for what he had said and done. She should have hated him. But their relationship had once been too strong for anger or hate to take root inside of her. So she had spent years yearning for the closeness they had lost.

More often than she wanted to admit, she had reached for the phone to call him. On lonely nights, when she acknowledged her marriage was an empty mistake, she ached just to hear his voice. During happy times, when the dreams she had shared with him were coming true, she wanted him to share her joy. But her pride, unyielding and strong, always intervened before she gave in to the temptation to reach out to Jack. At the last moment she would remember the way he had rejected her. Though she couldn't hate him, she couldn't quite forget his cruelty. Even now, she wished she had been strong enough to do the rejecting.

No one would have been surprised if she had turned her back on Jack Dylan. His own parents had said his middle name was "Trouble." Jack had always asked too many questions, thumbed his nose at too many of Willow Creek's small-town conventions. He spent most of his youth knee-deep in mischief. But by the time the two of them were in high school, Marianne had made saving him her mission in life. She pushed and prodded; she allowed him to dream, then found ways to turn his wishes into realities. He wouldn't have his law degree if she hadn't convinced him that grades mattered or helped him apply for college scholarships and grants. Throughout all her efforts, he had exasperated and sometimes disappointed her. It would have made sense if she had given up on Jack. But in the end, he gave up on her. Gave up, before giving her a chance.

"So he has no right to be angry with me," Marianne murmured. The next time she saw him, perhaps at the welcome home party tonight, she would find a way to break through that anger, discover its source. It was either that or learn to ignore him completely.

But Marianne knew Willow Creek was too small for her to ignore Jack. He was now a prominent citizen, Jeb's partner, Delilah's friend and business advisor. And in all honesty, she didn't want to ignore him. When she decided to move home, thoughts of Jack had figured in her decision. In the days when he was her best friend, she had felt...safe? Complete? Confident? None of those words defined what he once brought her. But she wanted to capture that elusive feeling once more. She wanted Jack in her life again.

Though that resolve was firm in her mind, she wasn't up to another confrontation with him today. Avoiding the house, she decided to go in search of Laura. Delilah was probably right about her hiding out in the tree house. Smiling as she went down the porch's side steps and around the corner of the house, Marianne thought of the times, even as a teenager, when she climbed up to the tree house to sort out her problems. It was a hideaway she had shared with no one, not even Jack.

Lost in memories, she didn't see the kitchen door open in her path. She certainly didn't expect to plow right into Jack. His hands, still the broad, rough-textured hands of a farmer's son, settled on her bare arms as he steadied her.

Startled, she could only stammer, "I—I thought you were inside."

His green eyes glimmered beneath a tightly knit brow. "Is that why you're sneaking around this way?"

"Sneaking?" she repeated, irritated because she had in fact been trying to avoid him. "I do not need to sneak around my own home."

"This hasn't been your home for a long time."

His arrogant tone irked her even more. She forgot about mending fences and winning his friendship again. Sarcasm replaced her resolve to draw him out. "I'm sorry if my presence disturbs you."

"I'm not disturbed."

"Then why were *you* sneaking out the back door?"

"I wasn't sneaking."

"It looked that way to me."

"Why would I sneak out?"

Marianne lifted her chin. "You tell me."

"I'll tell you," Jack began, his tone terse. "I'll tell you exactly what…what you…" The words sputtered to a halt.

They stood for a moment, their jaws squared, their gazes locked. Then Marianne realized Jack still gripped her upper arms. Before she could step back, he let go of her. His hands fell quickly away. He stepped back like a man who had moved too close to a flame. Indeed, for the space of a heartbeat, she felt a sudden unexpected heat zigzag between them. She thought the cold fury in Jack's eyes melted. Tricked by that illusion, she swayed toward him. But he was in motion. Without another word or glance, he disappeared around the corner of the house.

She pressed one hand to her abdomen and stood unmoving until she heard a car engine roar to life in front of the house. Tires squealed against asphalt. Marianne jerked around, stunned by the familiarity of the noise. She held her breath while Jack's car blasted down the street, the sound fading like far-off but potent thunder.

The sound reminded Marianne of her father. When Elliot Cole used to take off in one of his drunken rages, he always drove like a madman. His car's engine had sounded like Jack's. Loud. Impatient. As if he hoped the speed and power of the automobile could somehow outrun his anger.

Now it was Jack who was running. Jack, who with his rebellious brilliance, had always reminded her of her father. Jack, who if today's demonstration was a true sample, was as full of suppressed rage as Elliot Cole ever was.

This wasn't the Jack that Marianne had known before she left town. This wasn't the man Delilah and Jeb had talked about through the years. He was angry with Marianne, furious that she had come home. And despite the way they had parted, she couldn't understand his fury. But she needed to.

Forgetting Laura for the moment, Marianne opened the kitchen door Jack had exited and crossed a small mudroom. She wanted to catch Jeb and Delilah before they left for their barbecue. Even if she had to tell them what had transpired between herself and Jack in the past, she was going to find out what was going on with him now. But in the doorway to the sunshine-filled kitchen, Marianne drew up short.

She caught Jeb and Delilah. Caught them, indeed.

The two lifelong *friends* were in each other's arms.

Chapter Two

A jovial crowd spilled out of Delilah's house and onto the porch as Jack went up the front steps for the second time that day. Earlier, he told himself he would skip Marianne's coming home party. But then Jeb called to say the occasion had become an engagement party for himself and Delilah, and Jack knew he couldn't stay away. He could wish, however, that Marianne might have gone back where she belonged.

Smiling at his own foolishness, he replied to a chorus of greetings and made his way through the crowd and into the house. The rooms were bursting with well-wishers. People sat on the steps in the foyer and filled the large front parlor. Well over a dozen revelers populated a bay-windowed and rather warm dining room. Delilah and Jeb had gone public in a big way, Jack thought with approval. After keeping their romantic relationship a secret for quite some time, they deserved some hoopla.

A slap on his back nearly sent him careening into the food-laden dining table, while a booming voice asked, "Well, what do you think?"

Turning, Jack grinned at an older man whose own face was split by a wide smile. Jack stuck out at his hand. "Congratulations, boss."

Jeb Hampton's splendid laughter suited his six foot four height, his husky frame and the thick and curly white hair that crowned his head. He pumped Jack's hand with enthusiasm. "What's this 'boss' business?"

"Your name is still above mine on the door at the office."

"Not for long." Ignoring the crowd that pressed in around them, Jeb made one of the sweeping gestures that had cemented his statewide reputation for courtroom theatrics. "I think Delilah and I are going to retire and cruise around the world."

Marianne materialized at her uncle's side. "Sounds like a grand idea." She ducked under Jeb's arm and planted a kiss on his cheek, but her gaze locked with Jack's. "Isn't that what they should do?"

Her appearance rendered Jack incapable of a reply. He didn't want to stare at her, but that was all he seemed able to do. Jeb covered some of the moment's awkwardness with more of his laughter, but Marianne waited expectantly, looking at Jack. Someone else in the surrounding group called out to her, and he was saved from any fumbling attempt at conversation. While uncle and niece were drawn across the room by friends and neighbors, Jack tried, but failed to look away.

This morning, in her shorts and T-shirt, Marianne had looked like the girl he had known. Tonight, she was the woman he had lost. It wasn't just that her hair or her makeup were different. It wasn't that she now wore a slim jade and red sundress that emphasized her every lush curve. The change went much deeper. The transformation had to do with polish, an aura of sophistication and charm.

She holds her head like a princess, Jack thought, watching Marianne listen with patience and apparent interest to one of her uncle's long-winded cronies. In the years she had spent away from Willow Creek, her innate confidence had been buffed to its present sheen. No doubt, she had distinguished many a Washington social event with the same easy grace she used now.

Studying her animated features, Jack's admiration mixed with something else. A darker emotion. The anger he had felt earlier today swept through him again. But he was determined not to surrender to it. The past was over. Done with. Through. He didn't need explanations from Marianne about anything she had done. She owed him nothing. There was no reason to shake things up. His life was just fine as it was. He was staying away from her, away from her daughter, away from dangerous questions and even more frightening answers.

He turned, wanting to put some distance between himself and her, but a hand slipped into his.

"Don't you have a kiss for the bride-to-be?"

He summoned a smile for Delilah, whose eyes sparkled up at him. After pressing a kiss to her flushed cheek, he whispered, "It's about time the two of you decided to make this official."

"You were good to keep it a secret these last few months."

Jack shook his head. "I never could understand the need for secrecy. You and Jeb should have been together years ago."

"Oh, Jack, you know small towns. At least you know this one. With Jeb and me being…well, with all our family ties and with…" She paused, as if searching for the right words.

Finally she said, "There were other considerations over the years, and I guess I thought people wouldn't understand us coming together after all this time and at our ages."

Jeb had confided his feelings for Delilah to Jack several months ago. He said he had loved her "forever." Jack didn't know what had kept them apart, but he sensed it was a painful subject for them both. He didn't pry then or now.

"Marianne discovered how we felt today," Delilah said. "And it just seemed that the time was right to tell everyone."

Jack looked in Marianne's direction again. "So she was pleased."

The older woman chuckled. "Shocked, but yes, pleased."

He nodded, still watching Marianne, who remained engrossed in conversation across the room. She brushed a curling tendril of hair back from her forehead. He followed the movement of her arm, thinking how smooth her flesh had felt beneath his fingers this afternoon. Soft and firm, warm and golden, her skin was just as he remembered.

He felt the room shrink as he looked at Marianne. The temperature edged up a notch. The laughter of the crowd grew shrill. He shouldn't have touched her today. Just as he shouldn't be looking at her now. He swung his gaze back to Delilah, who watched him with an expression he couldn't read.

Softly, she said, "I really don't understand why she's come home."

Jack made his shrug deliberately careless.

"I thought she had everything she ever wanted in D.C.— an outstanding career, a beautiful child, nice home, friends, the excitement of being in the capital."

Because Delilah seemed to expect some sort of comment from him, Jack made a sound that was somewhere between a grunt and a clearing of his throat. He tugged at the collar of his knit shirt, irritated by the heat and the noise, though it was the conversation that really bothered him. He could live the rest of his life without hearing how perfect Marianne's life with Kyle Wingate had been.

But Delilah didn't pause. "I'm worried that this move was a mistake, that Marianne did it for me. She says not, but I don't believe her. What do you think?"

Jack looked at her in surprise. "Why should I know why she's home?"

"Because you were close before she left," Delilah said. "Because you..." She stopped, as if reconsidering her words. Then she sighed. "I'm just worried, I guess. I'm afraid Marianne won't be happy here. Laura certainly is miserable."

The child's name caught Jack's attention. "She is?"

"Oh my, yes." Delilah shook her head. "It'll pass, I hope. But Jack I wish you would..." She paused as someone in the kitchen doorway called her name.

"Would what?" Jack prompted. But Delilah's attention was now focused elsewhere, and she left him standing beside the table. He looked around, thinking he might see Laura. Instead he found Marianne advancing on him.

"You're not eating," she said, gesturing toward the table.

He tried not to look directly at her. "I've had dinner."

"But there's some of Delilah's buttermilk pie here—"

"I had dessert, thank you."

Ignoring him, she lifted a huge wedge of pie onto a glass plate. "Oh, come on, you always had room for this."

"Well, I'm not hungry now."

She frowned at him. "There's no need to snap at me."

"I just don't care for any pie." Exasperated, he glanced around, thinking someone would interrupt at any moment.

But the room, so crowded a moment ago, was emptying. No doubt everyone was as warm as he was.

"Are you watching your waistline or something?"

His hand went automatically to the belt of his jeans.

And Marianne giggled. Quick as the change of expression, the Washington sophisticate became the schoolgirl of their youth. The past and the present mixed, drew Jack in. He wasn't sure which aspect of her was more alluring. Perspiration beaded on his forehead as he tried but failed to turn from her eager, glowing features.

She picked up the pie and a fork. "If you're not eating, that means there's more for me." Grinning, she carved herself a generous bite. "Sure you don't want this?"

Jack didn't answer. He had all he could do to try to ignore her pink, slightly parted lips.

A look of pure ecstasy spread across her face as she swallowed. "Now this is something you can't get in Washington, D.C."

He muttered a reply.

"Oh, D.C. did have its fine points, I suppose," she continued, cutting herself another bite. "I did find a bakery that made a carrot cake almost as tasty as Delilah's, but all in all, the place was lacking when it came to good basic food."

"Is that why you came home?" he asked. "To get some decent baked goods?"

She laughed again, her eyes crinkling at the corners, black lashes sweeping upward in the way he remembered all too well. Tender memories and gentle emotions tumbled through Jack. He steeled himself against the onslaught, sharpened his voice. "While the pies may be good, you're not likely to win a Pulitzer prize here in Willow Creek."

Her blithe expression sobered. "Possibly not."

"Possibly?" He gave a short laugh. "Reporting who won the Civitan Club's July 4th essay contest isn't exactly like covering the White House."

Marianne set her plate on the table, all trace of mirth gone now. "I didn't cover the White House."

"You know what I mean."

"Do you know what I did in D.C.?"

"Sure I know. Everyone in town knows you were an award-winning reporter, then you had your own column. It all worked out. Just like you always planned." He didn't want to sound bitter, but he knew he did. "Except for the Pulitzer prize. But then, you're only thirty. If you go back to D.C., I'm sure you'll do it yet."

A troubled line appeared between her eyebrows as she studied him. "I don't worry too much about prizes anymore."

"Oh, really?" he drawled, a calculated bit of disbelief in his voice. "When did this happen? You were always so focused on your goals."

"Having a family changes your priorities."

A family. The thought of her and Kyle and Laura as a family twisted inside him. But he maintained control of the resulting fury. "It seems to me you've been pretty successful at having a family and reaching your professional goals, as well. I'm not surprised. I always knew you could do it all, have it all."

"You say that like I've done something wrong."

"Absolutely not," he protested. "In fact, I salute you. You've done everything I expected you to do. Except for coming home, that is. I can't see how coming back here to run the paper fits in with everything else you've accomplished."

"I think it fits very well," she said, her chin lifting to a challenging slant. "Did you ever read my column?"

Dozens of times, Jeb or Delilah had passed a clipping of one of her stories on to him. Jack had read each of them time and again, though he hated himself for doing so. "Of course I saw it. Like I said, everyone in town knew about Marianne Cole making good."

If she caught the sarcasm in his tone, she gave no sign. "If you read it, you know my column was about ordinary people living ordinary lives in the midst of today's complex world. The things I wrote about weren't so very different from what the paper here always covered."

"The only difference is that Willow Creek isn't part of *today's complex world*," he mocked. "People here are still just born, they just live, and then they just die."

"Sounds complex enough to hold my interest."

"As I recall, it didn't do much for your father's interest."

She sucked her breath in. "I'm not like my father."

"Aren't you?" Jack pressed. "You inherited his talent. And you took the road out of here, the road he wanted to take himself. I wonder what he would say about you coming home."

Jack saw the wounded look in her eyes and was instantly contrite. He, more than anyone, knew how much of Marianne's ambition had been motivated by her father's unhappiness. He knew how miserable Elliot Cole had been, how terribly his misery had hurt his daughter. Jack shouldn't have reminded her of that. "Listen—"

She cut him off with a cool, "Excuse me."

But he caught her elbow before she could walk away. Just like this afternoon, the feel of her skin burned straight into him, burned through doors he had thought sealed against Marianne's special fire. Touching her, even casually, was torture, but he held on. He made himself look in her eyes as he said, "I didn't mean to bring up your father. I'm sorry."

She studied him with the same head-up, straight-shouldered intensity she had exhibited her entire life. Her eyes didn't soften when she said, "I'm sorry, too." Then she walked away.

Muttering a curse, Jack swung around to face the dining room table again. He felt like a heel. No, worse than that. He felt like the awkward, tactless farm boy he had once been. Growing up, when he found himself threatened or in an unfamiliar situation, he had been incapable of just walking away. He just blundered through, inevitably running headfirst into trouble. He thought he had developed some finesse. This morning, for instance, he had known enough to get away from Marianne. Tonight, he should have left the moment she came near him. But no, he had to stand here, look at her, talk to her, touch her... *burn* for her.

"Fool," he murmured, thrusting a hand through his hair. He took a deep breath and looked down, gathering his composure. A soft close-by murmur made him glance up.

He found Willow Creek's two most notorious gossips beside the table, staring at him. He cleared his throat, feeling more like a callow youth than ever. "Hello, Miss Louella, Miss Clara." Despite years of marriage and widowhood, both women were always addressed as they had been as young women.

Clara arched one brown, penciled-in eyebrow. "Jack Dylan, who are you calling a fool?"

He forced himself to pick up the plate Marianne had set down. "I'm just foolish about this pie."

Laughing, Louella slid a hand down an ample hip. "I must say, I am, too."

Clara sniffed. Behind rhinestone-studded glasses, her black eyes were just as shrewd as they had been when Jack was in her third-grade class. She was one teacher who never put up with any of his shenanigans. Not surprisingly, she caught him off balance with her question. "So what do you know about Marianne Cole coming home?"

"Sister," Louella admonished in a voice as sweet as her sibling's was vinegary. The smile she gave Jack bordered on coquettish. "Don't mind Clara. Just because you and Marianne had your heads together in here doesn't mean you know what she's really doing back in town." She leaned forward, expression sharpening. "But what do you *think* is the real reason?"

"Actually, I don't—"

"As I remember," Clara cut in, a considering gaze sweeping him from head to toe. "You and Marianne used to have your heads together all the time."

Louella chuckled. "Oh my, yes. I remember the two of you coming into the diner when you were in high school or home on your college breaks. You used to sit back in the corner booth, and heavens, you did some talking. If you recall, on more than one occasion I had to ask you to go home so we could close up."

"Folks thought you must be sweet on each other," Clara added. "But of course, every chance you got, you went out with Sally Jane Haskins." A slight pinching of her already-thin nostrils betrayed her disapproval. "And Marianne had her pick of boys, of course."

She could certainly do better than a no-account county boy. Jack silently added the words he was sure she was thinking. Her expression and what he read into it, negated his degrees and his profession and left him feeling he had dirt caked on his shoes and straw in his hair.

"Jack and Marianne were just friends, Sister." Louella slanted her body toward Jack again, patently eager for whatever crumb of information he could impart. "You were *just* friends, weren't you?"

Jack didn't realize he was backing away until he felt the wall behind him. The room was now even warmer. Miss Louella and Miss Clara's faces appeared too large for their bodies as they peered expectantly at him. He had to escape. Clutching his pie plate, muttering an excuse about needing water, he fled the room, but not before he saw the two sisters exchange I-told-you-so looks.

He had no idea why they thought he knew more about Marianne's return than anyone else. But it was an opinion shared by half of everyone there. Around every corner, he found a group waiting to quiz him about Marianne's *real* intentions. He kept saying he didn't know and kept receiving skeptical glances in reply.

For nearly half an hour, he heard what good friends he and Marianne used to be. He listened to dissertations on how wonderful a life Marianne had been living away from Willow Creek, how hard it was to imagine her settling down here. Even though he also found it difficult to accept that she had come home to stay, the attitudes of everyone else bothered him. To hear these people tell it, all of them, including him, had lived pretty insignificant lives when compared to the adventures of Marianne Cole Wingate. Up until today, he had considered himself a successful, productive person. It was disconcerting to hear otherwise.

But when he wasn't hearing about Marianne, he was watching her. In a house as large and as crowded as this, he should have been able to avoid her. Instead, they kept bumping into one another. She gave him guarded, angry glances. He moved away, feeling irritated with her and with himself.

He should have gone. But each time he started for the door, someone else stopped him. And besides, he didn't like thinking that he had to leave. These were his friends. They belonged more to his life than to Marianne's. She had left them all behind. But tonight, as he moved through the crowd, he felt like an outsider, the way he used to feel. And he didn't like that sensation. Not one little bit.

So he stayed, bouncing from room to room like a man trapped in a pinball machine. Finally, he settled in an empty corner of Delilah's study. Partially hidden by a carved wooden screen, the leather chair he chose was out of the flow of party traffic. He settled back, realizing he still carried the uneaten piece of pie. The plate had been a useful prop as he dodged questions and tried to avoid Marianne. Though the pie looked less appetizing than before, he lifted a bite to his mouth. His tongue touched the sweet, delectable morsel about the time he remembered this was Marianne's fork. At the same moment, she appeared in the doorway from the foyer.

Simply sharing her fork shouldn't have brought Jack such a crazy, intense feeling of intimacy. But it did. Marianne remained in the doorway, talking to the former principal of their high school while she pretended not to look at Jack. But her pretense was useless. Their gazes kept tangling and untangling like bare, charged wires, making sparks whenever they touched.

Jack thought once again about leaving. But stubbornly, he stayed right where he was. He finished the pie, remembering how Marianne's mouth had closed over the creamy filling, thinking of the way she sighed in pleasure as she ate. His body stirred in response to his thoughts, in response to the current of awareness rocketing between the two of them.

He tried looking away. It didn't work. So he stared blatantly at her, hoping she could read his mind the way she had when they were younger. He wanted her to know every erotic thought he had about her. He wanted to shock her. He wanted her to feel uncomfortable, to walk away. But she wasn't looking at him now. She was laughing with a group of friends. The sound broke over him like a sudden summer storm, leaving him harder than a touch ever could. He didn't want this attraction, these emotions. But he couldn't look away, couldn't stop remembering another summer night when the two of them were lovers. If only he hadn't memorized her every movement, her every sigh, her every tempting, arousing glance.

While he watched, she drifted into the study, surrounded now by women who had been schoolmates of theirs. One of them, married to a successful businessman, had propositioned Jack at the country club's spring charity gala. Another was a client whose messy second divorce he had handled. Jack had been her friend as much as her lawyer, and as a result, he knew secrets that would come as a surprise to even Miss Clara and Miss Louella, who prided themselves on knowing everything about everyone in town. But the women with Marianne, who had both shown an inordinate amount of interest in him in the past, ignored him now. They were engrossed in the details of a party Marianne and Kyle once attended at some foreign ambassador's residence. They wanted to know about her trip to Europe. They giggled over an interview she had conducted with one of Hollywood's current studs.

Jack listened, too. Delilah's pie became a hard pile of bricks in his stomach while he listened. All the dreams Marianne had dreamed with him had come true with Kyle Wingate.

Finally, the divorcée asked the question that everyone had been addressing to Jack. "Lord, Marianne, why in the world would you give all that up to come back here?"

Why indeed? Jack thought, his gaze locking with Marianne's once more. Whether or not she had the hidden agenda everyone seemed to suspect, he didn't care. All he knew was that her presence made him miserable. Turned on and miserable, all at once. His face burned. His belly ached. He felt inadequate, just as he had felt the day he threw her into the arms of another man. And he had sworn never to feel like that again.

Not waiting to hear Marianne's reply to the woman's question, Jack left the room. He headed for the front door, but Miss Louella and Miss Clara were lying in wait. Everywhere he looked, someone called to him. So he went up the stairs. To the second floor. To the third, where no one else had wandered, where the lamps burned softly, where it was quiet and smelled of the rose potpourri he remembered so well.

Once, he had been as familiar with this house as he was with his own. He was pleased to see Delilah hadn't changed much in the years since he had ventured up here. The third floor had belonged to Marianne all the time Jack had known her. Half of the attic had been remodeled into a bedroom, a bath and sitting room, plus a small screened porch. He used to come up here to sit and talk with her, even though Delilah had said it wasn't proper and that Jack should be entertained in the parlor.

Entertained. He laughed at the old-fashioned word.

From the darkened screened porch, which lay to the right of the sitting room where he stood, he heard a squeak. Even up here, he couldn't escape the party.

"Hello?" he called, hoping he hadn't interrupted some lovers' tryst. When there was no reply, he turned to go down the stairs again. It wouldn't do to cause anyone embarrassment.

Then a tentative voice said, "Hello." He turned back around as Laura appeared in the doorway from the porch.

Jack was struck anew by the child's similarity to her mother. Tonight, Laura wore a party dress, light blue with a white ribbon sash. The braid from earlier today was gone.

Her hair hung in curls on her shoulders, just as Marianne's had at her age. In the dim pool of light from a nearby lamp, her eyes looked suspiciously red, as if she might have been crying. Jack didn't want to care about her tears. Long ago, he had decided he never wanted to know Marianne's child, never wanted to give her a face, a personality. But now, looking at her in the familiar confines of this room, a yearning started in his gut. Like a low hum, it spread upward.

"This is my room," Laura said.

Jack grinned at her very proper, grown-up tone. He replied with suitable formality. "I apologize for intruding. This used to be your mother's."

"She gave it to me." There was proprietorial hostility in the words, even though she advanced toward him a bit.

Jack stayed where he was, not wanting to seem in any way threatening. "I always thought it was a pretty special place." One evening in particular, this room had been magical.

Laura said nothing, her lips pursed as she stared at him with palpable distrust.

"Do you like it?"

She shrugged.

"I guess it's not as nice as your room back home."

"Well..." She crossed her arms and seemed to be considering the subject. "I didn't have three whole rooms to myself at home."

"Three rooms. That's pretty great." He shoved his hands into his jeans' pockets and took a step forward. Thinking of what Delilah had said about Laura being unhappy, he searched his brain for something that might be of interest to an eight-year-old girl. "I expect your friends are going to enjoy coming up here for slumber parties."

"I don't have any friends here."

"You will."

She shook her head with a stubbornness that reminded Jack anew of Marianne. Though something painful twisted inside him, he made himself smile. "I know someone about your age," he said, thinking of Sally Haskins's little girl. "Maybe I'll bring her over."

"No."

"Are you sure? Her name's Betsy, and I think she would like this room." He looked around, his gaze lighting on the elaborately dressed dolls that lined a low bookcase to his left. "I know she'd really love these." He stooped to examine them.

Apparently overcoming her distrust a bit, Laura crossed to his side. "My daddy gave me all of these. Every trip he took without me, he brought me a doll." Lifting a kimono-dressed figure with a delicate porcelain face, she said, "This one came from Japan. That's where Daddy died."

The simple, matter-of-fact way she said her father was dead shocked Jack. While she told him about the other dolls, he studied her small, perfect profile. She was so neat. Her words were so precise. He thought it must be very difficult for a little girl to maintain such a level of poise. He wanted, quite suddenly, to hear her laughter. He wanted to be the one who made her laugh.

"Were you my mother's boyfriend?"

Her question came out of nowhere, startling Jack out of his reverie.

"Mom and Aunt Delilah said you weren't," Laura continued, her blue eyes intent on his. "But I think they were fibbing."

"You should believe them."

He couldn't tell if it was disappointment or relief that crossed her face.

"Your mother and I," he said, "were friends. We used to come up here and sit on the porch and drink Cokes and look at the moon. That's why I know your friends are going to like coming up here with you."

"The moon's big tonight," Laura said. "Wanna see?"

He followed her out to the porch. Sure enough, the moon was full, hovering over Willow Creek like the giant wheel of Swiss cheese Jack had believed it to be as a boy. The night sky was pale, lit by that big, distant globe.

"You can see the clock," Laura said, pointing across the treetops to the town square's singular spire. As if on cue, the clock struck ten times. Laura moved away.

Jack turned around. "What's the matter? Don't you like our clock?"

"It sounds spooky."

"Oh, no, it's not spooky," he said. "Your mother and I climbed up there and reset it once."

Laura's retreat halted. "Why'd you do that?"

"To see if we could."

Her nod showed she understood such youthful logic. "Did you get in trouble?"

He grinned, remembering that crazy Halloween night when he was seventeen. Too old for such stunts but determined to fulfill a dare from a friend, he had dragged Marianne along as a lookout for the sheriff. She spent the whole climb to the top trying to convince him to forget it. He thought with Marianne Cole along the sheriff would go easy if they were caught. And he'd been right.

"What happened?" Laura urged. "Did you get arrested?"

He laughed. "Well, the sheriff pulled up in front just as we came out of the building, and a dog chased us down the street, and your mother tripped and fell facedown in a mud puddle. I fell down on top of her. And that's when the sheriff caught us."

Laura laughed then, a delightful, throaty giggle. The sound, like her mother's laughter, spurred a reaction in him. She came back to stand beside him, and in a splash of moonlight, Jack saw that her too serious expression had been transformed into that of a carefree little girl.

The hum that had been spiraling up through him suddenly surrounded his heart.

His throat tightened, and it took every ounce of control he had not to reach out for her. All these years, he had told himself it didn't matter that Laura belonged to someone else, that he couldn't miss what he had never known. But now he knew. Listening to her giggle, he knew all he had missed. He made himself join his laughter with hers, liking the way the sounds blended and mixed.

But inside him beat an old, old question.

Why'd you do it, Marianne? Why?

By eleven o'clock, the party was winding down. But Jeb and Delilah were still going strong, talking and laughing with some of their closest friends in the study. Marianne wandered from room to room, her feet aching, wishing they would all go home. Stifling a yawn, she pushed through the front screen door, thinking she might find Laura out on the porch. Or Jack, maybe. His big, red car was parked out by the curb. But the porch was empty.

Marianne hadn't seen her daughter since well before Jack appeared at the party. Everyone had asked after Laura, but Marianne had never found a moment to go looking for her. She had decided this afternoon not to push Laura into accepting her new home. In time, Marianne was certain the child would grow to love Willow Creek. Just as Marianne loved it.

Stepping out onto the front lawn, Marianne took a deep breath of the warm evening air. It was so quiet here. No sirens in the distance. No planes streaking overhead. No traffic. Just the low song of crickets, the faint buzz of voices from inside the house and the sound of a child's laughter trickling down from upstairs.

Stepping out into the yard, Marianne looked toward the third floor. Lights glowed in the windows, but she couldn't make out anything or anyone else. There was only Laura's laughter. Bright. Sparkling. More uninhibited than it had been since Marianne decided to move to Willow Creek. Glancing at Jack's car, Marianne thought she knew the source of the giggle. She smiled, her earlier displeasure with Jack disappearing as she thought of him coaxing this laughter from Laura.

She went in the house and up the stairs. On the second floor, she slipped off her red, strappy sandals and crept upward, remembering to avoid the fifth step, which had always squeaked. In the small sitting area at the top of the stairs, she paused. Through open French doors, she could make out Laura and Jack side by side in a wicker settee on the screened porch. She grinned. It was just like Jack to have open doors when the air conditioner was running.

"Your mother had never milked a cow before," he was saying while Laura giggled. "She kept squeezing and squeezing and nothing was coming out. And Old Daisy was getting madder and madder. Your mother's face was red and she was cussing—"

"Mom says ladies shouldn't ever curse."

"Oh...well, I mean...she was really mad at Old Daisy—"

"What'd she say?"

"I don't curse, either," he said, pretending affront.

"Oh, tell me, Jack, tell me—"

"Yes," Marianne interrupted, stepping onto the porch. "What'd I say, Jack?"

He stood abruptly, smoothing hands down his denim-covered thighs. "I was just telling Laura—"

"Did you mention that Old Daisy hadn't given milk in at least two years?"

"No—"

Marianne came and stood behind the settee. "Did you mention she eventually kicked me in the behind?"

Laura laughed even harder. "Sounds like Jack tricked you."

"Yes," Marianne agreed, tousling her daughter's hair. "Jack was very good at tricking me and getting me in trouble."

The child twisted around to face her mother. Marianne could see her eyes were bright, her cheeks glowing. "He told me about climbing up in the clock and setting the barn on fire and getting caught in an ice storm and—"

"Now, now," Jack cut in. "Don't tell her everything, Laura. I'm sure there are some secrets your mother wants to keep."

The sharpness in his voice made Marianne glance at him in surprise. It seemed that just because he had been up here making her daughter laugh didn't mean he was going to be nice to her.

Ignoring him, Marianne said, "It's time for bed, Laura."

"Aw, Mom—"

"Now, come on. I didn't make a fuss when you left the party and came up here. So let's not argue about this, okay?"

Laura pushed out her bottom lip, but agreed. She gave Marianne a hug, then turned to Jack. "Can I really go out to your farm?"

"Your farm?" Marianne asked.

"My parents'," he explained. "Pop hasn't been the same since Mother passed away, but my brother Brad has pretty much taken over the place, keeps it and Pop going."

Marianne remembered Jack's mother as a small, energetic woman, made to seem even tinier next to her tall husband and eldest son. "I was sorry to hear about your mother, Jack." She thought the words seemed rather inadequate. She should have contacted Jack four years ago, when his mother died. "Delilah told me, of course. I should have called—"

"We got your flowers," Jack cut in.

"Brad's wife sent a thank-you note." Marianne couldn't say how much she had hoped to have a note from Jack instead.

"Lainey's good about those things."

"How are she and Brad?"

"Busy. They've got twin sons now. Two years old."

"Little Brad?" Marianne shook her head, thinking of an earnest, chubby boy several years younger than herself. "I bet he's a great father."

Jack shrugged. "Yeah, in between working himself to death on the farm and holding down another job over at the chair factory, he has a little time to be a good father. Brad's life is... well, *complex*."

His reference to their earlier discussion wasn't lost on Marianne. She felt a pinprick of annoyance, but didn't give in to it. Instead she turned back to Laura. "Off to bed. I'll come tuck you in."

Jack started toward the door. "I'll see you soon, Laura."

Marianne knew it would be better if he left, but perversely, she wanted him to stay. No matter what he said or did, she couldn't stop wishing they could mend this rift between them. "I wish you'd wait," she said before he reached the sitting room.

He hesitated, but nodded. In less than ten minutes, Marianne settled Laura in bed and rejoined him on the porch. He stood, his back to her, looking out at a landscape still touched by moonlight.

Crossing her arms over her midriff, Marianne came to stand beside him. "Laura was half-asleep before she got her pajamas on. I guess those stories you told wore her out."

He said nothing, and she turned to study his strong profile. They were close enough for her to see the silver hair at his temples, close enough for her to feel the heat that came off his body. Even as she acknowledged the warmth, he moved away and faced her.

"Delilah says Laura isn't too happy about moving here."

"She'll adjust."

"It's a big adjustment so soon after her... after Kyle's death."

Marianne bristled at the note of censure in his voice. "Kyle died nearly eighteen months ago. Laura has begun to heal. I think she'll do even better here, in a new place, without so many memories."

"Maybe those memories are important to her."

"Her memories of Kyle are going to fade in time, anyway. She was too young when he died for it to be otherwise. And at least here, she and I will be with relatives. I want that for her. I want her to know something about tradition. And I think Willow Creek is a better place to grow up than D.C. All things considered, I had a pretty good childhood here."

"You spent all your time wanting to leave," Jack reminded her tersely. "Have you forgotten?"

"No, I haven't," Marianne shot back. "I did leave. And someday, if she wants, Laura can leave, too." She struggled not to grow angry. Why was everyone questioning the wisdom of this move? To her, it made perfect sense. "I believe Willow Creek is what both Laura and I need right now."

"Even if she's miserable?"

"It'll pass. I know my child—"

"And she's none of my business, right?" Jack challenged.

"I didn't say that. All I'm saying is that this was a safe place to grow up. I think it still is."

"Wouldn't Laura be safe anywhere with you?"

The weariness that had been Marianne's companion for months assaulted her anew. Sighing, she sank down on the settee. "I didn't feel safe in D.C. anymore. I kept thinking about this house, this street, the way it never really changed. There's something special about that kind of stability, Jack. It's lacking in big cities. That's why I wanted to come home, to bring Laura here."

"A visit might have served your purpose. You wouldn't have had to uproot Laura."

This time Marianne gave in to the irritation his disapproving manner aroused. "Why is it that you have to be so rotten to me, Jack? I thought if I came back here you and I could be friends again. But I was wrong, wasn't I? Wrong!"

Her outburst was met with silence. Jack stared at her for a moment that stretched to two before he looked away again. Even though she could see that his jaw set and his back stiffened, he said nothing. She wanted to ask him why he was so furious with her. But she was afraid of the answer, afraid they might have to discuss the night their friendship had changed forever. Marianne had invested a great deal of time and energy in trying to forget that night. She wasn't up to dissecting it now. She just wanted to pick up as if nothing had happened. On a snowy winter afternoon in February when she had decided to make this move, she had foolishly believed going forward without confronting the past would be possible.

Quite obviously, Jack didn't see it that way.

She started to speak again, but then swallowed the words. She hated feeling she had to be so careful with Jack. Once, they had been so open with one another. So free. She wanted to tell him how empty and lonely her life had become, even before Kyle's sudden death. She wanted to say she had yearned to come home for years and years. She wanted to explain how her accomplishments, which Jack had spoken of with such sarcasm, had come to mean so little. She wanted Jack to help her understand why her dreams hadn't turned out quite as planned.

Thwarted dreams were one thing she thought Jack might know something about.

Softly she asked, "Why did you stay here?"

He shrugged. "Jeb gave me a job."

"You could have gone anywhere when you got out of law school."

"I decided to stay here."

"But why?"

"Because I wanted to." With a suddenness that startled her, Jack whipped around. "Marianne, you did what you planned. I did as I wanted. Okay?"

"But Willow Creek wasn't your dream. Why did you stay?"

The question vibrated across the hot, still air while Jack sucked in his breath. Marianne's perfume mixed with the scent of roses, the smells of a summer night. What he wanted to say was that Marianne was the only dream that ever mattered. But he couldn't reveal that to her. Hell, he didn't like admitting it to himself.

"Jack?"

He sighed. The anger he had felt toward her all day long evaporated, replaced by a sad, empty ache. "I like my life here, Marianne. I like my work. I'm happy." Until he said the last two words, he didn't realize how patently untrue they were.

Marianne was silent. Jack could feel her doubts just as surely as if she had spoken them aloud. But she didn't. While they stood looking at each other in the semidarkness, whole conversations were played out in his head. In his mind, he asked her hard questions and got straight answers. Silently he was able to say he wanted to be her friend again, too. Her friend and much more.

But in reality, nothing was said. The two of them stayed as they were, unmoving and mute, while a cloud scuttled across the face of the moon.

"I should go," Jack said as the porch grew darker.

This time Marianne didn't protest. She stood. "Thanks for making Laura laugh."

Remembering Laura's uninhibited giggle soothed some of the newly raw places in Jack's heart. "I would really like to take her out to the farm."

"Any time. It's good of you to be so kind to her."

He gave her a sharp look, irritated anew that they had to play this little game. His voice was rough as he said, "It's no problem, Marianne. After all, Laura is . . . she's . . ."

He pushed a hand through his hair, exhaled deeply. "She's . . ."

Puzzled by his hesitation, Marianne prompted, "She's what, Jack?"

His words came out in a rush. "She's . . . she might have been mine."

Shocked, Marianne didn't let out her breath until she heard the front screen door slam behind him.

Chapter Three

Marianne had forgotten how quickly the rain could roll in over the mountains west of Willow Creek. Sunday served as a reminder. The day started clear enough. Bright sunshine illuminated her favorite stained-glass window at church, a soothing sight to match the pastor's message of hope. Looking at that window, listening to the uplifting sermon, Marianne felt her worries drop away. But by midafternoon, the sky was dark. The storms descended, full of booming thunder and brilliant lightning. Then the rain set in, falling in sheets, rushing in the gutters of the old house, sounding, as Uncle Jeb put it, "Like it might pay the town a long visit."

And by then the weather suited Marianne's mood. Indeed, the steady drone of rain provided a fitting accompaniment to the memory of Jack's voice when he had spoken of Laura last night.

"She might have been mine."

Five words. A simple statement, reminding her they had been lovers for one night. One unforgettable night.

Standing in the bay window of the dining room, Marianne watched the downpour pummel the zinnias in the garden of the house next door. She felt beaten down, herself. How foolish she had been to think anything between she and Jack could be as it was before. A fire, unexpected and hot, had flamed between them nine summers ago, sending their friendship up in smoke. The sparks remained even now. She felt them whenever Jack looked at her. Indeed, whenever she looked at him. Marianne didn't deny the heat, but she wasn't sure she could handle the blaze they might kindle now any better than she had handled it in the past. She was older and wiser and also much less naive about the way men and women can hurt one another.

Her relationship with her late husband had been lukewarm at best, but they managed to inflict maximum misery on one another. It seemed to Marianne that a union with more fire would definitely carry even more pain. She already knew Jack could hurt her. She couldn't bear to give him that sort of power again.

When he'd walked away and left her to deal with the ashes of their relationship, she had been in agony. The whole summer had been full of emotional upheaval, some concerning Jack and some not, but his rejection had clouded her judgment with sudden, intense pain. Her wedding plans to Kyle had been set in motion long before the summer, before the trouble between she and Jack began. For heaven's sake, it was Jack who introduced Kyle to Marianne in college. Jack who had pushed them into dating, encouraged their romance. None of them suspected everything would change in the space of three short months. Kyle never knew. Marianne realized soon after they married that she was cheating Kyle, cheating herself, perhaps cheating Jack. But in her confusion in those last days before the ceremony, marriage to Kyle had seemed like the most reasonable course of action. After all, Jack didn't love her, didn't want her. In fact, his final words to her that summer had been to urge her to go forward just as she had planned.

So she had married. Left town. Had a child. And through all of Marianne's and Kyle's failures, she thought Laura had been a bright, shining success. When it came to her daughter, Marianne had wasted little time over the years in thinking of what *might* have, *could* have been.

But now here was Jack. Intense, passionate Jack. With five simple words he had filled Marianne with questions. What would it have been like to have shared her pregnancy with him? Without a doubt, Kyle had been solicitous and proud. But under the same circumstances, Jack would have probably been overprotective of her, would have strutted like some triumphant, delighted rooster over the knowledge that he, supreme male that he was, had planted his seed inside her. Marianne managed a smile, thinking of how joyously insufferable Jack might have been as an expectant father. He would probably have been worse after the child was born. When Laura was a baby, Kyle had displayed plenty of excitement over her first gurgles and steps and words. But Marianne could just imagine Jack's kinetic exhilaration over the same events. She had no doubt he would think no child equaled the accomplishments of his own.

Kyle and Jack were so very different that it seemed wrong somehow to be comparing them, but Marianne couldn't help herself. Until now, she had never questioned Kyle's ability or his actions as a father. But Jack's words, "She might have been mine," made her wonder and question and wish.

Oh, Lord, how she wished. As she watched the rain fall from the heavens and into rich, Tennessee soil, she allowed herself to make the wishes she had long ago set aside. She wished Jack had wanted her. She wished she hadn't let him walk away. She wished she had more than one night's worth of memories. And she wished she knew how he might have looked when she presented him with a child.

Yearning rolled inside Marianne, carving hollow spaces in her heart. She hated herself for wishing to undo a past that couldn't be changed. But most of all, she hated herself for still wanting Jack, for not having learned from her past mistakes. When sex rose between them, consumed their innocent friendship, was when all their troubles began. She had to be out of her mind to wish for that sort of anguish again.

Muttering an admonishment to herself, Marianne turned from the window and went to the kitchen. She called up the back staircase for Laura. Delilah and Jeb, who had been talking wedding dates when Marianne wandered into the dining room, were now at the dinette table with the big Sunday newspaper from Knoxville, Tennessee, spread between them.

"I want a banana split," Marianne explained to them as Laura came bounding down the stairs. "And I'm taking Laura to the Dairy Bar to get one. I think it's time she experienced that particular Willow Creek tradition." She paused as a terrible thought struck. "The Dairy Bar is still in business, isn't it?"

Delilah made another mark on the crossword puzzle in front of her. "Yes, and the banana splits are still bigger than any I've had anywhere else."

"Sound like a good deal?" Marianne asked her daughter, who responded with enthusiasm.

Jeb nodded toward the window, where rain still streamed, then peered at them over his half glasses. "Why don't you wait till it slacks a bit?"

Marianne shook her head. "You always said I wasn't sweet enough for a little rain to melt me."

His agreement was a low rumble in his throat, and he turned back to his paper, grumbling, "Be careful, and don't call me if you land upside down in a ditch. I'm no ambulance chaser."

That gruff admonition made Marianne think of the past. Most Saturday nights when she had prepared to go out on a date or with Jack and other friends, Jeb had been here with her father and Delilah. He had always said these same words to her. Hearing them now brought a big rush of happiness. Despite her troubles with Jack, she was glad to be home. She dropped a kiss on the top of Jeb's head as she headed for the door.

"Laura," he said, not looking up. "See that your mother behaves."

Laughing, Marianne grabbed an umbrella in the mudroom and took Laura's hand as they hurried through the rain to the car. She made a slight detour on the way to the Dairy Bar in order to show Laura more of Willow Creek. They had been too busy settling in to do much exploring thus far.

Unfortunately the rain did little to enhance many of the places they visited. Marianne was dismayed by much of what she saw. Because the residential section near where they lived still retained its comfortable, cared-for look, she had assumed the rest of the town had fared as well in the last nine years. She was wrong. Terribly so. Afraid of what she might find, she avoided the section of Main Street where the newspaper office was located. Tomorrow morning would be soon enough to see how that particular memory had stood the test of time. Some of her earlier happiness had disappeared by the time she pulled her cream Toyota Camry to a stop in front of the Dairy Bar.

The restaurant, which according to Delilah had once been a drive-in complete with roller-skating carhops, was located on what was commonly called "the wrong side of the creek." But everyone in town had always come here. And Marianne had never really thought of her hometown as a divided place. She had gone to church and school with children from both sides of the creek.

The Dairy Bar sat on a small knoll, just past a bridge, so that most of the downtown area and the better residential section could be seen from the parking lot. As a matter of fact, Delilah's house occupied a similar elevation, so that in addition to the town clock, Marianne had grown up seeing the Dairy Bar's flashing neon lights from her bedroom windows. She had no idea why this prime location had become an ice cream and hamburger joint.

"It's bright," Laura commented, gazing up at the two-story building's orange-and-yellow neon sign and the lights that lined the front windows.

Blinking, Marianne decided the lights were brighter than when she was a girl. But if the sign was more garish, the restaurant certainly looked neater. The paint was fresh, and checked curtains hung at the windows. It was good to see one of her favorite spots hadn't succumbed to the decay affecting other businesses they had passed.

Marianne was laughing, advising Laura to go for extra hot fudge when they came through the door. Her laughter died when she looked straight at Jack. His big, red, unmistakable car hadn't been outside, but here he was.

He was sprawled in the first booth to the right of the door. A dark-haired girl who looked to be about Laura's age sat across from him, and on the table between them was a Monopoly game board. They were the restaurant's only occupants that Marianne could see.

Holding a handful of pink play money, Jack stared at Marianne, but offered Laura a grin and a wink. It seemed to Marianne that a special sort of understanding arched between him and her daughter.

The little girl with him twisted around to give them both a considering glance. Laura waved at Jack, but moved closer to Marianne. "Mom," she said, tugging her arm. "Put down the umbrella. It's bad luck to leave it open inside."

"Oh, Laura, you don't believe that," Marianne admonished even as she did as she was asked.

"You'd best believe it, Marianne. Bad luck is something you don't tempt."

The slow-as-sweet-sorghum drawl drew Marianne's attention to the counter in front of them. Recognition came immediately. "Sally Jane Haskins."

"Marianne Cole."

Together, the two women said, "You haven't changed a bit." Then they burst out laughing.

Happy to have someone other than Jack to concentrate on, Marianne quickly crossed the green and black checkered tile floor to the counter. "But you really haven't changed at all, Sally. You still look fabulous." The other woman still had skin as flawless and delicate as a magnolia blossom. Her hair was still a soft ebony cloud around her face. Her eyes still a startling, translucent gray. Now, even more than when they were in school, she reminded Marianne of a young Elizabeth Taylor.

"But I look terrible," Sally protested, straightening the collar of her cotton shirt and smoothing back her hair. "My weekend counter help skipped out on me, so I had to work late last night and then get up this morning early, and I know I'm a wreck."

"You manage the Dairy Bar now?"

Sally smiled proudly. "I own it."

"No kidding. That's fantastic. I must say you've done more for the place than Old Man Koontz ever did." Marianne glanced around the restaurant once more. The aromas were the same as she remembered, a combination of onions and ice cream. But the interior sparkled as it never had in the old days. "I hope business is booming. Aunt Delilah tells me the banana splits are better than ever."

"Keeping this place going in this town isn't easy. But I'm determined to make it a success."

Marianne looked at Sally with renewed approval and some surprise. Granted, she and Sally had never really been close friends, but the other girl had never struck Marianne as the entrepreneurial type. If she had given the matter any thought back then, she probably expected Sally would marry some local boy and become a contented wife and mother. Marianne had always liked Sally's manner, a mixture of brashness and genuine warmth. But she knew there had been whispers about her, hints that she was too warm with the boys. Sally had sometimes run around with an older, tougher crowd. But even as a teenager, Marianne had chalked much of the talk up to classmates' jealousy over Sally's astounding looks and the boys' resulting attention. Sally had never lacked a date. As a matter of fact, the boy on her arm had often been Jack. Remembering school dances and Saturday nights, Marianne glanced in his direction.

He was looking at her, even though the little girl with him admonished, "Pay attention to the game, Uncle Jack."

Uncle, Marianne repeated to herself. Perhaps Jack was still the man often seen at Sally Jane Haskins's side. Sudden jealousy surged through her. She turned back to the counter, only to see a speculative expression on Sally's face.

"Mom," Laura spoke up. "Aren't we going to order?"

Summoning a smile for Laura, Marianne asked for a banana split and a hot fudge sundae, then added, "Sally, this is my daughter, Laura. Laura, this is Miss...uh, Mrs...."

"I'm still just Sally Haskins," the other woman supplied smoothly. "And you can call me Sally, Laura. That's my daughter Betsy over there with Jack. I know you've met him."

So she knew, did she? That meant Jack had told her. Marianne darted another look at him.

"Me and Laura are old friends," he said, grinning at the child again.

Sally took two glass bowls from beneath the counter. "Why don't you go over there and sit with Betsy, Laura? She's your age, you know."

Laura looked uncertainly at the other little girl, then up at Marianne. "Mom?"

"It's fine with me."

"You come, too."

"I'll bring your order over," Sally offered.

Marianne realized the only way she was going to avoid sitting with Jack was to make a big deal out of refusing. So she took Laura by the hand, and soon found herself seated beside him.

Wouldn't you just know it? I start out trying to get away from my memories of this man and end up sharing a booth with him.

Trying to ignore the way Jack's leg brushed against hers beneath the table, Marianne concentrated on the two little girls seated across from them. Jack performed the introductions, and Marianne greeted Sally's daughter. Though the child's features weren't much like her mother's, she did have the same gorgeous dark hair. However, her eyes were a mischievous warm brown. She wore neat denim overall shorts, very similar to a pair Laura had at home. And her dark hair was caught up in a stylish, lopsided ponytail. On her wrists were bangle bracelets that matched her fuchsia knit blouse and jangled as she folded the Monopoly game board and put tokens and play money in a box.

Marianne recognized the approval in Laura's gaze, and thought the same could be found in the covert looks Betsy sent Laura's way. Perhaps Marianne's yearning for a banana split had been providential. Here was a little girl who just might replace D.C.'s often-quoted and much-missed Alissa Johns.

Beside her, Jack cleared his throat. "So, Laura, what have you been up to today?"

"Nothing."

"We went to church," Marianne offered.

With the candor of the very young, Betsy said, "Mom says that some old biddies might throw her out if we ever darkened the door of a church in this town."

Astounded, Marianne gaped at the child. She felt rather than saw Jack's struggle to smother his laughter.

Sally, who was approaching the booth with their ice cream, flushed scarlet. "Betsy Haskins!"

"That's what you said, Mom."

"Do you have to repeat everything I say?"

"Oh, man," Betsy groused. "Can Laura and I take her sundae over to another table? I want to show her where that man shot a hole in the wall last week."

Church biddies and gunshot holes. Marianne closed her mouth, and wondered if Betsy would be Laura's salvation after all. But before she could protest, the two girls scampered away to examine the scene of the crime. Laura's final bit of shyness was overcome by curiosity. Sally set Laura's sundae down at another booth, then deposited Marianne's order and took a seat herself.

Jack's shoulders were now shaking with suppressed laughter.

"Just stop it," Sally hissed at him. "You're half the reason she's so dam . . . I mean, darned impossible."

He gave up the struggle not to vent his mirth.

Two spots of color burned on Sally's high, fine cheekbones as she looked at Marianne. "I'm sorry, but Betsy is eight going on thirty-eight."

"It's okay," Marianne said, although she wondered if it was.

Between whoops of laughter, Jack gasped, "I don't know what was funnier . . . what Betsy said or Marianne's face when she said it."

"Oh, hush," Marianne told him, attacking her banana split with more force than was necessary.

"Believe me," Sally said earnestly. "I don't think everyone in church in this town is a biddy, and there haven't been that many guns fired in here—"

"Many?" Marianne repeated, nearly choking on her ice cream. She ignored Jack's renewed laughter. "You mean it's happened more than once?"

"Oh, no, but . . ." Sally glanced at Laura and Betsy, who were now seated at a nearby booth. "I'd rather not go into any of it, especially with those little pitchers over there perked up."

"I heard that, Mom," Betsy said.

Sally rolled her eyes. "Just be nice and talk to Laura. When she's finished eating, why don't you take her up to the apartment and play Barbies or something." She glanced at Marianne. "If that's okay, that is."

Marianne found Barbie much more acceptable than bullet holes and gave her permission. The girls left Laura's sundae almost untouched and dashed around the counter. Their laughter continued as they clomped up unseen stairs.

Marianne knew a friendship had been born; she recognized the harmony in the sound of their giggles.

Chin in hand, Sally gave Marianne a look of genuine appeal. "Please don't think I'm running a madhouse here. The gunshot incident was an accident . . . sort of. It was—"

"Just one of her admirers acting up," Jack supplied.

"You're making it sound even worse," Sally protested.

"No one should come in here with a gun like that," Marianne said, aghast. "The whole time I lived here in Willow Creek, I never heard of anything like this."

Jack's lip curled. "You lived on the wrong side of the creek, Miss Marianne Cole. You couldn't be expected to know about it over there, but guns were known to go off over here all of the time."

"Now wait a minute," Marianne said. Jack's depiction of the "here" and "there" of Willow Creek was at odds with her own memories.

"It was never that bad," Sally said, rising as some customers came through the door. "And it's not bad now. It's just that things . . . well, they happen."

Marianne digested that explanation along with her ice cream while Sally returned to her station behind the counter.

Jack sprawled back against the end of the booth, his back against the window, his tanned, muscular arms folded so that his green T-shirt stretched tight across his chest. He drew one leg upward, till his knee touched the back of the booth.

Because he was facing her now, Marianne couldn't help but notice his jeans were as tight and well-worn as ever. The seams were faded to white, especially at his crotch. She glanced away, berating herself for noticing those particular seams and the apparent fullness beneath his zipper. Mouth suddenly dry, she took a sip of the water Sally had brought with her ice cream.

"Doesn't sound so safe around here, does it?" Jack challenged.

"There's trouble, and danger, everywhere," she replied. For instance, if she allowed herself, she could see trouble in his green eyes, could find danger in memories of how his strong arms had once held her.

Don't do it, she told herself. *Don't even look at him.*

Heeding that advice, she moved away from him slightly. She straightened the crease on her white cotton slacks, fussed with a button on her tangerine-colored blouse and tried once more to concentrate on the suddenly tasteless food in front of her. She toyed with the idea of getting up and sitting across from him, or even finding Laura and leaving, but didn't want to betray how uncomfortable his proximity made her. Eager for something, anything, to take her mind off the man who was so disturbingly near, she watched while Sally flirted easily with one of her customers.

"Sally really hasn't changed," she murmured after several moments of silence passed.

Jack had been wondering what was going on behind Marianne's straight-backed, tense exterior. After what he had said last night, he didn't blame her for being tense. He had spent a long, sleepless night regretting those words. For what purpose did they serve now? His questions were just going to upset everyone.

When Marianne came through the door here and saw him, he halfway expected her to turn around and leave. He hated himself for feeling so damn relieved when she didn't. God knew, he wasn't inclined to get overly chummy with her, but unfortunately, he wasn't satisfied with the distance between them, either. Just like last night, he knew he ought to leave right now, before they headed into rocky waters.

But his other inclination was to stick it out and see if they couldn't reclaim some of the easy camaraderie of old.

His glance followed hers to where Sally stood. "So you don't think she's changed, huh?"

"No, and I like that. She's still just herself. Just as warm and uninhibited as ever."

He stiffened at her choice of words, became defensive. "She's not a slut, you know."

Marianne looked surprised. "I never said she was."

"Everyone in high school thought so."

"Did you ever hear me say that?"

"No, but—"

"Then I probably didn't think it." She glared at him. "After all, you were privy to most of my thoughts and opinions back then."

"Privy?" he repeated.

"Yes, *privy*. It means—"

"I know what it means," he cut in tersely. "I have a college degree the same as you." He should have known any conversation between them couldn't remain simple for long. "It just didn't sound like something you would say. It's so formal."

Marianne sighed, looked away, then abruptly turned back to him as if deciding she had to pursue this line of talk. "Perhaps the word struck you as odd because you're *not* privy to all my thoughts and opinions anymore. Maybe we no longer know each other at all."

It dismayed him to think how right she was, how much of her life he had missed. The knowledge knocked whatever irritation he had felt right out of him. He slumped back against the window. "You're right, of course. We're virtual strangers."

Something in the glance that passed between them proclaimed his statement to be utterly false. Time might pass.

Surface appearances might change. But Jack would always know Marianne. On some deep level, where it mattered most, they would never be strangers.

Finally, Jack looked away from her. Struggling for composure, he sent greetings to the crowd of new customers who came through the door. There were nods in Marianne's direction and greetings. And raised eyebrows. Jack sighed. The news that he and Marianne had been sharing a booth would be all over town by tonight.

"I guess this really is still the place to go on a Sunday afternoon," Marianne murmured.

Recognizing Sally's business as the safest choice of topics open to he and Marianne, Jack agreed, "Sally's done pretty well for herself."

"Despite what the biddies think?" Marianne's tone was teasing.

He nodded. "Some folks can't get beyond rumors and trumped-up stories."

"I guess it doesn't help that Sally's an unmarried mother."

Jack realized that Marianne didn't know the whole story behind Sally and Betsy, but he decided not to enlighten her now. It was a complicated story and was Sally's to tell.

"Willow Creek can be an awfully narrow-minded place," was all he said.

"That's one of the negative things I remember," Marianne said softly. "I think Sally was plenty brave to stay here."

"Or plenty foolish."

"Foolish?"

"It would have been easier to leave."

"Perhaps—"

"Wasn't it easy for you to leave?" The question slipped out before he had time to consider it. Damn, but why couldn't he stay on some safe subject with her? Like tributaries of one giant, roiling river of questions, every conversation fed right into danger.

"Forget I said that," he said before she could answer. "It's none of my business."

"But, Jack—"

"Marianne." His gaze locked with hers. "Drop it."

She let out a frustrated breath. "Do you think there's anything the two of us can discuss without getting in trouble?"

The answer was probably no, but he did have something he needed to talk to her about. He had been planning to wait until she officially took over the paper, but now seemed as good an opportunity as any. "We could talk about the newspaper."

"What about it?"

"I suppose you know the shape it's in."

Not looking at him, she drew circles in the moisture that had collected on the Formica tabletop. "You mean the finances?"

"I mean the fact that you've got maybe six months to turn the thing around."

"I guess I shouldn't be surprised that you know that. Delilah's told me how much you've helped her recently."

"Delilah has turned to me *and Jeb* for advice more and more this past year. She's been struggling. Subscriptions and ad revenues are down. Last year, she poured more of her personal money into the paper than I wanted her to."

"I know all that. But I'm not worried."

He frowned at her. "Marianne, I don't know if you understand the scope—"

"Don't talk to me as if I'm a dunce."

"Marianne, there are considerations—"

"I understand the considerations," she said, her voice rising enough to attract the attention of some of the customers standing nearby.

"So Delilah has told you everything?" Jack asked quietly.

Marianne glared at him. "I know that we're in the red. I think that's all I need to know. I've got a few ideas about improving the cash flow."

Jack could see Delilah hadn't told her everything, certainly hadn't divulged what he had wanted her to do with the paper. Of course, if she had done that, Marianne might not have come home. Delilah said she didn't want her niece to feel she had to return to run the paper. But in a way, by not being completely forthcoming with Marianne, Delilah had forced her home. Jack wondered if Delilah was even aware of what she had done.

Whatever the case, he decided this wasn't the time or place to discuss his opinions on the matter. "Listen, I'll stop by the office tomorrow and we'll go over some things I think you should know."

"I'm sure Delilah will do that."

"I'll come by anyway."

Marianne looked irritated. "Jack, really—"

"What's the matter?" he demanded, stung by her hesitation. "Don't trust my advice?"

"It isn't a question of trust."

He barely acknowledged her protest. "You know, Delilah and Jeb and several other people trust me, even though to you I might still be the 'no account' country boy I was when we were kids."

He thought something akin to hurt flashed across her face, but the expression was quickly masked. In a careful, quiet tone, she said, "I never thought of you that way."

"Don't lie, Marianne. Good girls aren't supposed to tell fibs."

She leaned toward him, fury almost crackling in her blue eyes, though she kept her voice low. "Why are you trying to paint me as some kind of snob, Jack? First, you accuse me of not knowing what happened on this side of the creek. Then you think I'm judging Sally on the basis of high school rumors. And now you're saying I looked down on you. And that's just not true. I always cared about you. I always believed in you."

"Oh, yeah," he drawled, voice heavy with sarcasm. "I was your pet project, the bad boy you decided to give a little polish."

Face flushed, she started to swing out of the booth. "I don't know what happened to the Jack Dylan I used to know. But you're not him."

"Oh, yes, I am." Ignoring the line of customers who stood nearby, Jack's fingers closed around her wrist, keeping her from leaving. "I'm exactly who I was nine years ago, Marianne. But you didn't want to face who I was then any more than you do now. You wanted the pretty, polished-up version of me. Well, the polish only went so far." He dropped his voice. "But as I recall, you liked some of those *hard* edges well enough."

She snatched her hand away from him and got out of the booth. "You have changed," she whispered. "You're mean and bitter. Staying here did something to you, Jack. The same thing it did to my father—"

"Then you'd better be careful," he jeered. "You could wind up just like us."

She turned on her heel, almost plowing into Miss Louella and Miss Clara, who had just come in the door.

"Dear me," Louella said, pressing a lace-edged hanky to her throat. "You gave me a fright, Marianne."

"I'm sorry," Marianne said. "I was just...just leaving."

Jack looked up at Clara, whose gaze was darting between him and Marianne with unabashed interest. To Marianne, she said, "So you and Jack were having some ice cream, I see."

Marianne's lips tightened. "Laura and I came in for ice cream, and Jack just *happened* to be here."

The gossips' gazes met and clung for a long, significant moment.

"Oh, yes," Louella said. "Yes, we see. Ice cream on Sunday afternoon is almost a tradition. I like to come over here and see what the competition is doing. Of course, I always close the diner on Sunday."

From behind the counter, Sally called, "Hey, Jack, how about giving me a hand back here?"

"Sure thing," he answered, grateful for the excuse to get away from Marianne and from Clara and Louella's sharp-eyed glances. He pushed past Marianne. Impulsively, with the same show-off ease he had often indulged in high school, he vaulted over the counter.

Laughing, Sally applauded, as did most of the group waiting for their orders. Conscious of Marianne's perusal, Jack grabbed Sally and twirled her around a couple of times.

"Whoa, boy," Sally said, though her smile was flashing. "I wanted help making sundaes, not with a floor show."

"Sure thing, babycakes," he retorted.

Sally's smile turned to a startled frown, but he just picked up an order pad and asked the next customer at the counter, "What'll you have?"

For the next hour or so, Jack barely looked up. He deflected Clara and Louella's questions. Vaguely, he heard Sally call Laura and Betsy down from the apartment. He thought he saw Laura and Marianne leave. But for the most part, he concentrated on dipping cones, swirling whipped cream and ladling hot fudge. As the rain ended and darkness fell outside, the crowd peaked and gradually fell to nothing.

And as the whirl of activity faded, Jack's regrets over what he had said to Marianne grew. He didn't have long to think about it, however, because Sally had a thing or two on her mind.

She threw a wet dishrag right at his head, demanding, "What in the hell was that babycakes crap?"

"So you had ice cream with Jack yesterday?"

Startled by Delilah's question, Marianne looked up from the jumbled desk in front of her. "What?"

Delilah took one of the straight-backed chairs in front of her. "Frank Harvey just stopped by to place an ad for his hardware store. He said he saw you and Jack 'having sundaes and looking more serious than a couple of Democrats.' And that's a quote straight from Frank."

Marianne frowned. "Why are Democrats supposedly so serious?"

"Ask Frank," Delilah returned, laughing. "Why didn't you say you saw Jack?"

"I didn't think it was important."

"But why were you so serious?"

"Delilah," Marianne admonished. "We had ice cream. I don't know what else Frank Harvey was referring to." She shifted in her chair, as uncomfortable as she had ever been about lying.

The older woman regarded her with skeptical blue eyes. "You looked upset when you came home yesterday."

Marianne picked up the file folder in front of her. "You're imagining things."

Though Delilah's sigh betrayed her frustration, she didn't press. "Do you think you'll be okay here in your father's old office?"

"Of course," Marianne lied again. If the truth were known, she felt like an intruder here. This morning, when Delilah showed her into this office, she had half expected her father to greet her. Framed photographs and mementos he had collected still lined the low shelves and the one wall that wasn't windowed. She knew it was ridiculous, but she thought she could still smell his tobacco. And the big, leather chair she sat in bore the imprint of the years he had sat in it, supervising the paper's content. His old manual typewriter was on a stand beside the desk. Yellowing notes scrawled in his handwriting were still tacked to some of the folders Marianne had found in the drawers she had investigated thus far.

"I couldn't change anything after he died," Delilah murmured, leaving her chair. She stopped in front of the window that looked out on Main Street. "I gave the editor I hired another office, and I just shut this door and drew these shades. The only thing I did was have the place dusted every week. Last month, I came in here and tried to redo it for you." She laughed softly and gestured toward a half-filled cardboard box in the corner. "As you can see, I didn't get very far." Her voice and eyes filled with unexpected tears.

Marianne got up and put her arm around her. This emotion wasn't what she would expect from the strong, practical aunt she had always known, the woman who had seen to the business of this newspaper for nearly forty years. "Delilah, what's wrong?"

She shook her head, brushed away her tears. "Don't mind me, Marianne. I guess there's just been an awful lot happening the last few days. You and Laura home. And then

Jeb and I . . ." She managed a weak smile and straightened her shoulders. "Now that's enough sentimental hogwash. I came in here to see if you had looked over the financial printout I gave you."

Dropping back into her father's chair, Marianne groaned. "It's worse than I thought, Delilah."

"I tried to warn you," her aunt said rather defensively. "I told you we were in bad shape before you said anything about coming home."

She was right, of course. Marianne didn't feel as if she had been deceived. She knew nothing Delilah might have said would have kept her from coming home. But now she understood exactly what Jack had been trying to tell her yesterday. Until she went over the black and white and very red figures on their financial statement, she hadn't been aware of the scope of the problems facing the *Oxford County News*.

Like most small newspapers across the country, theirs had faced an uphill battle for the last several decades. Advertising and subscriptions alone hadn't been enough to keep up with escalating costs, including the very necessary expense of updating to computers several years ago. Their salvation had been that other small papers within this region of the state had paid them to use the *Oxford*'s press. But that revenue had shrunk as many of the other papers folded. Even the printing of high school newspapers from around the area, once a very viable source of income, had diminished with the advent of computers and desktop publishing.

"I think we have to raise the ad rates," Marianne said. She glanced toward the open door, beyond which sat a secretary and bookkeeper and lowered her voice. "We'll have to streamline operations."

Delilah frowned. "I agree, of course. But I don't know if the advertisers will accept another increase. Things haven't been so great around here lately, Marianne. The battery plant has had big layoffs. But you know that. You've been reading the papers I mailed to you all these years." She sighed. "I hate to think of laying off any of our people, too. It's not as if we're a big operation."

Indeed, Marianne wasn't sure who among their small group of full and part-time employees they could do without. "We could start putting the paper out only once a week," she suggested.

Her aunt's distress couldn't be hidden. She turned to look out the window again. "When your father and I took over the paper from your grandfather, it came out six days a week. We weren't making a fortune, but we were run off our feet, trying to keep up. Then the stove factory shut down, and we went to four times a week. Then three. And now just two. It hurts me to take it down to once a week, Marianne." Her hands clenched into fists at her side. "I can't tell you how much it hurts to see all your father's work, all of mine, come to this."

Marianne stared at the woman's ramrod straight back and wondered, as she had for years, if it was the newspaper that had kept Delilah from finding fulfillment in her personal life. Was it her unending dedication to this place that had prevented her and Jeb from marrying long ago? There was no doubt that Delilah had poured most of her life into it.

Marianne's determination to keep the paper going strengthened. "We won't take it down to once a week. And I'm going to find a way to eke some profits out of this sucker."

Delilah turned around. "But, dear—"

"I have money," Marianne cut in. "From Dad's insurance and from Kyle. I'll make an investment in the paper's future."

"No. You're not using your own money. That's for your security, for Laura's."

"Jack said you used your money."

Delilah lifted her chin. "He shouldn't have told you that."

"Why not?"

"Is that what you were talking about yesterday when Frank Harvey saw you?"

"I guess Jack thought I should know."

"What else did he tell you?"

"Why? Is there more?"

Delilah plucked nervously at her cream-colored linen skirt, but she was saved from answering by the ring of the phone. It was Laura. Since this was about the fifth time the child had called that morning, Marianne reacted with an irritated, "What is it now?"

"Mrs. Pervis is being mean to me."

Marianne sucked in her breath and counted to fifteen. Mrs. Pervis was Delilah's part-time housekeeper, whom Marianne had hired full-time to do most of the laundry, the cooking and to watch over Laura during the day. The woman was fiftyish, plump and grandmotherly, just about the sweetest person imaginable, and she had been working for Delilah for twenty-five years. She had come in last Friday, and had seemed to hit it off well with Laura, who was behaving like a brat today.

"Laura," Marianne said in her best authoritarian voice. "If you call me one more time with one more ridiculous complaint about Mrs. Pervis, you're not going over to see Betsy tomorrow like I said you could."

"Mom—"

"Get off this phone, Laura, and don't call again. Do you hear me?" With carefully restrained violence, Marianne put the receiver in its cradle.

"Perhaps you should go check on her," Delilah suggested.

"No," Marianne said. "I've always worked. Laura doesn't need me at home. And I have complete confidence in Mrs. Pervis's ability to handle her. After all, she raised six girls of her own. If there's a real problem, I know she will call me."

"Perhaps I'll run home, then. Tomorrow's issue is ready, and Friday's is well under way here."

Marianne had begun to see that Delilah would spoil Laura rotten if permitted. Today, however, she just didn't feel like fighting it. "Fine," she told her aunt. "I'll be here, getting settled in. But you can tell Laura that if she calls me or has you call me, that she is definitely grounded."

Chuckling, Delilah headed for the door. "I'll be sure and tell her."

Only after Marianne watched her aunt walk past the Main Street window did she realize Delilah hadn't divulged what else Jack might have been trying to tell her about the paper yesterday. He had said he would be in this morning, but after what had passed between them, she wasn't surprised that he hadn't shown up. She hoped and prayed he would stay away. With the paper's financial woes spread across the desk, with Laura behaving like a crybaby and with all the painful memories evoked by this office, the last thing Marianne needed was Jack.

But as she set to work cleaning out more of the desk drawers, she kept expecting him to appear in the doorway in his tattered, tight jeans and ripped T-shirt. Surely he wore more conventional attire to the office, although Marianne wouldn't put anything past him.

Lips pressed tight together, she tossed worthless note-filled steno pads in the trash and remembered the way Jack had vaulted over the Dairy Bar's counter. Like a child. And then he had grabbed Sally and called her "babycakes." How silly. He made her sick. And she didn't care if he was Sally's lover, either. Even though unwelcome visions of the two of them together had kept Marianne awake most of the night, she really did not care.

But those disturbing visions taunted her again as she reached the back of the desk's right-hand bottom drawer. Then her hand closed around a bottle. And all thoughts of Jack and Sally fled.

It was vodka, of course. Her father's favorite. But surprisingly enough, the bottle was two-thirds full.

"He probably forgot it was here," Marianne muttered.

Angered by her cynical thought, she threw the bottle on top of the overflowing wastebasket. She sat back, watching the dust dance in the sunbeams that slanted through the blinds.

She wasn't sure how long she sat immobile. But it was long enough to give in to memories of the way her father had wasted his life. Long enough to grow sad and despondent and to begin to question her own reasons for being here. Silently she echoed what everyone else had been saying, *"Why did you come back?"*

She wasn't startled when she looked up and found Jack standing in the doorway. Distractedly, she noted that he wore khaki slacks, a white shirt and tie, and a conservative navy blazer. And she realized she had been waiting for him.

Somehow, that thought seemed to answer her earlier question.

Why had she come back?

Because she had been waiting for Jack.

Chapter Four

"Marianne," Jack said, stepping into the office. "Are you okay?"

She nodded.

Unconvinced, but determined to get out what he had to say, he stopped in front of the desk. "I'm sorry about yesterday."

Her response was a blank stare.

Sally had said it might be a rough haul to convince Marianne he hadn't turned into an unadulterated jackass, but Jack plunged ahead. "I didn't intend to sound bitter or mean yesterday, didn't intend to call you a snob. You're not a snob, of course. You never were." He took a deep breath and went further. "And I know we've got stuff between us that you don't want to talk about. And that's okay with me. I accept that." He paused, reconsidering. "I accept it for right now, anyway. If we could, I'd like to just pretend yesterday, and Saturday night for that matter, didn't happen."

She still gave him no encouragement, still looked through him more than at him. Despite his resolve, Jack felt annoyance take hold. "Marianne, can you help me out here, maybe? I mean, I said I was sorry."

She blinked like someone coming out of a trance and began shuffling through the debris on the desk, looking everywhere but at him. "Okay."

"Okay?" he repeated, spreading his hands wide. "Just okay?"

"Yes. I accept your apology."

Puzzled, he frowned at her. "Marianne, what in the world…" Then he looked, really looked, at the office where he stood.

Though he knew Delilah didn't use Elliot Cole's old office, it never occurred to him that she might have left it just as it was the day the man died. Jack could well remember this room. There in the corner was the umbrella stand with the carved dog's head in the center that Marianne had always hated. On the shelves were old trophies for baseball and track. On the wall was the autographed picture of Pete Rose, which Jack had coveted as a teenager. The room was like a page torn from a time long past. Preserved forever. Right down to the liquor bottle lying on top of the full wastebasket.

Staring at that bottle, Jack thought he understood why Marianne seemed distracted and removed. She was sitting smack in the middle of memories. Some good, maybe. But some awfully bad.

"It's not easy being here, is it?"

She nodded. "I told Delilah it was okay, but it's not really. In fact, it's downright eerie." Her gaze went around the room. "Don't you think it's bizarre that this office could be just like it was, even though the rest of the world has gone right on? Why would Delilah keep it this way? It seems out of character for her."

"Perhaps this was her way of holding on to him."

The chair squeaked as Marianne leaned back and took a deep breath. "After he was killed, I thought she handled it so well. She stayed home from the newspaper for a week. Then she went right on, busy as always. She cleared out his room without saying anything. All of his clothes went to the church rummage sale. The rest she boxed up and put in the attic. Then she redecorated. Two weeks after his funeral, it was as if he had been gone forever. I remember wishing I could be like her. I wanted to just go on, too. But it was so hard."

Jack remembered how difficult her father's death was for her. It had been Marianne's sorrow, her inability to deal with her grief that had driven her into Jack's arms.

The air in the office pressed in on him like the heat of a long-ago August night. The memories were smothering. But all he had done for the past three days was remember. He found he couldn't stand it anymore.

"Let's get out of here," he said to Marianne.

"What?"

"Let's drive to the river, have some catfish for lunch."

She gestured to the heaping mound still left to sort through on her desk. "I can't go anywhere."

"Sure you can. I'm the newspaper's legal advisor, and I need to advise you."

"Jack, we shouldn't—"

"Please, Marianne," he cut in. "I promise to behave myself. I won't make you mad or ask too many questions or dredge up ancient history."

The pleading look in his green eyes and his promises to behave were exactly the sort of tactics he once used to lead her into a variety of scrapes. Marianne knew the innocent mischief of the past was nothing compared to the turbulent emotional territory they might venture into today. She had just admitted to herself that he was the chief reason she had uprooted her life and her child and moved home. The knowledge had left her dazed and unable to look at him for the first few minutes he stood in the office. She should send him packing. At least until she understood her own feelings toward him. But it was hard to resist Jack as he was now— the rakish, hooky-playing boy from their past. This was certainly an improvement over the surly adult he had been for the past few days.

"You haven't ridden in my car yet," he wheedled. "It's big and fast. And I bet you still like fast cars."

She did. Contrary to Kyle's preference for safe, speed-limit drives, she had never shaken her partiality to window-down, thrill-causing speed. The thought of just such a drive was far more appealing than an afternoon in this dusty, depressing office.

"Oh, what the hell," she said, reaching for her purse.

Jack's triumphant whoop brought the secretary to the door of the office, looking concerned.

Grinning at the woman, whom Marianne had known most of her life, she pushed Jack toward the front doors. "We'll be at lunch if anyone asks."

Too late, she wondered what the well-developed gossip network would make of that statement. For she knew it would soon be all over town that Marianne Cole and Jack Dylan were taking off in his big, red T-Bird.

She forgot to care once she was in that broad, front seat, once the wind was whipping through her hair. They literally blew through town, waving at Miss Louella who stood on the sidewalk outside her diner, blowing a horn at the usual crowd of retired men gathered on the town square. They crossed the creek, and headed onto familiar country roads. Jack put Springsteen in the tape player, cranked it up and pushed the big, powerful car toward the river. Farms flashed past. Barns and homes and livestock. Marianne drank in the beauty of the countryside, gave herself over to enjoyment of the sunshine and clear air.

Some twenty minutes after leaving town, they took an old wooden bridge over the slow-moving green water. On cue, in the center, the minute the county line was breached, they yelled together, just as they had when they were young. And then they laughed at their foolishness, giddy from remembered excitement. The county line, Jack used to say, was where the rest of the world waited. What waited on the other side was what had always tempted them both.

Today, the rest of the world was a tin-roofed restaurant perched on a bluff over the river. Marianne supposed a good, strong wind might blow the whole structure down. But one didn't come here for fancy amenities. The proprietor was a middle-aged man who greeted Jack like a bosom friend. The tables were made of rough-hewn lumber, slapped with wood preservative and long-since worn to a smooth shine. The chairs were mismatched and crude, as well, and Marianne snagged her hose right away. But the catfish was just as she remembered, flaky and almost sweet on the inside, coated with cornmeal batter, deep fried to a fine crackle. Without embarrassment, she licked her fingers after her third diet-busting fillet.

"Mrs. Wingate," Jack said. "I'd have thought you'd learn some table manners in the nation's capital."

"Must be the company I'm keeping that's made me revert to bad habits," she shot back, watching him devour buttered corn on the cob with a definite lack of finesse.

He put the cob aside and reached for another from the platter in the middle of the table. "Aren't you glad you came?"

She was too busy eating tangy homemade coleslaw to answer.

"Just because we're having fun doesn't mean I'm not going to talk business," Jack warned.

She swallowed. "I'll save you the preliminaries, then. You were right about the paper. It's in much worse shape than I thought."

His expression sobered. "I'm sorry to be right, Marianne. I wish you had come home to better news."

"I've just got my work cut out for me, that's all."

Jack studied her for a moment, wondering how she would take his next statement. But he couldn't hold back. She needed to know. "A company made an offer to buy the paper this last winter."

She gave him a blank look.

"It was a good offer," Jack continued. "I advised Delilah to take it."

"She didn't," Marianne replied needlessly.

"But I bet we could still interest them."

She wiped her hands on her paper napkin with a delicacy that had been missing moments ago. Her voice was similarly sensible and calm. "The newspaper has been in our family for four generations. My great-grandfather started it right after Willow Creek was founded."

"I know the legend," Jack said. "After the town sprang up around the creek and the railroad stop, Reginald Cole got off the train and decided to settle there. Without any idea that he could make it a success, he unloaded his printing press and started cranking out newspapers. It made him and your family rich."

"I'm not selling the paper," Marianne said with quiet finality.

"This company doesn't want to close the paper down, Marianne. They own a couple of other small newspapers across the southeast. You could probably still edit it if you wanted. I'm sure they would be more than happy to have an award-winning writer on the payroll, especially someone who's a member of the Cole family. Wouldn't you rather be writing and editing than dealing with finances?''

"This isn't about being on a payroll. This is about my heritage. Delilah's. And Laura's.''

"You don't know if Laura will give a hang about the newspaper business.''

"But that doesn't matter, either. When you've owned something for so long, when it's been a part of your whole life, you don't give it up easily.'' Elbows on the edge of the table, hands clenched, she sat forward.

"Jack, for four generations, my family has reported deaths and births and marriages. My grandfather wrote headlines about the end of one world war and the beginning of another. About a man on the moon. Dad wrote a whole series about Watergate from the local perspective that won the paper a big award from the state press association. Through that newspaper people found out about who won the pickle contest at the July 4th festival. It's so big and yet so small that it can't help but be worth saving.''

No one could listen to her soft, impassioned voice and not be affected. But Jack had to keep in mind what was best for her. "You sound like Delilah. Full of sentiment. I would have thought both of you were better businesspeople than this.''

"Maybe there are some things more important than business.''

Shaking his head, he reached for a napkin to wipe the butter off his fingers. "The paper is going to go bankrupt, Marianne.''

"Maybe not.''

He balled up the napkin and tossed it aside. "Up until this winter when Delilah said you wanted to come home, I wouldn't have thought you cared what happened to that blasted newspaper."

"I didn't."

"What happened? And don't give me that story about wanting to be safe, about bringing Laura back here to experience her roots." He held up his hand as she started to protest. "All that may be true, but coming home didn't mean you had to take over the paper. I'm sure your column was popular enough that you might still be doing it long-distance or perhaps syndicating it. Something made you want to come back to the *Oxford News*. What was it?"

She looked out the window, eyes narrowed as if gathering her thoughts. "It started before this winter."

"When Kyle died?"

Her denial was emphatic. "It didn't have anything to do with Kyle." Then she shook her head again. "Although maybe it did. Maybe if we had been happy..." Her words trailing away, she stared at Jack with eyes that grew wide and clouded with confusion. "No, that's not right...that's not what I meant, what I meant was..."

But there was nothing she could say that would take back that confession. Jack knew it was selfish to wish an unhappy marriage on anyone, but he couldn't stop the charge of elation that ripped through him. Despite his big corporate law job, despite an elaborate house, trips to Europe and invitations to ambassadors' homes, Kyle Wingate hadn't made Marianne happy.

She sat across from him, her expression guilty. "I shouldn't have said that."

"If you weren't happy why did you stay with him?"

"We aren't talking about my marriage," she said, firmly closing the door on that subject. "It wasn't the marriage

that made me want to come home. It was... this feeling."
She pressed a hand to her chest. "It was this overwhelming
homesickness. I didn't feel it when I first left. I guess I was
too busy with Laura and my work. But after nine years, I
just wanted to come home. I wanted out of the rat race and
the competition. And amazingly enough, I wanted to run
the *Oxford County News*. It's as simple as that."

"It can't be that simple."

Marianne avoided his glance. For there was more to it.
Jack had been a big part of her reasoning. But she couldn't
tell him that.

She brought the conversation back to the newspaper. "I
won't sell, Jack."

"Delilah has a say in this, too, you know."

"She wouldn't sell before."

"But I doubt she'll stand by while you sacrifice your own
financial security to save the newspaper."

Marianne wondered how he had figured out what she was
planning to do. "I wouldn't be foolish enough to endanger
Laura's future."

"Please don't risk any of your own money." Hands
clenched into fists, Jack gently thumped the table to em-
phasize his plea. "It's just not worth it."

"It was worth my father's life."

"Marianne..." he began.

"No," she cut in, unconsciously putting one of her hands
over his fist. "That paper claimed Dad's life. Bit by bit, day
by day, he died there."

"Because he hated it."

"I still can't let it go," she insisted.

"And you can't make it a sacred cause, either."

"But there's Delilah, too. Good heavens, Jack, it kills her
even to think of reducing the publishing schedule to once a
week."

"Delilah is going to marry Jeb. She's going to have the life I think she should have had long ago. They're going to retire and travel and enjoy one another. Hopefully, she'll be too busy and too happy to worry about the newspaper."

"But she'll be happier knowing that the newspaper is in my hands."

"No, that's not . . ." Jack's protest faltered as he realized Marianne's hand was now enfolded in his own. He looked down, noticed how pale her skin looked against his tan, admitted how right it felt to be touching her. Then he glanced up, and their gazes locked, only to spring apart as quickly as their hands.

Reaching for his glass of iced tea, he said, "I'm wasting my time trying to convince you to consider this offer, aren't I?"

"Definitely."

He set the glass down. "I guess we should go."

"Yes, back to town," she agreed. "It's nearly two-thirty."

But he wasn't ready to go back. Today, they had finally gotten past a hurdle, and he didn't want it to end just yet. "The day's already two-thirds wasted. Let's not go back."

"Jack—"

"Let's sit by the river. Watch it run."

She sighed in disapproval, but he saw the smile that crooked one corner of her mouth.

"I can tell you want to."

"Shouldn't you be in court?"

"Not today."

"Then aren't there torts or briefs or something you should be considering?"

"I'm considering stripping down to my briefs and going for a swim."

"Jack, stop it." Marianne glanced around the nearly empty restaurant, afraid someone might have heard.

"You think anyone here would be shocked by a little skinny-dipping?"

"No, but Miss Clara and Miss Louella probably have spies out watching us, especially after the way we tore through town."

Jack made a very rude suggestion about what the two sisters could do with their meddling, busybody ways.

And in the end, Marianne went along with him. They drove down the river, away from the bridge and the road that would take them home. He parked in a spot Marianne remembered, close to the water's edge, near a willow whose branches dipped into the languorous current.

She shed her lightweight cotton knit jacket, grateful for the white camisole underneath, and made Jack turn around while she slipped off her panty hose. Then, with her pleated navy skirt hiked up over her knees, she stretched out on the T-Bird's long, red hood. Jack had pulled a worn but clean blanket from the trunk to use as a cushion. She refused to speculate on why he carried the blanket or whom he might have shared it with in the past. The day was too nice to waste on such thoughts. The sun was warm but not uncomfortably so, the air still cool from yesterday's storms.

"You're gonna burn," Jack warned her, even as he stripped out of his tie and shirt.

Marianne sat up when he reached for his belt. "You're not really going in, are you?"

"Would it bother you?"

She lay back, closing her eyes and pretending indifference. "Do what you want."

"That's a dangerous invitation."

His voice was disturbingly near, so she opened her eyes, shaded them to get a better look at him, then wished she hadn't. Arms braced on the car hood, Jack stood over her. He hadn't taken off his pants, but he was naked to the waist.

His stomach was still flat, still defined by a washboard pattern of muscles. His chest was broader than she remembered, the curling black hair in the center thicker. And his shoulders were just as she remembered them, wide and straight and strong.

In a husky drawl, he said, "See something you like?"

She sat up again. "I thought you were going to behave."

"This is how I always behaved."

"No, it's not. Not with me. We never flirted."

He reached out, stroked her cheek. "Maybe we should have."

His touch set her pulse points thrumming, but she resisted their call. She closed her hand over his, pulled it away. "Please. Don't."

He stepped back, seemed about to say something, then reconsidered. "All right. I'll be good."

And he was. As one golden hour stretched to two, he kept things light. They talked about school, about friends who had moved away and stayed in town. They touched on his mother's death and his father's lingering depression. Whenever the conversation faltered, or they were headed up a dangerous path, it was Jack who pulled them back. Resolutely, they avoided talking of Kyle. Of Laura. Or of a nine-year-old summer.

"Remember when you decided to be my friend?" he asked as he sent a rock skipping out over the river.

"We've always known each other."

"Yes, but it was seventeen years ago that you really became my friend."

She smiled. "It was the July 4th festival."

"You were about thirteen."

"And you were already a hell-raiser. I think you were Sally's date that night. I remember the two of you dancing."

"But she got mad and went home."

"Why was that, anyway?"

He sent a devilish grin over his shoulder. "I'd rather not say."

"Jack! She was only thirteen, too."

"She was more developed."

"She still is."

"Shut up and stick to the story."

Laughing, he leaned against the car's front grillwork. "I decided to set off the fireworks a little early. Now that I think of it, it was such a stupid, dangerous stunt."

"Which I saw you do."

"I was sure you were going to tell the sheriff."

She sat up, crossing her legs. "He's the one who screwed up and left the stuff unguarded."

"That's because a couple of my buddies lured him away."

"I never knew that part of it."

"While he was busy with them, all I had to do was light a few fuses."

Marianne remembered that she had stood in the shadows, watching Jack, wishing she had the nerve to do something so bad, so forbidden. When the first of the rockets had taken off, Jack had started running and crashed right into her. They had steadied one another and looked up together as a waterfall of color lit the dark sky.

A sheriff's deputy had come puffing around the corner of a tent, demanding to know if either of them had seen anything. They said no. Then the officer had peered at the boy beside her, evidently noted how close they stood, and said, "Your Uncle Jeb's standing right over there, missy. And I'll bet he's looking for you." Nodding, Marianne pulled Jack away.

Remembering the man now, she said, "That deputy was always such a pompous ass."

Jack turned around to face her. "He just knew your family wouldn't want you standing in the dark with the likes of me."

"Is that why you stuck beside me the rest of the night? To show him?"

"Hell, no. I was afraid you would change your mind and turn me in."

Looking off across the river, she thought about what had happened next. She remembered the connection she had felt with Jack that night. They certainly knew each other before then, but had not been aware of one another on any significant level. He had always been just slightly off limits. Though he was brash and cocky, she had secretly admired his spunk. Marianne wasn't brought up to think of herself as better than anyone else, but she knew the distance between her house and Jack's family's farm covered more than miles. That night, however, they bridged the gap. They discovered a common disdain for Willow Creek. And an affinity for a lot more. Such as Springsteen, Delilah's buttermilk pie and science fiction. Marianne had realized right away that Jack was much smarter than he wanted everyone to believe. Funny how he had never hidden that side from her.

He laughed now, also remembering. "My buddies were flipping out. Didn't know what I was up to with you, of all people."

"They never understood that we were friends."

"No one did."

"Except maybe Kyle," Marianne said, without thinking. She waited for Jack to pounce on the subject, but he didn't. Instead, he turned around, threw a few more rocks in the river and soon had her laughing about something else. It seemed to Marianne that he was intent on making up for the unpleasant tension between them during the past few days.

Not that the tension disappeared. Quite the contrary, tension still ran between them like a stream of hyper-charged energy. She felt it when Jack brushed a wayward leaf from her shoulder. Or when they smiled into each other's eyes over some remembered escapade. Or when she caught a certain awareness in his glance.

Doggedly, she tried to ignore what they were building to. She told herself not to think about the immensely sexy way Jack's hair fell across his forehead. She didn't want to remember how his big, well-made hands had once felt on her skin. Or how his mouth tasted. Or how his clean, masculine scent lingered on her sheets after the one night he spent in her bed.

Marianne tried, and failed, not to think of any of this. But toward the end of the day, it seemed that sex was all she could think of. So she blamed it on herself and not Jack when he kissed her.

They were leaving when it happened. It was after five, and Marianne had to get home to Laura. Reluctantly she stepped into her shoes and got down from the car. Jack shrugged into his shirt. But he didn't button it, and when he opened her car door, she brushed up against his warm, muscular chest. He made a strangled sound, half groan and half sigh. She paused. Looked up. And his mouth caught hers.

After nine years of waiting, Marianne should have expected the powder keg that lit inside her. Jack's kiss simply blew her apart. One minute she was trying so hard not to think of his touch. And then his lips were on hers, his tongue was in her, and she became a trembling, aching bundle of want. They kissed deeply, until she broke away.

"We can't," she murmured, even as her fingers threaded through his dark, soft hair.

He nibbled at her chin. "Why not?"

"You know why."

But evidently he didn't, for he was intent on maneuvering her back against the car door. Hands brushed on her thighs. Gentle hands, sweeping upward, palms finally cupping her rear, slipping beneath her lace panties.

Her head arched back. He pressed his face to the hollow of her throat, murmuring sweet, unintelligible words, words she somehow understood. Then he kissed her again, the lightest, tenderest of kisses. And somehow that delicate touch made her wilder than all the openmouthed kisses that had come before. She opened to him, offered herself.

Pressed back against the car door, she parted her legs, slipped them around his lean, straining hips. She felt his hard length beneath his zipper, grinding against the scant barrier offered by the lace that covered her mound. It would take very little for him to be inside her. Marianne remembered how it had felt to accept Jack into her body, how he had moved and stroked, how she had stretched around him, how she had shuddered and shattered beneath him. She remembered how sex had changed everything between them.

With that thought, sanity returned.

Somehow, she pushed him back. Somehow, she staggered away from him and the car, toward the river. Gasping for air, she straightened her skirt, tried to smooth her tangled hair.

But Jack caught her arm. "What's wrong?"

"We can't do this."

He brought her hand to his chest, where the skin was hot to the touch, spread her fingers over his heart, which was racing. His voice was low and fierce. "I want you. You want me. And you don't belong to Kyle like you did nine years ago. You're not betraying anyone. So what's stopping us?"

"It isn't about belonging to someone else. It was never about that."

"Then what is it?"

She pulled away from him, stumbled away again. "This just isn't what I want."

He moved in front of her again. "That wasn't manufactured passion back there, Marianne. You can't lie to me about what you were feeling."

"But don't you remember?" she demanded. "Nine years ago we made love and I lost you. I lost my best friend."

He took her hand again. "Everything was different then. I was young and foolish and scared. You won't lose anything this time."

"This time there's nothing to lose. You're not my friend anymore. You said it yourself yesterday—we're really just strangers."

"You didn't believe that any more than I did. I saw it in your eyes yesterday. And today...today we've been the way we always were."

Frustrated because he was right, she pushed at his chest. "Yes. Today was the first time since I came home that we didn't snipe at each another the whole time we were together. And then what do we do?" She paused, brushing a hand over her face. "We start pawing each other like two animals."

"Jesus, Marianne," he protested. "It's not like that. I mean, haven't you felt it every time we've been together? It's this thing...you know...call it chemistry or pheromones or fate if you want."

"So does that mean we're supposed to just drop right down in the dirt and do it?"

He stepped back, stared at her. "Is that the way you see this?"

"I don't know," she said, shaking her head. "I know that there's something between us. I won't lie about that. But I just don't know if every impulse has to be acted upon. I mean, sometimes I've wondered if my life wouldn't have been different, *better*, if I hadn't been so impulsive with you that night after Dad was killed.''

"I'm sorry for your regrets, Marianne. From the beginning, I was sorry—"

"And what about your regrets? Weren't you just as sorry that it happened as I was? Didn't you wish we had stayed the way we were before? Didn't you ever miss my friendship the way I've missed yours?"

The questions stunned Jack because his answers weren't what he expected. All these years, he said over and over that he wished it had never happened. But now he knew that wasn't true. Holding Marianne in his arms, feeling her body accept his, guiding her first taste of real passion—those were sensations he knew he would never trade. Not for his peace of mind. Not even for the sake of their friendship. He had missed Marianne, of course. But simple friendship wasn't what he wanted with her. Not nine summers ago. Not this summer.

But Marianne's regrets were what had driven them apart. If she hadn't regretted what they had done, he would never have walked away and let her marry Kyle. He wasn't about to allow similar feelings to come between them again.

Right now, if he followed his impulse, he would kiss Marianne once more. After what had flared so quickly, so potently between them only minutes before, he had no doubt that kisses would lead to more. But he also knew Marianne would have the same profound regrets she'd had before, and he couldn't live with that again. This time, he was going to curb his impulses.

He drew in a deep, steadying breath. "Okay. You win. This isn't right. Not the right time, anyway."

Marianne touched his arm. "I don't know if it will ever be the right time."

He checked his instinctive protest. Nothing would be gained by pressing the point right now.

"Come on. I'm sure Laura and Delilah are wondering where you are."

He took her straight to the house, rather than to the newspaper office where her car was still parked. If Marianne had been thinking straight, she knew she would have protested. At the office, she could have combed her hair, repaired her makeup or at least put her jacket and panty hose back on. But at the house, she had to get out of the car, bare-legged, windblown and sunburned. She felt as if her entire afternoon was on display. On the porch of the house next door, she caught movement and knew she and Jack would be fodder for dinner conversation. Two kids on bicycles careened around the car, their necks craning. And from Delilah's came the sound of the front door slamming and Laura's voice, calling for her.

But as she closed the car door, Marianne turned to look at Jack, the first time she had met his gaze since they left the river.

"I don't know what to say," she murmured.

"Admitting that is a lot better than making something up." Briefly, his hand covered hers.

Then he wheeled the car around in a U-turn that defied its size and the narrowness of the street.

Laura reached her as Jack headed for downtown. Arms closing around her mother's waist, she said, "You're late."

Marianne absently smoothed her daughter's hair. "I'm sorry." Only half listening to Laura's complaints about Mrs. Pervis and the day, she walked toward the house.

Delilah stood at the top of the front steps. Her gaze swept Marianne from head to toe, not with censure, but with distinct interest. A smile quirked her lips. But all she said was, "Must have been some lunch."

* * *

The law offices of Hampton and Dylan were located on the second floor over the Town and Country Dress Shop. To outsiders, the combination might have seemed strange, but both establishments had been here longer than Jack had been alive. Even as a boy, he had liked this red-brick building that sat across from the courthouse square. He liked working here now. In fact, he preferred his office to his home, which still felt a bit temporary, even five years after he moved in.

The building's upper windows were long and narrow, softened by graceful arches at their tops. In the sixties, downtown landlords had given in to the urge to modernize, but Jeb Hampton had resisted. When the merchants' association began its downtown restoration a few years back, this building wasn't touched.

Tonight, as Jack stood beside one of his office windows, he could see the handiwork of the restoration project. Willow Creek looked much as it might have sixty or seventy years ago. But his mind wasn't on buildings or even on the desk full of work he had neglected by taking the afternoon off. He was remembering Marianne's mouth, the taste of her lips opening beneath his. Incessantly her kiss was all he had thought of since leaving her.

He was so caught up in his memories that it took a few minutes to realize someone was pounding on the office's rear door. Thinking of Marianne, Jack sprinted down the hall. But it was Sally who stood on the stoop outside.

"Did you get my message?" she asked, pushing past him.

Grumbling, he closed the door. "And hello to you, too."

"Did you get it?" she demanded again.

Upon his arrival at the office, Jack had picked up a stack of messages half an inch thick. Sally's had been among them, but he hadn't tried to call her.

"She's going to do it," she said now, a note of hysteria in her voice. "Renee is going to sue to get Betsy back."

Renee was Sally's younger sister and Betsy's biological mother.

Jack took Sally's arm, propelled her back down the hall. "Just calm down. Tell me what's going on."

He dropped into his chair while Sally paced in front of the desk. "Renee's new husband showed up at the restaurant this afternoon. He had Renee out in the car. So I went out." She stopped, hugging her arms to her middle. "God, Jack, I know she's using again. I could see it in her eyes."

Eight years ago, when Betsy was less than six months old, Renee went to prison for her involvement in a local drug ring. She had been in and out of trouble for years, so the court went hard on her. Betsy's father, whom Renee never married, was killed by police during another bust. Sally had been caring for Betsy, anyway, so Renee gave her custody, and eventually allowed her to adopt the child. After her release from prison, Renee dropped out of sight. Last year, she suddenly showed up again, married, living in Nashville and asking to have her daughter back. She had told her husband Sally coerced her into giving up Betsy.

"Just calm down," Jack told Sally now. "Maybe it's just another threat."

Sally shook her head. "Not this time."

Jack wanted to say Renee couldn't win. After all, a drug dealer with a history of substance abuse didn't sound like an ideal parent. But she was Betsy's real mother. And she was pretending to be rehabilitated. There were some people who would say she had a right to her child. Moreover, there was a history of bad blood between the sisters.

Before she knew he was involved in drugs, Sally had dated Betsy's father herself. And undeserved though it was, she also had a reputation. Some of the good citizens of Willow

Creek couldn't accept that her sensual looks and warm smiles didn't translate into loose morals. Jack would defy anyone to prove Sally's behavior was ever less than circumspect. But rumors died hard in a small town, especially when Sally had admirers bringing guns into the restaurant. Trouble did seem to follow Sally, which was why she had been so angry about his flirtatious behavior last night. He didn't blame her, and was sorry for what he had unthinkingly done. Betsy's well-being was at stake. No doubt any lawyer Renee hired would try to capitalize on Sally's reputation. From here on, Sally had to be very careful.

Jack had never taken Renee's threats seriously before now, but he saw that it was time to take action. "We'll get a private detective on Renee right away. If she's using again, we'll know it, and that will be ammunition to fight her. And I'll also ask for a restraining order to keep her away from you and Betsy. I hope you left Betsy somewhere safe tonight."

"Of course. Thinking that Renee might come after her is what scares me the most." Still agitated, Sally dropped into a chair in front of his desk. "I'm so glad you know what to do, Jack. I'll find the money to pay for this somehow."

"Don't worry about that. The important thing to do is stop Renee. If we make this hard enough, maybe she'll just go away."

Sally disagreed emphatically. "She means to go through with this. She's convinced herself that I stole Betsy from her."

Jack talked quietly and sensibly to Sally for several more minutes, again outlining what they would do to stop any claim Renee might make on Betsy. If it actually came to trial, he might call in an attorney specializing in family law. Sally said she wanted him in charge, that she trusted him. Finally, after a half hour or more of discussion, Sally's voice had lost its hysterical edge and she had a little more hope that the issue might die before going to court.

Sitting back in the chair, she took several deep breaths. "Talking to you about it makes me calmer. I was in such a panic when you didn't call me back this afternoon. Your secretary said she didn't know where you were. I thought you'd had it with me after last night."

Last night, when she was finished berating him for the "babycakes" remark, Sally had quizzed him about Marianne, about the vibes she had picked up between the two of them. Without explaining everything, Jack had admitted he and Marianne had a history, some unfinished business between them. Sally, in her usual straightforward way, said he should confront Marianne with whatever was bothering him, get it out in the open.

"I took your advice," he told Sally now. "I apologized to Marianne for acting like a jackass ever since she came home."

"What did she say?"

"We spent the afternoon together."

Sally's mouth formed a silent O as she sat back in her chair. Jack thought something akin to disappointment slipped across her features, but the expression came and went too quickly for him to tell. She said, "So did you get things straightened out?"

He summoned a rueful smile. "You've got enough problems without hearing about mine."

"That's true enough," she admitted while drawing a hand through her curling ebony hair. "But you seem upset. And you always listen to me, so..."

Jack had spent plenty of time listening and helping Sally over the past few years. He knew most people assumed they were more than friends. But even in high school, Sally never shared more than a few kisses with him. Maybe, a couple of years ago, they might have become lovers if he had pressed the issue. But that time had come and gone. He almost regretted that now. Maybe if he had allowed himself, he could have fallen in love with this lush, vibrant woman and he wouldn't be torturing himself over Marianne Cole. If he and Sally were lovers, he might be able to assuage the ache that was in his gut right now.

As soon as the thought hit him, he was ashamed. He hoped he wasn't the sort of man who would use one woman to forget another.

Sally got to her feet. "If you're sure you don't want to talk, I'm going home to Betsy."

"I'll walk you out."

After promising to find a Nashville private detective first thing the next morning, Jack put Sally in her car. He considered confronting the chaos of work on his desk again, but in the end he went home instead.

Home was a renovated white cottage not too far from Delilah's house. In fact, in the winter when the leaves were gone, he could stand on his deck and see the third floor. Too many times, he had looked through the trees and thought of Marianne's room. Where they had made love. The room that now belonged to his daughter.

His daughter. Laura.

He laughed bitterly, thinking of the innocent way Sally had urged him to confront Marianne about their past. That would be much easier to do if all that lay between them was a night of forbidden passion. But there was more. There was Laura.

Was Laura part of the reason Marianne had pulled away from him today? After all, if she got too close to him, she might have to admit that Laura was Jack's, that she had lied about her daughter's paternity all these years. For all her talk of impulsiveness and regrets, perhaps she was really just protecting her lies. But if that were the case, why had she come back here at all? Surely she knew he suspected the truth, especially after what he had said to her the other night. If he hadn't lost his nerve at the last minute on Saturday night, he would have said, "Laura is mine." So surely Marianne knew that sooner or later he was going to confront her.

Or would he? This was the dilemma that had been torturing him since the day he began to suspect Marianne carried his child. He could have confronted her long ago. But maybe he didn't want to see her scramble for answers and excuses. Or, as he had said to himself all these years, maybe it was best not to complicate matters by making claims and trying to assert rights. That argument seemed even stronger now that he had seen and talked with Laura. She thought Kyle Wingate was her father. And judging from her face when she showed Jack her dolls, she had adored him. What right did Jack have to destroy a little girl's illusions? That was the question that had kept him away from her.

Standing on his deck, cold beer in hand, he peered through the darkness, trying to see Delilah's house. But he couldn't make out even the lights. They were probably out. Laura was most likely asleep, perhaps curled up in the same bed where she had been conceived.

He remembered that night. The middle of a hot and dry August.

Unwanted memories tumbled through Jack's head. He took a deep swig of beer, tried not to remember. Still staring toward Delilah's house, he sat down in a cushioned redwood chair. He breathed in the honeysuckle-scented air and struggled not to think of the night he and Marianne made Laura.

But he couldn't put the brakes on his runaway thoughts.
He remembered how the whole thing started. Strange how
Laura's life really began with her grandfather's death.
With that, Jack let his memories take over....

Chapter Five

The grandfather Laura never knew was killed on a Thursday. Near midnight. At the end of July. Elliot Cole had been drinking, of course, and driving, two pastimes he had combined frequently and without tragic results for years. Only this night his luck ran out. His car wrapped around a telephone pole just off the two-lane highway between Willow Creek and Knoxville. The coroner said he died instantly.

The community reacted with suitable mourning to the death of one of its sons. But no one exhibited real surprise. Behind their hands and in low voices, they said it was a shame, of course, but it was a blessing, too, a blessing that Elliot Cole hadn't taken someone else to the grave with him long before this.

Jack could still hear echoes of their whispers as he stood behind Marianne's chair at the graveside service. He didn't think she had heard anything anyone said to her or around her for days. She had appeared dazed since hearing of her father's death. Today, her fiancé sat by her side, holding her hand, but Jack hadn't seen her speak to Kyle. Tonight, Kyle was going back to D.C., to his fancy new job. He would return here in three weeks to marry Marianne.

Thoughts of that wedding brought an uncomfortable tightness to Jack's chest. He tried to shake it off, tried to concentrate on the words of the minister who stood beside the flower-draped coffin. But he kept looking down at Kyle and Marianne's joined hands, kept wanting to pull them apart.

Jack didn't want these new and disturbingly intense feelings for Marianne. He had enough troubles without them. By day, he was working his tail off in Jeb Hampton's law office. Three nights a week, he was on the loading dock of the chair factory, trying to scrounge up enough money for his second year of law school. Whatever time he had left, he had to give to his father and brother on the farm. His days were long and exhausting, but he had his eye on the future. Rebellious rabble-rouser Jack Dylan had reformed and focused. His goals were set, and they would require all his concentration and effort. Two years from now, he wanted the same kind of job Kyle had accepted at the beginning of the summer. He wanted to get through the rest of his schooling. He wanted out of Willow Grove.

But he also wanted Marianne Cole.

Standing behind her chair, watching while her father was laid to rest, Jack finally had to admit the truth of the matter. It had taken most of the summer to get to this point.

The change started that February at school in Knoxville, when Kyle put a ring on Marianne's finger, and they set a wedding date. Jack liked and admired Kyle, thought him ambitious and intelligent. Though Kyle came from an affluent, politically connected background, he wasn't a snob. In fact, he had given plenty of advice and encouragement throughout Jack's first, tough year of law school. Up until that ring was presented, Jack had thought Kyle a perfect husband for Marianne. He was, above all, a good and kind person, and would provide her with the sort of stable, secure home life her childhood with an alcoholic father hadn't. Something happened when Jack saw that ring, however. His mouth went dry. His heart turned over. Every nerve in his body cried out in rebellion. It hit him in the gut. Marianne was really going to marry. And move out of his life.

Now, some three months later, it still didn't seem right. But then, the thoughts he had been having about her weren't right, either. She was his friend, and she belonged to someone else. Her face shouldn't haunt his dreams. His senses shouldn't leap at her smile. And thinking about her walking down the aisle to join her life with Kyle Wingate shouldn't fill him with such blinding, senseless fury. But it did.

And there wasn't a damned thing he could do about it. Except maybe stay out of Marianne's way. She was no longer just a friend in his eyes, but she was going to marry Kyle, so the safest course for all of them was for him to quietly fade from the scene.

With that in mind, Jack stayed behind Marianne until the graveside ceremony ended. He gave her one last hug. Then he went home alone. And tried not to think of her.

But his plan didn't work. For Marianne needed his friendship now more than ever.

"You're the only one I can talk to," she told him that night on the phone. "It feels so weird here in the house without Dad. Come over, Jack. Come talk to me."

And he went, of course. Because to deny Marianne anything was impossible. She had done so much for him, encouraged him, cared about him. Now, when she needed him, he had to be there for her.

Late that night, on the screened-in porch adjoining her room, she cried in his arms. Jack couldn't help but think Kyle should be here to help Marianne through this time. He even said as much.

But Marianne said Kyle couldn't help. "He didn't know Dad like you do. I never even told him that Dad was an alcoholic until the day after the accident. But you know everything. I don't have to explain it to you."

"I'm sure Kyle understands," Jack said, not quite sure why he was defending the guy who was going to steal Marianne.

"Maybe he does," she replied, sitting up and brushing tears from her cheeks. "But he had to go back to D.C., to his job. He's only been there a little more than a month and with the wedding coming up and our honeymoon, he can't stay here now."

Thinking of the wedding and honeymoon made Jack move away from her. "Maybe you should join Kyle now, get away from all this."

"I can't leave. There are all these plans for the wedding and Delilah needs my help at the paper until she hires a new editor and there's just all this... this *stuff—*"

"What stuff?"

"In my head. About Dad." She got up abruptly, arms wrapping around her middle. "I could have stopped him the night of the accident. I knew he was drunk. I should have hidden his keys, done something." Her voice broke on the last word.

"This wasn't your fault," Jack said, standing up and quite naturally pulling her back into his arms. At this moment, she just needed his comfort. Touching her now was innocent. "Your Dad has been gambling with his life for a long time, Marianne. Sure, you could have hidden the keys. I know you did that plenty of times in the past. But what would have happened the next time? And the next? Since he wouldn't get help with his drinking, he would have wound up drunk and in a car sooner or later. And the odds would have still caught up with him. I hate it. I wish he were still here, but this wasn't your fault. I don't think it was ever about you."

She tucked her head under his chin, drawing in a trembling sigh. "I know you're right, Jack, but I can't help thinking I made his drinking worse this summer."

"How?"

"All I've talked about is the job at the paper in D.C., about going away."

"He was proud and excited for you."

"And maybe a little jealous that I was doing what he never could or would."

Jack stepped back, staring down at her. "Do you really believe that?"

"Oh, I don't know." She groaned, burying her face in his chest. "I'm so mixed-up, Jack. About Dad...about lots of things. I don't know what I believe." Her arms crept around him. "I'm just glad you're here. And I'm glad both of us are getting out of this stinking, suffocating town."

Jack gathered her close. But there was guilt in the gesture. For he was suddenly aware of Marianne in ways that were inappropriate for one friend comforting another. Her hair smelled like strawberries. Her breasts pillowed softly against his chest. He felt every breath she took all the way to his toes, and his body stirred and hardened in response.

Ashamed of feeling this way when Marianne needed his friendship, afraid she would soon become all too aware of his arousal, Jack set her gently away from him. "I should go home."

"Please stay," she urged, tugging him back toward the settee. "I promise, I won't cry anymore."

"I don't care if you cry," he said quickly. "I'm not leaving because you cried . . ." He caught himself before he told her the real reason, that being with her made him crazy.

She curled into the end of the settee, hugging a cushion to her stomach. "Let's just sit here and look at the moon. Like we used to do when we were kids."

And like a fool, he stayed. That night. And nearly every night for the next two weeks. In fact, though he had been determined to put as much space between them as possible, he ended up spending every available minute with her. And it wasn't all tears and grief, either. Marianne needed Jack to take her away from her sorrow. To help her laugh again. If Kyle had been there, he might have drawn her out. But he wasn't there. And Jack quite frankly took advantage of his absence. He stole this time with Marianne for himself. Together, they went for drives. For swims at the river. For moonlit walks down the quiet street near Marianne's house.

Jack knew that when she married Kyle, she would be out of his life for good. Oh, she said differently. She said she would call and write, planned how they would visit. But Jack didn't know how long those promises would hold up once she was settled in D.C., being a wife, beginning her career. For the first time since the summer when she was thirteen, they would move out of each other's orbit. Even the year when he was away at school and she was here, they had stayed in close touch. Jack had dated a dozen girls since Marianne became his friend, but not one of them occupied his thoughts the way she did. But now it was ending.

So Jack saved up memories. Crazy memories. The sound of her laughter. The saucy wiggle in her walk. The number of freckles across her nose. As those hot, August days spun past, the two of them drew closer than ever before. Perhaps it was the sobering reality of death. Maybe it was their impending separation. But Marianne seemed to want to be together as much as he did. Unaware of how she disturbed his senses, she touched him, teased him, was all the things she had ever been to him. And yet more. Much more.

It was a dangerous line Jack trod, trying to be her friend but yearning to be her lover.

Sunday night before her wedding, they went for a drive. Deep into the country they went. More than once, Jack started to tell Marianne how he really felt. He wondered what she would do if he just kept driving, if he took her away. On Saturday, Kyle was supposed to carry Marianne off into her dreams. Jack wished he had something to offer her instead. But Marianne was headed to Washington, to a job with a major newspaper, to a life cushioned by Kyle's moneyed background and family connections. Comparing that to Jack's life, with two more years of school and a load of debt, was laughable. Jack had big hopes and little else. He had no reason to think Marianne would welcome a profession of love.

He didn't even know if it was love he felt. What was love? He had seen little of that emotion at home. His parents always seemed too overburdened with debt and responsibilities to be in love. Even Marianne and Kyle didn't appear to love each other the way Jack imagined it should be. They were so calm, so reasonable about their plans and expectations. Jack didn't think either of them burned the way he was burning for Marianne. If Kyle felt this way, surely he never would have left Marianne in Willow Creek for two and half months. If Marianne felt it, then why was it Jack to whom she had brought her tears and her sorrows? Why was she with him now?

He realized his feelings were probably more lust than love, but that didn't make them any easier to sort through.

Head throbbing with questions and doubts, Jack brought Marianne home. And of course they went upstairs, just as they always did. Her wedding dress was hanging in a corner of the sitting room, all pristine and white and virginal. He tried to ignore it, tried to ignore the impulse he had to take Marianne into his arms. He fought long and hard with himself. Even though he drank in her every movement, her every word, drank her in like a man who knew he would soon know drought, he resisted his impulses.

And then, when he was leaving, Marianne hugged him.

It was a simple, familiar gesture. But it was Jack's undoing. In response, he kissed her without thinking, a light touch that quickly grew to be more.

Marianne drew away from him, looked up at him, not really surprised. It was confusion she read in her eyes.

"I'm sorry," he whispered, his words stumbling over themselves. "I didn't mean that . . . I mean, I didn't intend for you to know how I felt . . . how I—"

Her lips silenced his. Her kiss was more curious than passionate, as if she was asking, "What is this?" But passion was the answer she received. It came so quickly, surging between them, rich and strong and too real to be denied.

If Marianne hesitated after that, Jack never remembered it. After that first moment, there was only the taste and feel of her. The two of them kissed and touched and explored. They communicated with whispers, sighs and quickly drawn breaths. Their bodies sang with unspoken emotion, finding a harmony that came from years of knowledge and a split second's worth of changing awareness.

In the bed she had slept in most of her life, Marianne gave Jack her virginity. The fact that she was still innocent said something to him about the tepidness of her relationship with Kyle. But he didn't think about that very much. For there was nothing tepid about the way Marianne moved beneath him, the way she touched him, with a mixture of wonder and delight. When he entered her, she wrapped her legs around him and thrust upward, meeting him, accepting him, with a joy that rang through his soul.

Only later, when they lay side by side in the tangled sheets, did she say the words that cut him to the core.

"What have I done?" she murmured, even as she turned in his arms again. "Oh, Jack, what have I done?"

The words pierced him, ripping the fragile beauty of what had happened between them. For what *had* she done? In six days, her dreams were set to take flight with another man. So what was she doing with Jack? Jack, the friend who knew all of her dreams but couldn't be part of them. Jack, the farmer's son who had nothing to offer but his plans and his passion.

With his heart on fire, he gave her that passion again. With her wedding dress hanging in the next room and another man's ring on her finger, he once more took her body to places he selfishly hoped she would never know again.

Then, while she slept, he drove away with her words pounding in his brain.

"What have I done?"

He went home, showered, tried to wash the smell of her from his body, tried to wipe away all memory of those hateful, hurtful words.

"What have I done?"

He was sure when she awoke, she would know what she had done, what a terrible error she had made. He was certain that the next time he saw her, she would tell him what they had done was a mistake. So he beat her to the punch. That morning, after he was sure Delilah was gone to the paper, he went back to the house and he told Marianne that the mistake was his. While she stood in the front doorway, staring at him with big, tear-drenched eyes, he gathered his pride around him and told her to marry Kyle.

"Go on with your plans," he said, his voice deliberately rough. "What happened last night shouldn't make any difference."

"It does to me," Marianne choked out. "What I did . . . what you did . . ."

"Wasn't something you should let worry you. Kyle needn't ever know."

She put her hands to her mouth. Jack saw that they trembled, but steadfastly ignored it as he turned away.

But she caught his arm, spun him around. "How could you do this?"

He closed his eyes. "It was just a mistake, Marianne. It shouldn't ruin your . . . *our* lives."

"Just a mistake?" she demanded. "That's what you call it?"

"Yes."

She slapped him then. Nice, obedient and kind Marianne Cole slapped him right across his face. But he barely flinched. Red-faced, she yelled at him, too, accusing him of taking advantage of her vulnerability, of using their friendship for something ugly and profane. Tears blurred her words, but he got the message.

And he took all the blame, agreed with her assessment of his actions and motives. Shoulders drooping as though they bore the burden of all she accused him of doing, he turned and walked away. That familiar front sidewalk had never seemed quite so long before. His footsteps had never been dogged with such bitter disappointment.

Five days later he stood across the street from the church where Marianne married Kyle, He stepped behind a tree when they came out in a shower of rice. He watched them drive away. Only then did Jack realize what he had done. He had thrown away his only real dream.

Thinking of Marianne in her white, virginal dress brought Jack out of his memories. The next time he saw her had been four months later. She had come home for Christmas. And she was pregnant. With Laura. With his child.

Yes, *his* child. Jack didn't need any confirmation from Marianne to reach that conclusion. He was privy to all of Marianne's hopes and dreams and plans before she married. He knew she had been ardently opposed to starting a family with Kyle right away. She was so determined about the subject that she took birth control pills for three months after her engagement, sticking with them even though they made her violently ill. Jack had been in her apartment when Kyle finally took the remaining pills and flushed them, promising if she was that emphatic about not wanting children, then he would take the responsibility for making sure there were no babies. Jack could even remember the three year waiting period she and Kyle had agreed upon. But four months after her wedding, she was pregnant.

Jack was positive Marianne's pregnancy was a mistake. *His* mistake. He just couldn't imagine Marianne changing her mind about children or see good old rock-steady Kyle going back on his promise. True, accidents might happen. But Jack's initial, gut reaction was to believe the baby Marianne carried was his. Later, when he heard Laura's birthday from Jeb and Delilah—a date almost exactly nine months after the night he and Marianne made love—Jack thought he had all the proof he wanted. He felt Laura was his, felt it in his heart. And he had believed it ever since.

He surged to his feet, angry as he had been back then. Laura was proof of their passion. Passion Marianne had regretted as surely as she said, "What have I done?"

He paced the length of his deck several times, his memories of nine years ago blurring with thoughts of what had happened between him and Marianne this afternoon. The passion had been there again. Quick and unsubtle. Too hot to deny. No matter what else Marianne had said today, she had not disavowed the heat they generated.

Of course, she had never denied it before. He denied it for her. He had stood on her front porch and told her that what had happened between them meant nothing, eager to say it before she could.

But he realized now why he had felt such disappointment when he left, when she allowed him to walk away. He had gone to her that morning, offering her a way out, but also hoping she wouldn't take it. In some dim corner of his mind, he had wanted her to say their lovemaking did mean something, to say she loved him. He wanted her to fight for him. That had been a foolish, selfish hope, especially since he hadn't been able to say he loved her. He still couldn't say it.

Love was just as elusive to Jack now as it had been then. The years since Marianne had gone away had brought him a few lovers, but no better understanding of true love. He understood physical desire, however. His continuing need for Marianne was proof of how strong that bond could be. She understood that, too. Else how could she have reacted to him as she had this afternoon? And perhaps the bond of passion was enough.

If it weren't, there was also Laura.

A child. And a bone-searing, heartbreak-surviving ache for one another. He and Marianne had more between them than many people ever found. Somehow, he had to make her see that.

For most of his adult life, Jack Dylan had been a man with an empty spot in his life. First, he filled it with school. Then work. But lately the emptiness had been more insistent. He always knew Marianne and her daughter were the missing pieces. He just never believed he could make them fit.

Until now.

Feeling like a man with a new mission in life, he began making plans.

"Mom! Mom, wake up!"

Laura's voice, loud and full of excitement, woke Marianne from a deep, exhausted sleep. It was Saturday morning after her first frustrating week at the paper. Five days after her disturbing interlude with Jack. The fifth morning in a row when all she wanted to do was pull the covers over her head. This time, that's exactly what she did.

"Mom! Get up!"

Growing really irritated, she flung the covers back. And was greeted by a cold, wet nose and a furious meow.

"Can we keep her?" Laura demanded.

Marianne blinked in confusion at a small, gray kitten and at her daughter, who held the squirming mass of fur over the bed. "Where in the world did this come from?" was all Marianne could think to say.

"From me."

With disbelief, Marianne lifted her head to look at Jack, who lounged in the doorway with negligent, confident ease. He wore his customary jeans with a neat, white button-down instead of the usual T-shirt. And he stood there as if he belonged, or had been invited, although she was just about as happy to see him as she had been to dream about him all week. He had some nerve, coming here like this, when she hadn't seen him at all since he sped away from here on Monday night. Not that she wanted to see him, of course, but...

Damn the man, anyway, she thought as he came into the room. Feeling as if she were caught in a Doris Day comedy, she pulled the covers to her chin and croaked, "What are you doing here? What time is it?" Difficult though it was from her horizontal pose, she squinted at the clock.

Laura said. "It's almost ten o'clock. Aunt Delilah said we could wake you up."

"Delilah sent you *and* Jack up here?"

"I came up on my own," he offered without a trace of apology. "I remember what a lazybones you could be on Saturday mornings, and I thought Laura might need a hand."

Groaning, Marianne pulled the covers over her head again. He acted as if they hadn't nearly made love. As if they hadn't prowled around one another for days before that. As if it were the most natural thing in the world for him to be in her bedroom, with her daughter and a cat in tow. Although maybe it was natural. This was Jack, and once upon a time he had been as unpredictable as they came.

To her dismay, she heard his footsteps cross the room. "Come on, Marianne. You know you can't hide under there forever."

Laura flung herself on the bed and bounced up and down. "Yeah, come on, Mom. Quit hiding and come help me name my kitten."

Someone, probably *not* Laura, reached under the covers and tickled the bottom of her foot.

That was enough for Marianne. "Get out!" she yelled, kicking, struggling out from under the sheets, tossing pillows. "Get out of here! Both of you! All three of you!" By the time she emerged from the covers, all she saw were Jack and Laura's retreating backs.

Thirty minutes later, after a calming shower, she crept down the back staircase toward the kitchen. She hoped Jack had regained his senses and left. But he hadn't. He sat at the kitchen table, sipping from a mug of coffee and advising Laura on names for the kitten.

"Who says the kitten's staying?" Marianne muttered as she stalked across the room to the coffeepot.

"Aw, Mom, please. Pretty please." Laura was sprawled on a rug, stroking the kitten, who was curled up in a spot of sunshine. "I really, really want to keep her."

"And I really, really wish Jack had asked me or Delilah before he brought her over," Marianne said.

Delilah, who sat studying a notebook calendar across the table from Jack, looked up with a distracted smile. "It's fine with me if she keeps the kitten, Marianne. I've sort of missed having a cat around since Old Gingersnaps left."

Spreading jelly on a piece of toast, Jack asked, "What happened to Ginger, anyway?"

"She moved on to greener pastures, I guess," Delilah said as she closed the calendar with a sigh. "Maybe we should make this one an indoor cat, not take a chance on her roaming off."

Marianne regarded them all with a frown. "Doesn't anyone care to know if I want this cat?"

"I think you're too grouchy to form a considered opinion," Delilah murmured, flipping through the calendar once again, a frown marring her forehead.

"Grouchy?" Grunting, Marianne sloshed coffee into a mug. "Why should I be grouchy? Just because I was literally dragged from my bed, from the best sleep I've had all week? Is that any reason to be grouchy?" She made a face at Jack's grin over the rim of the mug, but his smile just widened in response. What was wrong with him? she wondered. What was he doing here, acting this way?

"Oh, Mom, just have some coffee," Laura suggested with a very adult blitheness. "Betsy says her mom is always grouchy until she gets a shot or two of caffeine."

"A shot or two of caffeine?" Marianne repeated. After only two brief visits with her new friend, Laura was already quoting Betsy more than the nearly forgotten Alissa Johns. And the things Betsy came up with packed a lot more punch that anything from Alissa.

Laura got up, cradling the kitten in her arms. "I'm naming her Princess, and I'm taking her up to my room to see if she'll fit in my doll bed."

"You'd better take her outside first," Marianne warned, though Laura ignored her. She disappeared upstairs while Marianne sighed in frustration. "I have lost complete control of my daughter since coming home."

"Nonsense," Delilah said. "I find Laura to be a very agreeable child."

"Because you give in to her every whim."

Jack said, "I think—"

"Don't," Marianne cut him off. "Don't you say a word, Mr. Bring - A - Child - A - Pet - Without - Asking - Her - Mother. You should be ashamed."

"It's a nice little kitten," Jack said. "Born out on the farm. I thought it would be good company for Laura until school starts."

"Whereupon it will fall to me to do the feeding and cleaning up after said kitten, who will of course soon become a big cat who sheds on the furniture and leaves surprises on the floor."

Delilah tsk-tsked. "Goodness, Marianne, cats aren't that much trouble at all. You had three or four when you were a child."

But Marianne continued grumbling into her coffee.

"I can't think with this going on," Delilah said, getting up. "And I have to set a wedding date today or Jeb is going to call the whole thing off."

"What's so hard about picking a date?" Jack asked. "Jeb told me just yesterday that he would marry you any day you said. Just pick a weekend."

Delilah tossed him her calendar. "I challenge you to find a Saturday or Sunday that's not already full."

He quickly scanned the pages. "Here's one with nothing big going on. The end of August."

Delilah peered over his shoulder. "That happens to be the kickoff Saturday for the fund-raising drive for the new playground."

"So?"

"I'm in charge of that fund-raiser."

"Delilah—"

"Don't try to reason with her," Marianne said, considerably revived by the caffeine, just as Laura had predicted. "Delilah and I have been going round and round about this wedding date all week long. She insists it has to be on a day that doesn't interfere with any of her committees or clubs or charities."

Jack flipped the calendar shut. "Sounds like cold feet to me."

"That's absurd," Delilah denied. "I've waited over forty years to marry Jeb Hampton."

Marianne poured more coffee. "Then pick a date."

Color stained Delilah's cheeks as she looked from Marianne to Jack. But finally, she snatched up the calendar, seized a pencil and marked off the days. "All right, the last weekend in August, it is. I'll just go call Jeb and tell him the decision is made." Head high, she sailed from the room.

Jack and Marianne's gazes met, their smiles appeared and widened. Together, they said, "Nerves," and laughed easily until Marianne realized how she was beaming at him. Irritated with herself for forgetting to be irritated with him, she turned away, busying herself by buttering two pieces of bread.

He was the first to break the silence. "So. How are you?"

She slid two slices in the toaster oven, but didn't look at him. "It's been a busy week."

"You're settling in?"

"I got Dad's office cleared out and rearranged. It feels more like my own space now, especially since I have my own computer terminal. I'm taking over Delilah's duties, little by little figuring the changes in procedure that she's made since I left."

"Played hooky any more?"

The soft question brought her gaze around to his. Why did he have to mention Monday afternoon? Why couldn't they just pretend it hadn't happened? That's what she had been trying to do all week. She had almost convinced herself that the whole day had been a dream. During a long, sleepless night, she changed her mind about Jack being the real reason she had moved home. She decided she had been in an overly emotional frame of mind when she reached that conclusion. When Jack walked in, she had been overwhelmed with memories of her father and upset about the newspaper's many problems. She now knew that, other than her wishing to have his friendship once more, Jack had nothing to do with her decision to come back to Willow Creek.

As for what happened down by the river... well, she had admitted to the sparks that flew between them. Remembering them accounted for the better part of her sleepness nights this week. But she was well aware of what she had to do. She couldn't let those sparks get out of control again.

Any sexual involvement with Jack would lead straight to complications.

She didn't need any such complications now. She had a crippled newspaper to salvage. And a daughter to raise. Making a better life for Laura was the main reason she had returned to Willow Creek. She didn't need what Jack Dylan offered. Didn't need his soft, sexy drawl. Didn't need his insistent touch. Or his devouring kiss. Didn't need any of it, she told herself firmly.

"No hooky?" he repeated now, green eyes crinkling at the corners.

Damn him for those bedroom eyes, she thought, turning her back on him instead of answering. Doing her best to ignore him, she plucked a peach from the basket of fruit on the counter and moved over to the sink to rinse it.

But Jack got up and followed her, crowded her. "What's wrong? Can't we even talk?"

She struggled not to show how his closeness bothered her as she dried the peach on a paper towel. "Maybe we could if you were talking about anything interesting."

"I can't think of anything more interesting than what happened Monday."

His voice was low and seductive, playing expertly along her nerve endings. "Jack," she said in warning, stepping away from him.

"Haven't you thought about it?"

"Please stop."

He stepped closer. "I've thought about Monday all week."

"What is it you want me to say? I told you how I felt on Monday."

"You were upset then, overwhelmed—"

"And I'm getting upset now. Please just let Monday drop. I've been trying to."

His grin was triumphant. "So you *have* been thinking about it."

She made a soft sound of disgust and jerked her toast from the oven and onto a plate. "There's no way I'm going to get in to this with you again." She lowered her voice, glancing toward the door to the dining room through which Delilah had departed. "I'm not interested in a sexual relationship with you, Jack. Accept that or leave me alone."

His tone dropped to match hers. "You were plenty interested for a little while on Monday."

She wished she had the nerve to shove the peach and the toast right down his throat. But all she could do was glare. "Didn't you hear what I said? I'm telling you now and for the last time, we're not going to discuss this."

He didn't move from where he leaned against the counter. "The more you deny it—"

"I'm not denying anything," she retorted, voice rising. "I admitted to having..." She fumbled for the least descriptive word for her reaction to his kiss and his touch. "I admit to having *feelings*. I admit that I almost lost complete control of those feelings. But it's not happening again. Have you got that?"

"Seems a waste to repress those kinds of *feelings*."

He wasn't taking anything she said seriously. He acted as if this was a game. Some silly male-female thing where she played hard to get and he pursued her with all his might. He should know she didn't play games like that.

"Just shut up," she said. "And go away. I don't remember inviting you here."

"Laura did."

"And when did she do that?"

"I came over and saw her and Mrs. Pervis this week."

"She didn't say anything to me about it."

"It was no big deal."

She frowned in the direction of the staircase. "Laura usually tells me everything."

He looked sheepish. "I did tell her that I was bringing the kitten over. And I might have mentioned that it might be better if it was a surprise."

Rolling her eyes, Marianne carried the toast and fruit to the table. The last thing she wanted to do was sit down here with him, but if she knew Jack, he wasn't about to leave. He was having too good a time, trying to rattle her. Her best defense was to remain as cool as possible. And if she was completely honest, she rather preferred his flirtatious innuendos to the sort of barbs they had traded all last weekend. She had hated seeing him so angry and bitter, so like her father.

She took a seat at the table. "I might have known you would be the one to encourage my daughter to keep things from me."

For a moment Jack's expression sobered. He looked ready to say something, but didn't. He just plucked a peach of his own from the basket and sat down next to her.

She sighed. "Don't you have somewhere else to be?"

"That's not very hospitable of you. And after I gave you a cat."

She smiled with sarcastic sweetness. "I would tell you how grateful I am, but Delilah taught me never to use words like that."

He leaned close. "Oh, come on, let it rip. Let some of those suppressed feelings out, Marianne."

Just smiling in reply, she bit into her peach. Juice rolled down her chin. Before she could reach for a napkin, Jack cupped her face, his thumb wiping the sticky sweetness away. Then he licked that thumb. Calmly. His gaze holding hers. As if there was nothing out of the ordinary about such an intimate, suggestive gesture.

"What's the matter?" he asked after several moments had passed in which Marianne was unable to move. "Peach too ripe? Try mine." He held up the fruit he had selected and put it close to her mouth. "Go on, take a bite."

She stared at him and at the peach and back again. Then she stood, sending her chair crashing to the floor. She was so angry she trembled. Or perhaps she was turned on. She didn't know which emotion applied, and she didn't much care.

"I think you should go," she managed to grind out.

His expression was all innocence. "Leave?"

"Jack—"

"But I was going to ask you out."

His audacity left her sputtering. Marianne didn't know if she had ever sputtered before.

"Actually, this invitation is for you and Laura," he continued. "I want you to come out to the farm tomorrow for a picnic. Then we'll come back into town for the July 4th festival."

"No."

"But, Mom, please." Laura and her kitten stood in the doorway to the dining room.

Marianne wondered briefly how long her daughter might have stood there before she turned to Jack, demanding, "Did you tell her about this before you asked me?"

"I just heard him ask," Laura said, coming into the room. "Can't we go?"

"No, we can't," Marianne replied, her mind racing for an excuse. "Delilah and Jeb were talking about a picnic with them." They hadn't really but that didn't mean Marianne couldn't arrange one.

Laura's face fell. "But I want to go to the farm."

"Jeb and Delilah are invited, too," Jack put in.

"No," Marianne said again, frowning at him. "Not this time."

"But, Mom," Laura said, her eyes welling with tears.

Her daughter's use of such methods to get her way was beginning to irritate Marianne to no end. "Crying won't work, Laura. You know it never works with me."

But Delilah appeared then, demanding to know what was the matter, asking why Marianne was being so obstinate about a simple picnic. Between her questions, Laura's spoiled tears and Jack's smug smile, Marianne felt thoroughly trapped.

Which was probably the reason she ended up in Jack's arms, dancing under a July 4th sky. Dancing, but doing her damnedest not to enjoy it.

GOOD NEWS! You can get up to FIVE GIFTS—FREE!

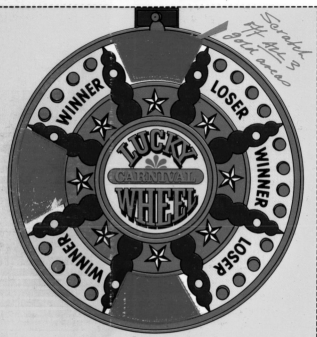

HOW TO PLAY:

1. With a coin, carefully scratch off the 3 gold areas on your Lucky Carnival Wheel. You could get one or more free Silhouette Special Edition® novels and possibly another gift, depending on what is revealed beneath the scratch-off areas.

2. Return your Lucky Carnival Wheel game card, and we'll immediately send you the books and gift you qualify for ABSOLUTELY FREE!

3. Then, unless you tell us otherwise, every month we'll send you 6 additional novels to read and enjoy, months before they're available in stores. You can return them and owe nothing. But if you decide to keep them, you'll pay only $2.71* each—plus 25¢ delivery and applicable sales tax, if any.* That's the complete price, and compared to cover prices of $3.50 each in stores—quite a bargain!

4. Your satisfaction is always guaranteed and you may cancel at any time just by dropping us a note or by returning any shipment at our cost. Of course, the FREE books and gift remain yours to keep!

No Cost! No Risk! No Obligation to Buy!

PLAY THE

LUCKY
CARNIVAL
WHEEL

GAME . . .

GET AS MANY AS FIVE GIFTS FREE!

PLAY FOR FREE! NO PURCHASE NECESSARY!

Chapter Six

The band hired for the July 4th festival's street dance called themselves country. But Jack could hear their rock and roll roots in two hard-driving guitars and a female vocalist who came on like a cross between Janis Joplin and Patsy Cline. They played the sort of music that made hearts pound and bodies move. Even those who weren't dancing were bobbing and swaying.

Jack had pulled a reluctant Marianne into the enthusiastic crowd on the second song, and they hadn't stopped moving since. His face was heated and damp. Her long, white knit top was plastered to her back, as well. But he didn't want to stop. They moved well together, with instinctive rhythm. Spinning and twirling in the humid night air with the rest of the crowd, Marianne looked downright happy.

"Careful," Jack shouted over the music as he swung her around. "Keep smiling like that and people might think you're really my date or something."

She glared and he laughed, just as he had been laughing at her frowns all day.

Since noon, when he had picked up her and Laura for the picnic out at the farm, Marianne had quite carefully informed everyone who would listen that she and Jack weren't really together.

She told Jeb, "Laura begged so hard to go out to the farm that I couldn't refuse."

To Jack's family, she explained, "I just had to come out and see all of you. It's been so long."

To Miss Clara and Miss Louella and everyone else who had greeted them with speculative glances, she said, "Isn't Jack the nicest old *friend*, escorting me and Laura this way?"

Jack wasn't quite sure why she was so determined to make it clear they weren't embarking on any kind of relationship. Unless, of course, it was really herself she was trying to convince.

On the stage set up on the broad courthouse porch, the band brought a particularly energetic song to a close, and the vocalist said, "How about if we slow it down here for a while?"

A cheer went up from the dancers, but Marianne moved away.

Jack took her hand. "Where are you going?"

"I'm hot."

"It's a slow one. You'll cool off."

Though she protested, he kept a firm grip on her hand and hauled her closer. Her back was poker stiff, but he put his cheek against her hair and forced her to move with him. The song's melody was slow and sad, a modern country tune following those classic country themes of loving and losing. The singer put just the right amount of suffering in her voice, and the band proved themselves as adept with a ballad as with a dance beat. Gradually, as the music washed over them with soft, seductive ease, Marianne relaxed and moved with the same grace she had been showing all night.

Jack turned his cheek further into her hair, inhaling her special scent. He told himself not to get too close. What he wanted to do was wrap his arms around her, bury his face in her sweet-smelling hair and move in the intimate, swaying way couples all around them were moving. But he knew Marianne would never submit to that.

Monday night, he had decided to take a new tack with her. Instead of pushing her so hard to confront their painful past, he was determined to take it easy and slow. He would be easy and flirtatious and fun. Nothing too heavy. No earnest talks about their past and future. That would come later. First, he would charm her and woo her and wriggle his way into hers and Laura's lives. His plan was set. And today, he thought it had gone fairly well.

Yesterday, there was that breathless moment when he brushed the peach juice from her face and sucked it off his thumb. This afternoon on the farm, they had stood together watching his brother Brad lead Laura around on a pony, and Marianne forgot her stiff and angry pose. Face glowing with delight at Laura's pleasure, she took his hand and squeezed it. Later, as she bit into his sister-in-law Lainey's fried chicken, she gave him a smile of pure joy. Tonight, at one of the festival's craft tents in the nearby city park, she oohed and ahhed over an intricately carved wooden Santa and told Laura a story about caroling in Jack's old Mustang when they were teenagers. All three of them had laughed together. In perfect harmony, Jack thought.

These moments had been fleeting. Marianne always remembered to pretend to be irritated with him. And that's
when he just grinned. No matter how she tried to disguise
her reactions, he knew his plan was working. He figured a
week or more of this would be all it took.

Only he found it difficult to keep his mind on any plan
with Marianne in his arms this way. Sighing as she moved
against him, he drew them closer together.

"Jack," she protested, stepping back.

"Sorry. It's just such a sad song."

Marianne looked skeptical.

"I'm sorry," he repeated as he brought them together
again. Not too close, of course. Just so her cheek touched
his shoulder. Just so her legging-clad thighs brushed against
his. Sighing again, forgetting the plan once more, his lips
skimmed the top curve of her ear.

This time she pushed out of his arms. And stalked off into
the crowd. He caught her on the sidewalk between the dry
cleaner's and Louella's Diner.

She snatched her arm away from his grasp and hissed,
"Just stop it, Jack."

"We were just dancing."

"I don't want to dance like that with you."

He spread his hands wide. "Like what?"

"Stop this ridiculous game," she retorted. "I know what
you're trying to do."

Through the years Jeb had often told Jack that a smart
attorney, like a gambler, knew when to hold back and when
to lay all of his cards on the table. Jack had learned his les-
sons well. So he dropped the innocent act now with Marianne. Glancing around at the neighbors and friends
gathered on the periphery of the dancers, he drew her toward the front of the diner, where the crowd was thinnest.

He kept his voice low. "I don't see what's wrong with wanting to dance with you that way. I don't know what's wrong with wanting you, period."

"Because I don't—"

He cut off her denial by touching his fingers to her lips. "Don't, Marianne. Don't you dare say you don't want me, too."

The light spilling from the diner window turned her hair into a red gold halo around her head as she looked up at him. Her eyes were wide and blue and troubled, but she made no further attempt at denials. She looked vulnerable and confused, two emotions he could well identify with. Instinctively, without thinking of the people who stood around them, his fingers slipped down to cup her chin and he leaned forward. But she ducked away before he could kiss her.

"Well, hello there," she said brightly to someone behind him.

Jack turned to find Delilah and Jeb giving them a quizzical once-over. Defying that look, he casually draped an arm around Marianne's shoulders. "Hey, you two, I wish you could have made it out to the picnic."

Marianne bore his arm without protest, but her foot came down on his as she added, "Yes, it was a wonderful day. I so enjoyed seeing Jack's father and brother. Laura had a terrific time. I'm glad I decided to go... for her sake."

Pain shot up Jack's leg as she ground her sandal heel into his toes, but he struggled not to show it. "Enjoying the music?" he managed to ask.

"A bit loud for us," Delilah replied. "We're thinking of going home."

"Oh, don't." Marianne eased her torturous pressure on Jack's foot and stepped forward. "Come on, stay with us.

Laura's around here somewhere with Betsy and Sally. We'll watch the fireworks together.''

Jeb and Delilah exchanged glances, and the older man said, rather unconvincingly, "I have a bit of a headache. I think I want to go home. Lie down."

"Well, then, Delilah—"

"Now, Marianne," Jack cut in. "Why don't you just let these young folks go on about their business? I think they have some fireworks of their own on their minds."

Jeb guffawed. Delilah actually giggled. Marianne flushed.

At the risk of further injury to his foot, Jack placed his arm around her again. "I'm sure we'll find something to occupy us until the fireworks start."

The quizzical look reappeared on Jeb and Delilah's faces as they said goodbye and slipped through the crowd. Once they were out of sight, Marianne rounded on Jack again, shrugging out from under his arm.

"What is wrong with you?"

"Me? You almost broke my foot."

"I should have. The way you're acting is going to have everyone in town talking about us."

"So?"

"So I have a business to run."

He frowned. "Why would what happens between us have any effect on the paper?"

"You know small-town minds."

"It's not like we're committing adultery or anything."

"But do you know how many times this week I've been referred to as Delilah's niece or Elliot's little girl? It's difficult to do business with people who don't see you as a businessperson."

"That'll pass."

"Maybe so. But if you keep up this ridiculous act of yours, everyone's going to be calling me Jack Dylan's lover."

Indignation sparked in him at her scathing tone. "Would that be the end of the world?"

"I'm trying to be taken seriously around here."

"And being associated with me means you won't? I'm not some hayseed—"

"Don't you dare try to make me out as a snob again, Jack," Marianne interrupted, her eyes flashing. "You know I'm nothing of the sort, and I resent you continuing to accuse me of it. All I'm saying is that I have enough to contend with without a bunch of gossip about me right now. And aside from the paper I'm trying to revive, what if Laura heard something, started asking questions?"

"Would that be so bad?" Jack demanded.

"She's eight years old," Marianne retorted. "And she still misses her father. I don't think she's ready to start hearing about her mother and some other man."

His eyebrows drew together. "I don't think I'm just any man to Laura."

"I know she likes you, Jack, but—"

"But what?" Her pretense at not understanding his meaning tipped his irritation into out-and-out fury. With a muttered curse, he gripped her shoulders. "Why don't we cut out the lies? Let's be truthful for once and for all. I don't care what you tell Laura right now about me. She *is* just eight years old, like you said. But between you and me, let's have some truth for a change instead of this game you play."

Marianne just stared up at him with a puzzled frown. "What game are you talking about?"

He glanced around. A crowded street full of interested ears was no place for this discussion. "You know what I'm saying," he muttered.

"You're talking in riddles."

"God, Marianne, have you avoided the truth so long that you believe your own lies?"

She twisted out of his grasp. "All I'm interested in avoiding is you." She backed away. "I want you to leave me and Laura alone."

Furious now, he once more drew her back. "Don't give me orders, Marianne. I'll gladly leave you alone if that's what you really want, although I don't think it is. But I'll see Laura if I want to."

"Why? To use her to get to me, the same as you did yesterday and today? No, Jack, I want you to leave her alone, too."

He fought an urge to shake her and settled for gripping her hand tightly between his. "I'm not using Laura. Can you make the same claim for yourself?"

She snatched her hand away. "You're not making one bit of sense, Jack, and I'm tired of listening to you. I'm finding my daughter and going home."

This time, she disappeared in the crowd too quickly for Jack to catch her. He didn't really try. He was so angry that staying with her much longer, especially in a public place, was dangerous. He was liable to say more than he should.

So much for the plan, for keeping it light and flirtatious between us, he thought as he strode away. He should have known it wouldn't work. Nothing between him and Marianne could ever be that simple.

He moved down the street, barely nodding at the many greetings tossed his way. He didn't feel like being pleasant or chatting neighborly. He stopped on the corner, surveying the crowd pouring into downtown for the upcoming fireworks show. These people represented all walks of life. Businessmen, farmers, and factory workers. Senior citizens, teenagers and toddlers. This was one of the biggest nights of the year in Willow Creek, had been so, long before the July 4th when Jack had set off the rockets early. Remembering that night only made him think of Marianne, made him frown deeply.

But then he saw a familiar face in the crowd.

A face that wiped all thoughts of Marianne away.

Marianne made her way slowly down the sidewalk, doing her best to ignore the curious glances thrown in her direction. *Damn Jack, anyway.* He had been acting like a fool ever since yesterday. Flirting with her. Touching her. Dancing that way with her. And he had been using Laura, no matter how he denied it. Well, that was going to end. Laura already thought him thoroughly terrific. She would be disappointed when he stopped coming around, when there were no more trips to the farm as the two of them had planned today. But that was the way it had to be. This silly game Jack had been playing was over.

Marianne just wished she understood what he had said to her. He accused her of using her own daughter. But to what end? And what truth was he pushing for? She had admitted to being attracted to him. More than admitted. She had almost made impulsive, irresponsible love with him. And she had told him with candid, open honesty that she didn't feel she could handle the consequences if she gave in to those impulses. Couldn't he accept that? They were two adults. They should be able to keep things under control. In time, when they conquered that mutual attraction, perhaps their old comradeship would return. After all, it wasn't as if Marianne was the only available woman in town. Judging from the glances sent Jack's way this evening, there were lots of females willing to be more than friends with him.

Ignoring the jealous surge such thoughts sent through her, Marianne continued moving through the jammed street, on the lookout for her daughter and friends. She wanted to go home. The music, so pleasant only moments ago, was giving her a headache now. Jack's puzzling accusations were eating away at her, too. She wanted to get away from the acquaintances she felt compelled to greet with a smile.

Sally appeared at her elbow just as Marianne was about to make a second trip around the town's central square. "Have you seen the girls?" the other woman demanded breathlessly.

"I thought they were with you."

Sally wiped a trickle of perspiration from her cheek. "Betsy wanted to go back to the craft booths to induce me to buy an expensive lace hair bow I had already refused to get. We had our usual tussle about it, then we were standing, talking to friends, and I looked around and she and Laura were gone. I figured she went back to the booth. But no one there has seen either girl." She looked near tears. "I've looked everywhere. I don't know where they could be."

"I'm sure they're fine," Marianne soothed, not worried at all. She refused to believe anything bad could happen to two little girls in Willow Creek.

But Sally was frantic. "You don't understand. I can't let Betsy out of my sight."

"But why?" Marianne said, picking up on the woman's tangible panic and fear. "What's wrong with Betsy?"

"It's not that...it's..." Sally broke off. "Oh, hell, Marianne, it's too complicated to waste time on explanations. Let's just find them. *Now.*"

They struck off in opposite directions, Marianne moving toward the stage, where she planned to have someone make an announcement before the fireworks started. She was certain Laura and Betsy or someone who knew them would hear, and the girls could meet her up by the stage. Before she could get through the crowd, however, rockets began exploding overhead. Recorded music blared an accompaniment from the public address system, and her progress was slowed considerably by the crush of people near the courthouse square. Knowing there would be little chance of an announcement until the show ended, Marianne concentrated on scanning the crowd for the two small girls. She was sure Sally was alarmed for no reason.

It wasn't until she surveyed the myriad faces around her, so many of them unfamiliar, that Marianne felt the first pinprick of fear. She didn't know these people. How could she be certain one of them wasn't some sort of child molester? Monsters like that could exist anywhere, just waiting to take advantage of two lost little girls.

Where *was* Laura? She was a city-reared child. She knew better than to wander off by herself, even if Betsy didn't. There were no guarantees against tragedy just because this was a small-town, all-American July 4th celebration.

Rapidly becoming as frantic as Sally, Marianne pushed her way through the crowd, ignoring the irritation of those around her. "I've lost my daughter," she shouted again and again. "I've lost my little girl and her friend. Have you seen two little girls wandering around by themselves?"

People reacted with concern, but no one had seen Laura or Betsy. Tears of frustration filled Marianne's eyes. She blinked them away, trying to remain calm.

Taking pity on her, a young father passed his own small son to his wife. "Come on," he told Marianne. "Let's get up there and have them make an announcement."

"The show—"

"Doesn't matter. Let's find your kid."

But before they could move, the music ended abruptly and Marianne and Sally's names were called from the stage. Fireworks still exploded overhead, but the show's emcee asked for the two women to come forward and claim their lost daughters.

Marianne moved rapidly through the crowd as the music resumed. Looking up, she could see Jack coming down the steps of the courthouse. He was carrying Laura, her legs hooked around his waist and her head on his shoulder, while Betsy clung to one of his jeans' pockets. His gaze met Marianne's across the heads of the people who separated them, and he turned to say something to Laura.

She looked up, saw Marianne, too, and screamed, "Mom," loud enough to be heard over the noise of the music and the crowd.

Marianne ran the last few steps that separated them when she saw the tears streaming down her daughter's face. But her anxiety wasn't over. For, as Laura moved from Jack's arms to her mother's, Laura choked out, "There was a man, Mom. He chased us."

Beside Jack, Betsy began to cry, as well.

Stroking Laura's hair and murmuring words of comfort, Marianne stared at Jack in shock, hoping he was going to say it wasn't true. Then Sally pushed past her and grabbed Betsy, who repeated what Laura had said.

Jack bent his head to Sally, and in a temporary lull in the patriotic fanfare of music, Marianne thought she heard him shout, "Renee is here. I saw her."

And Sally's face drained of all color.

Marianne lifted a ceramic pot and poured a third cup of herb tea for Sally, who sat on the couch in Delilah's parlor. "Drink this. You're still white as a ghost."

The cup rattled in the saucer as the other woman accepted it. Marianne placed a comforting hand on her shoulder.

A sheriff's deputy, Webb Forrester, a square-jawed, ex-football star who had attended high school with all of them, was perched on a chair across the room, flipping through a notepad. "Is there anything else you can tell us?"

Jack turned from the front window. "I don't think so. Like I said, I thought I saw Renee in the crowd—"

"Thought?" Webb repeated. "Earlier you said you did in fact see her."

"I saw her. I know it was her."

"You're *sure* it was Renee?"

"If it wasn't Renee, she has a twin."

"But by your own admission, it's been a while since you had any contact with her."

"Webb, I'm nearly positive it was her," Jack said, an edge of irritation in his voice. "I saw Renee, tried to follow her, but the crowd was too thick. Eventually, I ended up behind one of the craft booth tents over in the park. That's when I saw the girls running across the grass."

"And someone was chasing them?"

Jack's forehead creased in concentration. "It was dark. I thought I saw a shadow in the trees behind them, but I can't say I'm sure. The place was pretty deserted since most everyone had moved to the square for the fireworks show. My main concern was for the girls. I called out and they ran toward me."

Webb stroked his chin thoughtfully. "They didn't say anything about seeing a woman."

"Renee has a husband," Sally said. "He's come with her every time she's shown up to talk to me about taking Betsy back."

Webb flipped back through his notebook again and read aloud the description Sally had already given of Carl Phelps, Renee's husband. "This doesn't sound anything like the man the girls described."

Marianne sighed. "The girls were so frightened, Webb. And it was nearly dark. I don't know if they can give you a good description." Laura and Betsy had said a man came up to them out in the center of the park where they were eating an ice-cream cone. They said he was friendly at first, but the more he talked the "creepier" he made Laura feel. Marianne had taught her to run away from strangers, especially those who made her uncomfortable. So she grabbed Betsy's hand and they ran through the trees near where the craft tents had been set up. And the man chased them. Marianne swallowed hard at the thought. The idea of someone chasing her daughter still terrified her.

The deputy shook his head. "You'd be surprised how accurately kids can remember faces, Marianne. But just because this doesn't sound like Renee's husband, doesn't mean she wasn't involved. And that sounds possible, especially since Sally has reason to think Betsy's mother—"

"I'm her mother," Sally cut in. "Renee gave up all claim to her years ago."

"Sorry," Webb murmured. "Since Renee has threatened a custody suit—something she must know won't be easy since she gave Betsy willingly up for adoption—it's not impossible that she would try to snatch the child instead. Sally, has Renee ever come right out and said she was going to take Betsy?"

"No, but I've thought she might."

"There's a restraining order in effect against Renee right now," Jack said. "Sally reported Renee and her husband coming to her business and harassing her on at least three occasions."

"That order would help if Renee had gone near the child." Webb shook his head, looking frustrated. "But right now, since Jack didn't see the man, and the girls can't give us any description that links Renee or her husband to the incident, and since there's been no out-and-out threat to take Betsy, I don't see that we can do much more than call up Renee and ask a few questions."

"She'll lie," Sally said. "I'm sure she's on the road back to Nashville right now, planning her lies. You should call her now, before she gets home. Then you can ask her to prove where she's been."

Webb got to his feet. "Be assured that we will contact her, Sally. But you should also be aware that this man could have had nothing to do with Renee. He could be your standard, garden-variety weirdo."

An unknown deviant lurking out Willow Creek's city park frightened Marianne even more. She'd moved away from D.C. in order to avoid this sort of thing. She made a silent note to do a story on the subject of child molesters in an upcoming issue of the paper.

"I'd suggest you keep your daughters close by for the next little bit," Webb said, pulling on his hat. "We'll keep our eyes open, too. Please call us if you see anyone suspicious again."

Marianne saw him to the door, returning to a room where silence reigned. Jack stood looking out the window again, while Sally sat, staring down at her teacup.

At the fireworks display, all any of them had wanted to do was get the girls to a quiet and safe place. They had come here because it was closest. And Jack had called the sheriff's office, while Sally and Marianne calmed their daughters. The deputy had arrived at the same time as Delilah and Jeb, who now had both girls out in the kitchen, doling out leftover peach ice cream. Webb had questioned the girls first. It was during his talk with Jack and Sally that Marianne had learned the truth about Betsy's parentage and about the situation Sally was facing in regard to her sister.

Now Sally placed her cup and saucer very carefully on the wooden tray Marianne had set on the oval coffee table. "I'm sorry, Marianne. I'd do anything if this hadn't happened to Laura. Betsy usually knows better than to run off like that." She sighed. "And I usually don't let her get away from me, either."

"They can slip away pretty fast," Marianne said, crossing the room to sit down beside Sally. "You couldn't have known Renee would turn up tonight or would try to pull a stunt like this."

Sally's pretty mouth twisted into a bitter line. "I knew she would come," she whispered. "I just didn't know when." She put a hand over her face, but she didn't cry. In fact, though she trembled and was pale, she had been oddly calm ever since they arrived at the house.

Marianne's heart turned over for the other woman, but she didn't know of any words that would offer real comfort. What Sally was facing was truly terrifying.

Taking a deep breath, Sally raised her head and got up from the couch. "We should go home and let you put Laura to bed."

Marianne rose, too. "I think you and Betsy should stay here. A sleepover will help take both girls' minds off of that man. And surely you will feel safer here with us."

"I couldn't impose on you any more than I have already."

Jack left his post by the window. "You should stay, Sally."

It took a few minutes, but between the two of them, they managed to persuade Sally that this was the best place for she and Betsy for the night.

She went out to the kitchen to tell the girls while Jack and Marianne stood, just looking at each other. Somehow, the angry words they had traded earlier that evening seemed trivial in comparison to all that had happened since.

After several uncomfortable moments, he cleared his throat and moved toward the foyer. "I should go home."

She didn't try to stop him, although she really didn't want him to leave. What could she say? That even though she'd ordered him to leave her alone earlier tonight, she now wanted his company?

At the front door, he stopped. "Are you sure you'll be okay here tonight?"

"Don't worry. I bet the girls will be out like lights pretty soon. We'll bolt the doors and the windows."

They stepped out on the porch and down the steps, and even though the night was muggy, Marianne shivered as she looked up and down the dimly lit street.

"What's wrong?" Jack asked.

"It doesn't feel as safe as it did this afternoon."

"I'm sure this wasn't some unknown pervert. It was Renee I saw, and from what Sally has said, this is the sort of stunt she and her husband might pull."

"How can someone that unbalanced hope to regain custody of Betsy?"

"Who knows what goes through a mind like hers."

Behind them came the sound of running footsteps, and they turned as the screen door flew open. Hair streaming behind her, Laura bounced out on the porch, calling Jack's name. Marianne's heart jumped into overdrive. Jack dropped to one knee and caught Laura, holding her at arm's length while he demanded, "What is it? What's wrong?"

"Weren't you going to say goodbye?" was Laura's comeback.

Marianne's pulse regained its normal speed while Jack's shoulders slumped in relief.

He ruffled Laura's hair. "I thought you were too busy scarfing down ice cream for goodbyes."

"But I had to say goodbye. You saved my life." With the same melodramatic flair she had been exhibiting of late, Laura flung herself into his arms before he could say a word.

Jack hugged her back. Hard. In the light from the porch, Marianne saw his eyes close, saw the fierce look of love that settled on his features. Yes, she realized with surprise, *love*. She couldn't mistake his expression for anything else, and that look set her pulse pounding once more. Jack's dark hair pressed so close to her daughter's tangled, red-gold curls brought a lump to her throat and an overwhelming yearning for impossible might-have-beens.

Marianne thought his smile trembled as he set Laura away from him. His fingers were gentle as they slipped down Laura's arms and grasped her hands. "I didn't save you, honey. You were smart enough to run away when you got scared. I'm mighty proud of you for that."

"Mom taught me that." With one hand still in his, Laura reached out to her mother with the other. Marianne's fingers closed around hers, and Laura beamed up at the two adults she linked.

Marianne looked from her daughter's earnest, sweet face to Jack's. He was looking at her daughter with hungry, heartbreakingly tender eyes. By virtue of that look, Marianne felt as though she glimpsed a hidden corner of his heart. But she wondered what it meant. What did Jack really see when he looked at her daughter? What was it he wanted?

"Go to bed," he said, dropping Laura's hand to touch her hair once again.

Grinning now, as if she hadn't been in terrified tears only an hour before, she skipped up the stairs, but turned back once more. "I'm going to show Betsy the moon from my porch, just like you told me to. It's not so big tonight, though."

The moon from her porch. How well Marianne remembered looking at that same moon and dreaming aloud with Jack on dozens of summer nights just like this. She looked at him now, wondering when he and her daughter had discussed the moon.

Jack gave Laura a final salute. "Sleep tight."

Calling for Betsy, Laura ran back inside.

"Phone if you need anything," Jack said, and started to turn away.

On impulse, Marianne called out his name. He stopped. And before she could allow herself to hesitate, she closed the space between them, murmuring "Thank you" before she kissed him. It was meant as a simple, grateful kiss, but it surprised Marianne by becoming much more powerful, much more meaningful, although she couldn't for the life of her say what that meaning was. Jack looked about as startled by the kiss as Marianne felt.

He was still standing on the sidewalk when she ran indoors. She was running from her feelings as much as from him.

Chapter Seven

Like a lid closing over a pot of boiling water, July hunkered down on Willow Creek in its usual fashion. The days were given three descriptions by the residents—hot, fiery hot and downright sweltering.

But there was nothing new in the weather. Nothing unusual in the bumper crop of corn, or the zucchini and tomato pie Miss Louella added to the diner's menu. Nothing novel in the after-the-4th sales held in the recently built strip mall out by the interstate. Nobody was even surprised when Sally Jane Haskins's no-good sister filed for custody of little Betsy. Nothing that happened to Sally had surprised anyone in years. And even the coupling of Jebediah Hampton and Delilah Cole lost its impact. Theirs was an old scandal. No, the only fresh development in town centered around Jack Dylan and Marianne Cole Wingate.

Jack felt the speculation. It was a tickle on the back of his neck, a faint ringing in his ear, a taste in his mouth. He felt it when he sat down beside Marianne and Laura at a Dixie Youth baseball game. He heard it coming in waves from the neighbors' houses when Marianne and Laura stopped by his place one night. He swallowed it along with his coffee and pie every time he had lunch at the diner.

Along about the fifteenth of the month, he toyed with the idea of renting a billboard near the town's busiest intersection, over by the Wal-Mart, so he could be certain few people would miss it. In big, bold letters, he wanted to write, Folks, When You Figure Out What's Happening, Let Me Know!

Since the night of the festival, there had been a definite warming in his relationship with Marianne. Not a genuine heating up, mind you. Just a certain . . . reluctant acceptance. She had obviously forgotten that she told him to stay away from her and Laura. But she had also apparently set aside all memory of their necking session down on the river. And as for that sweet, eloquent kiss she had given him on the night of the 4th, *that* had passed into the same oblivion she had established for their more distant past. The boundaries of what they could and couldn't discuss were unspoken and yet clear. The ground rules for what they would and wouldn't do were even more distinct. Jack accepted them without argument.

Of course, it helped matters that he no longer wanted to talk about certain aspects of their past. At least not right now. He figured if he had lived without Marianne's revelations concerning Laura's paternity for nine years, a little more time wouldn't hurt. "The truth would out itself in time," as his mother used to say. And the passing of that time was now made sweeter by Laura's presence in his life.

He wondered how he had lived all these years with his daughter in the world and yet unknown to him. If Jack had it to do over, he would storm the Georgetown home where

Marianne and Kyle and Laura had lived as a family. He would claim the child he had fathered. But the past, as he had been telling himself since the first day Marianne came home, was gone. For now there was just July, a warm, full month of discoveries about a little girl who shared his gene pool and had claimed his heart simply by virtue of who she was.

As for that other matter, that nagging, lingering attraction that ran between himself and Marianne, Jack did what he could to ignore it. He certainly didn't play any more games; he formulated no more grand plans for making her accept the logical and no doubt satisfying outcome of such a strong, mutual affinity.

But he was only human. And it wasn't easy to ignore what was so obvious. So, he stood just a little too close to Marianne after Sunday dinner at Delilah's, so close he unintentionally breathed in her perfume, became unintentionally hard. Had to go to the office. Bury himself in some dry law books. Had to jog around the block when that didn't work.

But a few days later he lingered on the steps of the courthouse and watched Marianne's progress down Main Street. He admired the way the sun shone through her thin, cotton dress and highlighted the ripe curves of her woman's body. After that particular, forgetful moment, he had to go in the men's room and throw cold water on his face. He was late for court, was chastised by the judge, but felt it was damn well worth it.

And on the evenings that he dropped by to see Laura on one feeble excuse or the other, he almost always allowed himself to be drawn into an intense conversation with Marianne. She talked about business problems, and he offered advice. Or he talked about politics, and she offered opinions. Or they both talked about, or rather argued about subjects ranging from Atlanta Braves baseball to the correct way to brew a pitcher of iced tea. The results of those discussions were the same as that assailing him when he stood too close or watched her walk down the street. It was small comfort to know her mind turned him on as much as her body. He supposed that made him a modern, sensitive male. It also left him—as he and his high school buddies used to so sensitively put it—hornier than hell.

The best solution was to stay away. But that meant staying away from Laura. And he had done enough of that already.

Laura couldn't help but draw them together. If she went to the Dairy Bar with Jack, she usually wanted her mother along. Or when she cajoled Marianne into renting a movie, she invited Jack to join them. Those nights, she sat between them on the couch, a big bowl of buttered popcorn in her lap for all of them to share. Or she fell asleep before the movie was over, her head in Marianne's lap, her feet tucked under Jack's hip. He thought he could spend a couple of years just watching her sleep. He had missed so much. But strangely enough, he was no longer angry with Marianne about what he had missed. He just wanted to be part of the future.

When he was being really honest with himself, he admitted that the hoped-for future included the mother, as well as the child. That's why he made every excuse he could to be with them, both of them. And in the process provided fuel for the Willow Creek gossips.

Many nights after he came home, Jack sat out back, imagining phones ringing across town, folks reporting to one another on the moves he and Marianne had made that day. He could hear them asking, "What do you think's really going on between those two?"

Not nearly enough, Jack wanted to shout from the rooftops. Not nearly enough.

* * *

On what the locals would a call a sweltering day in early August, Marianne sat at her desk, giving desultory attention to the editorial she was writing for the Friday edition. Since the paper's editor-in-chief had left last winter, Delilah had written these columns. But since Marianne was now officially at the helm, it was time she started making her mark.

Marianne had been looking forward to this moment, but now the words weren't coming. Perhaps it was the heat, or perhaps she had spent too little time on writing and too much time on the business side of the paper of late, but her mind felt as if it were clogged with cotton. Frowning, she lifted her face to the cooling breeze generated by the fan mounted on the wall above the door.

"Francine?" she called to the secretary who sat outside her door. "Do you know if that air conditioner repairman is ever going to come check our system?"

The woman rolled her chair backward until she was framed in the doorway. "He came yesterday. He said everything was fine."

"But I'm melting in here."

"Well, it always seems hotter in your office than anywhere else. It always has. That's why your father had that fan installed."

"Francine, don't you think there's something wrong about a air-conditioning system that cools every room in the building save one?"

"You want me to call that repairman back?"

Marianne sighed. "Yes, call him back. And this time tell me when he comes."

"I would have told you before, but you had gone out with Jack."

Blinking at the woman's choice of words, Marianne repeated, "Out with Jack?"

"For a meeting, I think you said."

"Yes," Marianne replied evenly. "That *is* what I said. Jack is the paper's attorney. We had a meeting yesterday."

Perhaps it was a trick of the midafternoon sun coming through the newspaper's front windows, but it seemed to Marianne that Francine's mouth lifted slightly at the right corner. "Yes, I know. That's what I said."

"No, you said..." Realizing the futility of what she was trying to prove, Marianne let her words trail away. Francine had said she was out with Jack, not that she was in a meeting with him. The two statements had very different meanings. But if she tried to explain them now to Francine, she would exacerbate what was already a problematic situation. So Marianne just summoned a polite smile. "Please call the repairman again, Francine, thank you."

The woman rolled her chair back into place, and Marianne heard her punching numbers into the telephone. Francine Newberry had been working at the *Oxford County News* for nineteen years. She was efficient on the phone and a whiz of a typist. But she also remembered when Marianne wore braces, a fact she liked to recall every chance she could. It was that familiarity, which probably accounted for her easygoing manner and her apparent inability to regard Marianne with a modicum of seriousness. And Francine wasn't alone.

That attitude was what Marianne had been laboring under for more than a month now. She had hoped it would get better, but it was getting worse. Her prediction had come true. On top of seeing her only as Delilah's niece and Elliot's daughter, everyone in town thought she was having some hot, flaming affair with Jack.

Oh, no one, not even Delilah or Jeb, said a word about it. But Marianne could tell what everyone was thinking. It was in the way Francine said she was "out" with Jack. It was a raised eyebrow when she and Laura happened to meet him at the supermarket. Or the way people had appeared in store doorways along Main Street when she walked over to Jack's office yesterday afternoon.

She was well aware that she could end the speculation and gossip by not seeing so much of Jack. Three and half weeks ago, she had intended to do just that. Even after the 4th, after kissing him and running from what he stirred inside her, she told herself to just stay away from him. But that hadn't worked. Laura wouldn't have it.

Laura had turned Jack into her hero. Marianne couldn't object, since he made her daughter laugh in a way Marianne hadn't heard since before Kyle died. Laura's petulance and her complaints about moving to Willow Creek were gone. Betsy had helped ease the transition. But it was Jack who had sealed the deal. He had convinced Laura there was magic in simply gazing at the moon. He made her see adventure in capturing lightning bugs in a jar. He demonstrated there was more fun in a Dixie Youth ball game than an afternoon at some big-city mall. Jack had revealed to Laura all that was good about living here. He did so with such enthusiasm that Marianne wondered when he had started loving those things he once had scorned.

What had happened to his dreams? she wondered now as she tilted her face up to the fan once more. When she left Willow Creek, he was headed back to school with plans for a career in international law, a career much like Kyle's. He went back to school, but he stayed here instead of pursuing the dream they had discussed so many times. And on the night of her coming home party, he told her he liked what he did. He said he liked his life, was happy.

But Marianne wasn't sure she believed him. From that very first day, she had sensed a restlessness in him. If his life here was so good, why after five years, hadn't he unpacked all the boxes in his house? True, she had only seen his living room for a brief moment or two when Laura induced her to take him a piece of buttermilk pie. But that house didn't have the feel of a real home. His Spartan bachelor quarters raised even more questions in Marianne's mind. Jack's relationships with Betsy and with Laura proved he liked children. Why hadn't he married, had a couple of kids? And with a mind as quick and agile as his, why did he settle for a straightforward general law practice in a small town?

Perhaps he had found it easier to remain in a familiar world than to branch out. It was true that Jack had a keen understanding of the people here. He had already given Marianne more on-target advice about running the paper than either Jeb or Delilah. But Marianne's father had understood this town, too. At Jack's age, maybe Elliot Cole had thought he was happy. Maybe the anger and the bitterness had come later.

"Just stop it," Marianne told herself. She focused on her computer terminal once more, trying to clear all thoughts of Jack from her head. She was marginally successful for almost fifteen minutes. Until Lolly Kingston showed up.

Lolly, who was a few years younger than Delilah, ran the Town and Country Dress Shop. For nearly half a century, Lolly and her mother before her had been clothing Willow Creek's more affluent women. And today, as was usual, Lolly was dressed in a manner that exemplified her current stock. Her pleated linen skirt was gray, her soft crepe blouse gray and lavender, her shoes and stockings bone. She looked cool and efficient as she took a chair in front of the desk, and she made Marianne feel warm and wilted in her own blue cotton blouse and skirt.

"I'm not trying to cause any fuss," Lolly began.

Marianne knew immediately that a fuss was exactly what she was after. Saying one thing and yet meaning the complete opposite was something she knew to be a Willow Creek trait.

Lolly touched the triple row of Barbara Bush pearls at her throat as if for reassurance. "I mean, I know you're still just settling in here, Marianne, just getting used to being back home. And I don't like complaining. I tried to see Delilah, but I understand she's only here a couple of days a week now."

Marianne straightened her shoulders. "She is retiring, you know."

"Yes, and you're taking over." Again, the words stated a fact, but there was disapproval and perhaps a faint edge of disbelief in her tone.

"Is there a problem with something, Mrs. . . ." Marianne caught herself, changed her address to just "Lolly." Because she had grown up calling her Mrs. Kingston didn't mean she had to continue. They were both businesswomen now, on the same level.

"Yes, Marianne, I'm afraid there might be a bit of a complication." Lolly thrust an envelope forward. "It's this past due notice. I don't understand it."

Politely, Marianne took the envelope and examined the bill. The Town and Country Dress Shop was three months in arrears. "Are the figures wrong?" She knew they weren't, but there was no sense irritating the woman even more.

"No. But we've never received a notice like this from you all before."

"We're instituting some changes in billing procedures," Marianne explained. "You see?" She held up the note that had been attached to Lolly's bill. "We explained the change in this letter."

"Yes, I read your note," Lolly said, making it sound as if Marianne had penned some scurrilous missive.

Nothing could be further from the truth, Marianne thought. Upon examining the newspaper's books, she had discovered some significant monies outstanding in the accounts receivables column. It seemed there were some accounts who paid their bills just any old time. Even Delilah, who had handled most of the advertising for as long as she could remember, wasn't sure why those clients paid as they did. Her only explanation had been, "That's the way we've always done it." Marianne, who had hired an eager young salesman to take over that aspect of the business, wanted such practices cleaned up. The bookkeeper and Delilah and Jack had cautioned Marianne about making too many waves too fast. So Marianne had composed a polite little note about prompt payments, which was to be included in the first batch of past due notices. Those notices had gone out in the mail yesterday.

"Lolly, I didn't intend my note to upset you."

"Oh, I'm not upset."

That meant she was really angry, Marianne knew. She tried to soothe the situation. "When I looked at the books and saw that the dress shop was behind, I thought there was mistake, that you just needed a little reminder—"

"But we're not behind," Lolly interrupted. "We have never failed to pay our bills. My family has never been that kind."

"I didn't mean to imply—"

"For as long as I can remember, we have paid our advertising bills every four months. Three times a year, on the button, I write you all a check. We handle it the same way with the radio station. And until now we've always done it here. You can look it up in your books, I'm sure."

Too many of those 120-day-cycled accounts was one of the reasons the newspaper suffered from a cash flow problem. Keeping her smile in place, Marianne tried to explain. "It would just help matters here, in our bookkeeping system, if we could expect payment each month."

"But that's not how I make my budgetary plans, Marianne, dear," Lolly retorted sweetly. "Mother set up the schedule years ago. It has to do with when our major shipments of stock come in, when the insurance is due—that sort of thing."

Marianne started to say that Lolly's budget wasn't her problem, that the newspaper had bills and insurance premiums to meet, as well. But she bit back the words just in time. The Town and Country Dress Shop might not be the biggest advertiser they had, but they were steady. It wouldn't do to tick Lolly off.

The other woman stood up, startling Marianne. She hadn't thought their conversation was near an end. But Lolly did. "So I'll just forget that." She pointed at the bill Marianne still held.

"Well—"

"And you can expect a check at the first of September."

"Yes, but—"

"I just knew if I came over here and explained things, you would understand." She turned to go while Marianne was still grappling with a way to make some sort of an objection.

Lolly then paused in the doorway, as if struck by inspiration. "Marianne, we have some lovely summer things still left and they're on sale."

All Marianne could manage was a weak, "You do?"

A beatific smile wreathed Lolly's face as she tipped her head to the side and studied Marianne. "In fact, I think there's a peach-colored, polished cotton in your size that would look just darling with your hair and eyes."

"Is there?"

"You could wear it to the country club dance next weekend. You know we always keep things casual at the club in the summer. You and Jack are coming to the dance, aren't you?"

"Jack?" Marianne repeated. She wasn't sure whether she was irritated by the woman's assumption or relieved that someone had actually coupled their names out loud. "Jack and me?"

Lolly's laughter was a delighted trill. "My goodness, Marianne, dear, don't look so surprised. You know how dress shops are. Everybody comes in, talking about this and that and what's happening. Miss Louella told me you and Jack were seeing each other."

"Did she?"

"And I saw you and your little girl with him at my grandson's ball game. Don't you remember? You and I talked."

Marianne didn't remember, but that was no surprise. She had spent most of that game trying to ignore Jack's smile, Jack's clean-cut profile, Jack's effect on her senses.

"Now don't forget to stop in and try on that dress," Lolly said, wiggling her well-manicured nails in goodbye as she backed out of the door. "It's forty percent off, so someone else could snap it up."

Then she was gone, leaving Marianne to try and assimilate everything that had transpired. There was little time for that before the phone rang.

It was Milton Lonas from the Farmer's Co-op, explaining that his was a seasonal business. In the next few months, as the crops continued to come in, the farmers would be paying him, and he would get current with all his bills. He said this was something Delilah had always understood.

Marianne had barely hung up when Frank Harvey from the hardware store stopped by. "To pay my bill in person," he said with a little sniff. He had a big end-of-the-summer sale coming up and he didn't want to take a chance on the paper not running his ads.

"But Harvey, we wouldn't do that," Marianne stammered.

He gave her a hard look. "I wasn't so sure when I opened my mail." But before he left, he patted her on the shoulder.

All in all, Marianne had six calls or visits in reaction to her "new billing procedures." The bookkeeper reported three more, but courteously refrained from any I-told-you-so speeches.

Delilah, who stopped by to show Marianne the fabric for her wedding suit, clucked in sympathy over the afternoon's events. "Change comes hard around here."

"But paying your bills on time is just a part of business."

"Honey, these people think they are paying on time. It's just on *their* time."

Marianne threw up her hands in disgust. "They're making it awfully hard to keep this ship afloat."

"I warned you," Delilah said softly. "Putting the paper back on solid footing isn't going to be easy. Do you want me to come back in a little more often?"

"Of course not."

"I hate seeing you so frustrated, dear."

Delilah's concern made Marianne feel like a child who was having difficulty with a school project. "Business is supposed to be frustrating," she snapped. "Did anyone come in and hold your hand all these years?"

Her aunt took a step backward. "Well, there was your father—"

"Yeah, I bet he was a lot of help."

"Marianne." Her name was a quiet rebuke.

Instantly contrite, Marianne shoved a few damp tendrils of hair back from her forehead. "Oh, don't mind me. I'm just stewing over the way everyone talks to me. No one takes me seriously. Milton explained things to me like I'm slow or something. Frank patted me on the shoulder. And Lolly prattled on about some adorable little peach frock for me to wear to the country club dance with Jack."

"Um-mm," Delilah said, then quickly began bundling her ivory brocade back in its bag.

"What does 'um-mm' mean?"

Her aunt nervously smoothed hair that needed no smoothing. "Nothing, dear. I just didn't know you and Jack were going to the dance."

"We're not," Marianne protested. "That's just the point. Jack and I aren't doing anything together, even though most of the town thinks we're making mad, passionate love every chance we get."

Delilah gave her a steady look. Then she crossed the room and closed the office door. "Don't let the gossips get to you, Marianne."

"Tell me how." She shuddered. "I just hate being watched like this. Good Lord, just because Jack's a man and I'm a woman and we've spent a little time together doesn't mean anything." It did, but she didn't care to discuss that with her aunt right now.

Very pointedly, Delilah said nothing.

"Have you been listening to what everyone is saying?"

"Heavenly days. You live under the same roof with me. What I think about you and Jack has nothing to do with what anyone else in this town is saying."

"What are they saying, exactly?"

Delilah's lips twitched, but she suppressed the smile. "Most people think the two of you make a pretty nice pair."

"Maybe they do too much thinking."

"And what are your thoughts on the subject?"

"I think..." Marianne thrust a hand through her hair, considering her words. She blew out a frustrated breath. "I think I don't know what I think. But I hate the gossip!"

"Well, it's not as if it's really malicious. It's more what I would call..." She paused, as if searching for the right words. "It's sort of the town's proprietary interest in two of their own." Delilah moved to the window that faced Main Street. Arms crossed, she looked out on a familiar, end-of-the-workday scene. "In a town this size, everyone tries to know everyone else's business. God heavens, girl, there was plenty of talk about you and Jack that summer before you married Kyle. You spent all your time with him."

Marianne was startled. "But we were friends. We had been friends forever."

The look Delilah gave her made Marianne wonder exactly what her aunt knew about the way that summer ended.

"I wish all these people would find something to do other than talk about me."

"Surely you knew this is the way it would be if you moved home."

"I didn't think of any of the bad stuff." Leaning forward on her desk, Marianne cupped a hand under her chin. "I thought of the oak tree in our front yard. And the roses next door. And the way you tuck little bags of potpourri in the linen closet so that the sheets always smell like springtime."

Delilah turned to smile at her. "You could have bought potpourri in D.C."

"It never smelled as sweet as yours."

"Oh, Marianne," her aunt murmured, sighing. "In your head, you painted a pretty picture of home. You left out the ugly parts. Like gossiping neighbors. Just ignore them." Once more she hesitated, as if picking and choosing her words carefully. "I've been deadset against meddling in this, but I'll say right now that if there is something between you and Jack—don't let the gossip around town influence your actions. You and Jack should have nothing to hide. And even if you did—" She broke off, shaking her head.

"What?" Marianne prompted, though she feared what Delilah might say.

"Just don't let what everyone else says or thinks make a difference. I made the mistake of listening too much to the opinions of others."

As long as she could remember, Marianne had thought of her aunt as strong and independent, a single-minded businesswoman who wasn't influenced by anything more than her own conscience. Marianne thought she had lived her life on her own terms, not bowing to the popular notions that a woman of her generation should marry and raise a family. But it seemed Delilah had some regrets. And Marianne was sure those regrets had something to do with Jeb.

Delilah cleared her throat, then began, "Your grandfather wanted me to marry Tom Nations." Marianne recognized the name of a prominent local physician. "But I didn't love Tom. I was in love with Jeb. And he was married to someone else. To sweet little Nina Franks."

Jeb had been a widower for so long that Marianne barely remembered his wife's name. "What happened?"

"We had what I guess you could call a flirtation. Jeb was unhappy, and I was very young." Her eyes narrowed, as if to block out a painful memory. "By today's standards, the whole thing was really quite innocent. But there was a scandal anyway. People embellished freely on the truth. Just like you, I hated their speculation. I wanted the talk to end. So Jeb stayed with Nina. And pretty soon I gave up pretending to be a debutante on the lookout for a man and became what we used to call a spinster. Disgusted, your grandfather put me to work at the paper.''

"So working here wasn't your idea?''

Delilah laughed. "Oh, it was very definitely my idea. I had to beg to be hired. Your grandfather didn't think women belonged in the workplace. And he usually got his way. God knows, he held your father down. But this was one thing that I bucked him on. He wanted me to marry, or to ship off to some other city so he wouldn't be disgraced, but I wouldn't do it. I figured this was the family business and I was family. So I worked here for forty years.''

Marianne sat quietly, digesting the story. "I don't understand,'' she said finally. "You said you made the mistake of listening to the opinions of others. Sounds to me like you thumbed your nose at them all.''

"Oh, no, I didn't,'' Delilah murmured. "If I hadn't worried about what everyone in this town was saying, I'd have run off with Jeb, just as he wanted. I'd have made love with him in that motel where someone saw us meeting. I'd have borne his children and grown old with him. I wouldn't have waited forty years to know what it's like to... to really love him.''

Her fervor brought tears to Marianne's eyes. She glanced down, blinking them away.

"You and Jack have nothing to hide like Jeb and I did,'' Delilah said. "You're both free. So if there's something happening between you, I hope you won't let a bunch of small-town gossips hold you back.''

"Gossip isn't holding me back,'' Marianne denied. "It's just that I'm trying to be businesslike and earn everyone's respect around here, and it's hard when I know they're all talking. And there's Laura and—''

''And perhaps you're looking for a good excuse to avoid what's really keeping you from Jack.'' Delilah's assessment struck too close to the mark for Marianne to deny it.

The older woman chuckled. ''It's really easy when you can blame your hesitation or your unhappiness on something other than yourself. It's much harder to face the truth.''

Marianne could only look at her, amazed by the woman's sharp insight.

Suddenly all business, Delilah gathered her purse and packages from a nearby chair. She blew a kiss in Marianne's direction and bustled toward the door, reminding her that she and Jeb were taking Laura for hamburgers and the latest Disney movie out at Willow Creek's new two-theater complex.

When she was gone, Marianne tried to block out her words. She attacked her editorial with new vengeance, but the tiny green cursor on the computer screen seemed to be screaming, ''Truth, truth, truth.'' For the first time in her entire professional life, Marianne felt completely blocked.

Five o'clock arrived, then six, and the building emptied. The quiet settled like a thick fog. And still she stared at the empty computer screen, growing angrier by the moment. Her mind was too jumbled to produce any coherent thoughts.

Back in D.C., when she had imagined herself coming home, this wasn't the way she saw it. In her dreams, she planned to rescue the newspaper's dwindling revenues with fresh ideas and hard work. As a civic leader, she had fantasized about spearheading initiatives for better schools and health-care facilities. As an editor, she had hoped to build the newspaper into one of the most respected publications of its size in the country.

Intellectually, Marianne knew one month wasn't enough time to begin realizing any of those dreams. But right now she felt so hopeless, so inadequate to the task. Today proved how resistant to change the people in this town could be. Marianne had never dreamed it would be so hard just to institute standard billing procedures.

Muttering a curse, she flipped off the computer and left, locking the big double-glass doors of the building behind her. It was now after seven. Dusk was beginning to fall. Most of the downtown businesses were dark. At night, the energy of the town shifted toward the newer discount department stores that had sprung up out near the interstate. Only the diner looked busy tonight. On the other side of the creek, the Dairy Bar sat on its rise overlooking the town, its neon lights glowing in the haze that lingered after the day's heat.

Marianne considered going over to see Sally. They had become friends since the night the girls were chased in the park, and Sally could use good friends nowadays. The police had been unable to link Renee or her husband to the park incident. Furthermore, Jack had reported just last evening that the court was going to hear Renee's petition to rescind Betsy's adoption. He had hoped the case would be tossed out, but some judge evidently thought there was merit in Renee's accusations against her sister.

So, yes, Sally could probably benefit from some company right now. Only Marianne didn't feel like cheering anyone up. She was restless and tense, still angry from her frustrating afternoon and somewhat melancholy after what she had learned from Delilah.

Glancing around the courthouse square, her gaze settled on a lighted window over the Town and Country Dress

Shop. Jack's office. Through the long, gracefully arched window, she could see him sitting at his desk. Her initial reaction was to head in that direction, tell him her troubles. But the "truth, truth, truth," screamed by her computer wasn't forgotten. Delilah had talked about confronting what really kept Marianne from Jack. But she just wasn't ready. She might never be ready.

She didn't want to go home, however, so she was just standing in the muggy early evening air when she saw the faces turned her way in the front booths of Louella's Diner. That dinner group, assembled so neatly, watching her with such unabashed interest, sent a fresh surge of fury through Marianne. She toyed with making an obscene gesture in their direction. She wondered what they would do if she strode in the front door and announced that she and Jack would be having sex in his big, red car tonight and they were all invited. Or maybe she should tell the truth about nine years ago. What would they do if they really had something to talk about?

Give 'em something to talk about.

The words to a popular song played through her brain while she stood tapping her foot on the sidewalk. Good advice, she thought. Tossing her head, she started toward Jack's office. When she passed the diner, she waved. She kept her chin up, her footsteps purposeful, as she opened the brass-trimmed black door beside the dress shop's entrance. Her confidence didn't flag while she mounted the steps and pushed through the second set of doors to the office. Only when Jack called out, "Who's there?" did her bravery desert her.

"Anybody there?" he said again as she stood uncertainly in the dark-paneled, leather-chaired waiting room. She heard his chair squeak, heard his footsteps, then saw him coming down the hallway toward her.

Jack paused in the arched doorway. Marianne was the last person he expected to see. It wasn't unusual for a client to drop by after the accepted business hours. When someone was in trouble in a small town and needed an attorney, they might not want to come in the front door in the middle of the day. But Marianne wasn't a client, though the stricken look on her face said there might be trouble.

"Jack," she said, taking a deep breath. "I've come by to add some fuel to a fire."

"Pardon?"

"If you'll look out your window and over toward the diner, you'll see about a dozen faces pressed to the glass. No doubt they are discussing whether or not I came up here to seduce you."

He considered not taking the bait, but couldn't. "Is that why you're here?"

"Of course not."

"Oh, come on." He took her hand. "Let's go smooch in front of the windows."

"Jack," she protested, though she laughed as he dragged her down the hall.

Once inside his office, he let her go. But he ignored her objections and flipped off the overhead light and the lamp on his desk. "We'll really have 'em guessing."

"I can just imagine what they're saying."

"Probably speculating on whether we'll do it on the floor or the couch."

"You're right. They're probably taking bets." Marianne's voice caught on the last word, and her sharply indrawn breath vibrated across the darkened room. The humor was missing when she said, "God, Jack, what have I done?"

Those words, the same ones she had uttered nine years ago, stole Jack's laughter, too.

Chapter Eight

Light pooled on the desk as Jack touched the base of the desk lamp again. "Maybe adding fuel to their fire isn't so smart."

"You're right." Marianne stood just inside the door, shifting uncertainly from one foot to the other. "They just made me so mad, sitting over there, watching me."

He made his shrug careless. "Think of it this way. What else is there to do on a Tuesday night in Willow Creek? You remember. You used to be about that bored with the place yourself."

Marianne stepped forward, blue eyes troubled. "You're angry with me for coming up here, aren't you?"

"Not angry, just..." Rubbing a hand across the tensed muscles in his neck, he shook his head. "It's just been a long day." He gestured toward his desk. "I'm working on Sally's case."

"Surely it will turn out all right. Who would take that child from the only mother she's ever known?"

"I don't think there would be a question if Sally were . . . well, if Sally were someone other than who she is. If she were happily married to some upstanding citizen."

"Why haven't you volunteered?"

He looked up in surprise.

"I'm sorry." Marianne tossed her purse down beside the overstuffed sofa that filled one wall of the spacious office. "That was a foolish thing to say, except that—" She broke off, shook her head.

"Except what?"

Her words came out in a rush. "Except that you and Sally are obviously close. Betsy adores you. I guess I've wondered why you haven't gotten together."

He considered that a moment, "There's a little matter of love. I don't love Sally."

"People don't always marry for love." There was an edge to Marianne's voice that Jack wasn't sure he had ever heard before. Before he could reply, she apologized again. "This is none of my business. I'm no better than those people down at Louella's."

He rubbed his neck again, just as happy not to get into an intense discussion about love and marriage with her tonight.

Prowling restlessly around the room, Marianne ended up in front of a window. She crossed her arms, made a frustrated sound. "I can't make out much from here, but I bet they're just all a-twitter down there. Miss Louella is probably busy making phone calls. They'll most likely make a party out of the night, sell tickets, run specials on drinks and food."

Her preoccupation began to irritate him. "Why do you care so much?"

Marianne turned toward him. "You don't?"

"I know they're talking. It irritates me some. But it's just part of living here. I accept it. About the same way I accept that the city council will never put a red light at the corner of Hilldale and Vine."

"You didn't use to be so good about accepting things."

"And you didn't use to care so much about what everyone thought of you."

She swung away from him again, as if she knew he was telling the truth and didn't want to face it.

But Jack pushed the point. "The girl you were didn't care. She was friends with me when all her highfalutin friends wondered why."

"Jack, I've told you why I hate this gossip about us now," Marianne began, but her words trailed away, her gaze slid away from his. She remembered, all too clearly, what Delilah had said about making up excuses to avoid the truth. "I guess I am carrying on about this a little too much. But I still don't like it. It's just one of the bad parts of Willow Creek that I had forgotten."

"Just one part?"

Quickly she told him about her afternoon. The more she talked about Lolly Kingston and Frank Harvey, the angrier she seemed to Jack. He sat down on the edge of his desk, listened to her complaints about small-town minds and small-town ways, watched her pace around the office, growing more and more agitated.

"It's not working out the way I thought it would," she said, pausing in front of him. "This isn't the way I thought coming home would be."

"Marianne, I told you the paper—"

"Oh, it's not just the paper. It's everything." She gestured toward the window. "It's a man threatening my daughter in the park. It's having my personal business discussed in the diner. It's Delilah and Jeb and—''

''What about them? What have they done?''

She clasped her hands together, and the expression on her face was the same look she used to have when she talked of her plans when they were teenagers. ''It's just that I had this *dream*, Jack. I dreamed of Laura and I living in the house with Delilah. She would make everything nice, the way she did when I was small. Even when Dad was drinking, Delilah always had this talent, this way of making it all so right.''

''Will that talent disappear when she marries Jeb?''

''No, but I'm not going to live there with them.''

Jack's heart thudded. After a frustrating day, Marianne was obviously disenchanted with her move to Willow Creek, but surely she wouldn't, couldn't, go away again. A month ago, he had prayed for her to leave. Now he couldn't imagine it.

''Delilah and Jeb deserve to be alone. They've waited forever to be together. I don't want to crowd them. Laura and I are going to have to move out.''

Relief swept through Jack, only to be overturned by her next words.

''And if things don't work out here—''

He couldn't hear the last part of her sentence because the roaring in his ears was too loud. He came off the desk and grasped Marianne's arms, a movement of barely contained violence. ''You can't move again.''

Marianne just looked at him, openmouthed.

''You wouldn't, would you?'' he demanded.

''Jack—''

''Laura's just getting used to Willow Creek, for God's sake.''

''I know that, but if the paper—''

"If it folds? Is that what concerns you now? Why didn't you think about that before you came here, before you turned Laura's life upside down? Before you . . ." He swallowed, not trusting himself to say, *before you turned my life upside down, too.*

Hand at her throat, Marianne stepped back from him.

Jack found his voice again before she could reply. "What are you going to do, Marianne, keep moving until you find some perfect little world?"

"No, I—"

"There is no such place." His blood was pumping with anger and fear. Plain ordinary fear. It made his voice rough, left him wanting to shake some sense into her. "All your life you've talked about your *dreams*." He sneered the word. "First you dreamed of getting out of here. And then you dreamed of coming back. You can't spend your life chasing dreams, Marianne. Especially not at Laura's expense."

"What do you know about dreams? What dream did you ever chase?" Though her voice was trembling, her words were clear as glass, sharp as broken pieces.

He stepped toward her again. "I don't know how you of all people can stand in this office and say that to me. You know how hard I worked to get through school and to get here."

"To *this* office?" She laughed, a bitter sound. "I don't remember this office in *this* town being part of your dreams."

"We weren't talking about my dreams."

"Oh, yes," she said, her voice full of sarcasm. "Every time I ask what happened to your great and grand plans, you give me some song and dance about being happy. Then you change the subject. You're not getting off so easy this time."

"I don't have to explain myself."

She thrust her chin up. "Neither do I."

"But don't you see?" he said, frustrated by the way she had turned the conversation on him. "Don't you realize that you can spend your life chasing around, looking for happiness in some *place*? But happiness isn't a place, Marianne."

"How do you know? Are you so happy here that you can speak with authority on the subject? From where I sit, you don't look so damned content."

Her contemptuous tone sent heat streaking up his neck to his face. "And what makes you an expert on contentment? Seems to me you said it was unhappiness that drove you back here. So are you planning to drag Laura back to D.C. to see if it's any different? Is going back to your big job on a big-city paper going to make you happy this time? It didn't before."

He saw her hands clench into fists at her sides, but her voice was low and even. "You know what I think? I think you're jealous of me, of what I've done."

"Jealous of you?"

"Because you never went anywhere. Because you never took a risk."

"Why should I envy you? You came running back."

"But that was only after I went after my dreams." The muscles in her throat worked as she swallowed. "You never did half of what you planned, Jack Dylan, and it kills you because I did. You're eaten alive with jealousy."

The time had come to admit to that emotion. But not for the reasons she thought. Jack met her gaze straight on. "There's only one person I've ever really envied. And that's Kyle Wingate."

Marianne's eyes widened.

"Because you allowed him to be father to my child."

A full minute must have passed before Jack's words fully penetrated Marianne's understanding. *His child?* If she heard him correctly, he was claiming Laura as his own. She tried to speak, tried to come up with a denial, but his accusation had momentarily struck her mute.

Weeks ago, he said Laura *might* have been his. That was something Marianne would concede. Nine summers ago, Marianne had tried taking birth control pills in anticipation of her marriage. But they made her ill from the beginning, and she and Kyle had agreed to use another method, one he would provide. So when she and Jack had made love, they had been unprotected, and as she remembered, unmindful of the consequences. So, yes, she and Jack *might* have had a child.

Only they didn't.

Laura wasn't his.

Hands outstretched, Marianne took a step toward him. She couldn't think of any other way to say this but bluntly. "Kyle was Laura's father."

Deliberately or otherwise, Jack misunderstood her. "I know he raised her. I know he loved her. I know Kyle was a good man."

"Yes, but—"

"But I know he wasn't her real father."

"How?" Marianne whispered. "How do you know?"

"You weren't planning to have children so soon, remember? Kyle wanted a family right away, but you didn't. You were starting your career. You wanted to wait for children."

"That's right, but..." Marianne swallowed, unable to admit the guilt that had prompted her to forego birth control on her honeymoon, the guilt that made her give in to Kyle's wishes. That guilt had sprung from the night she had spent with Jack, from wishing it was Jack who held her under the bright Bahamian moon at the resort where she and Kyle spent their two-week wedding trip.

She tried again to make Jack hear the truth of what she was saying. She gentled her voice, kept herself calm. "I don't know how or when you decided Laura was your child, but she isn't. I know my own body, Jack. I'm the only person who could possibly know. And I'm certain Kyle was her father."

Jack's features hardened with disbelief. "You were pregnant when you came home that Christmas. I stood across the street from Delilah's and watched you walk up the front steps. I couldn't believe it when you turned to the side and I saw how pregnant you were. I knew then. I knew it was my baby."

Marianne remembered that Christmas well. She had wanted to come home to Willow Creek more than anything. She had been ill since the beginning of her pregnancy. Ill and bitterly unhappy. Her marriage, like too many things in her life, hadn't begun as she had expected.

She knew part of that could be blamed on her emotional state, on what had happened with Jack. But now she wondered how she could ever have been blind enough to think two such different people would be happy together. Kyle had been a traditional-minded man. Before their marriage, his quiet stability seemed a pleasant contrast to her father's volatile unhappiness. Kyle had been old-fashioned enough to want to wait until after their marriage to make love. And Marianne had agreed, been pleased, even touched by his reverence and respect. But she was not so pleased when she realized he fully expected her to give up her job and devote herself to him and their coming child. They argued when she wouldn't. Fundamental clashes about everything from their stolid sex life to social issues eroded the marriage from the start.

By December of that first year together, Marianne was already questioning the choice she made. She had begged Kyle to come home to Willow Creek for Christmas week, even though he preferred spending the holidays with his family in Maryland. He gave in, perhaps because of her pregnancy, because she was so miserable and swollen. At four months, she had been as big as some of her friends were at six months or more. All she had wanted for Christmas was to see Delilah.

And Jack.

"I called you," she said to him now. "I called and told your mother that I was in town and I wanted to talk to you." His mother had said he was working a holiday job in Knoxville near the law school and wouldn't be home until Christmas Eve.

Jack nodded, saddened by his memories of that day. "I came right over as soon as I got home. I walked halfway because I wanted to get my head on straight. I wanted to see you so...so bad." That last few words came out broken and choked. And he had to turn away from Marianne. Even now he didn't want her to see how much he had cared, how much he had missed her during those first four months when she wasn't a part of his life.

"Oh, Jack." She stepped close, her hands slipping into the crook of his arm. She leaned her cheek against his shoulder. "I wanted to see you just as much. I had missed you. I hated my life, and I just wanted..." She inhaled deeply. "I wanted you to be my friend again. I needed a friend."

"I just stood across the street," Jack whispered, remembering. "I stood. I saw you were pregnant. And I..." He stopped, shaking his head. "I went a little crazy, I guess."

"I called and called the whole time we were here," Marianne said. "You never called back. I thought you hated me."

He turned to her, his hands closing over hers, his voice growing fierce again. "I did hate you. I watched you walk in that house, at Kyle's side, with my baby in your belly—"

"But that's not true."

"Oh, God, Marianne, don't lie now. What possible reason is there to lie? Kyle's dead and I...I love Laura. For years and years, I tried not to think of her. But when I looked at her...when I talked to her, I fell in love. She's so like you, like the girl I...like you."

Marianne was shaking her head. "Please, Jack, you've got to believe me. Laura is Kyle's daughter."

He dropped her hands, bitterness rising like bile to his throat. "Have you been telling yourself that for so long that you believe it?"

"I believe it because it's true."

"Marianne—"

She tossed her head, her red gold curls glinting in the light from the lamp. "If you were so sure she was yours, why didn't you confront me years ago? Why did you just stand across the street that Christmas Eve?"

"The same reason I walked away from you in the first place. I didn't have anything to offer you. How could I compare to Kyle, to the life he could give you?"

"So you just walked away?"

"I ran away." The words were strained, as if he had to force them out. "I ran away because I thought it was the best thing for you."

To Marianne, that admission didn't sound like the person she had thought him to be. But then, after their friendship was changed that summer, he had changed, too, become a stranger. The young man who had stood on the front porch and told her their lovemaking was nothing hadn't been the Jack she knew.

Turning from him, she thought of the morning Jack had been so cruel to her, remembered how used she had felt. How inadequate. For her, making love with him had been a revelation. And so upsetting. Yes, it had been that, too. She had been confused about the shift in their relationship, about what it meant for her future, but she would never have called what happened between them nothing.

But Jack had. He had walked away. And stayed away. Even when he thought she carried his child. He said he did it for her, for what was best for her. But backing away wasn't what she would have expected of him.

Hugging her arms tight to her midriff, she stared out the window at the town she and Jack had once sought to escape. That December when she drove away with Kyle she thought she had finally left here for good. She had felt so betrayed when Jack didn't call her back. He had meant so much to her, and she was in so much trouble in her marriage. She had wanted Jack, wanted his friendship. But when he didn't call, she went home, she had Laura, and she worked at trying to be happy with Kyle, at building a career and a good life. Only when none of that worked had she come home again.

"Marianne." Jack's hands settled on her shoulders, his touch as gentle as his tone. "I'm sorry. I should have had the courage to confront you that day."

"The answer would have still been the same. I would have told you Laura was Kyle's daughter."

He turned her to face him. "I know you had to have been confused then. I mean . . . married to one man, carrying another's child."

She closed her eyes, started another protest.

He silenced her with a touch of his fingers to her lips. She looked up at him as he said, "It must have been hell for you. And naturally, you chose what seemed liked the safest, easiest—"

"I would never have lied about Laura for safety's sake."

"Yes you would." His gentleness disappeared, replaced by a bitter laugh. "You always chose safety first."

"How can you say that? I left, remember?"

"On your husband's arm."

"But Jack—"

He swept a hand toward the window, his green eyes glimmering dangerously in the dim light. "You wanted that big, wide world out there. But you wanted safety, too. So you chose Kyle as your vehicle. He was safe and secure. With him as your husband, you could take risks, but you had a net."

Only the net became a cage.

And the risks lost their appeal.

"You were always the same, Marianne. When we were kids, you played it both ways. You were a good girl. But you had me as a friend. With me, you could go along for the ride. The faster the better. Oh, you protested the whole way. But you liked the thrill. And there was always a net. No matter what we did, you were always nice little Marianne Cole. And your good name usually saved our butts."

He was right, of course. She had gone along on all their youthful escapades, terrified, but secretly thrilled to be breaking rules. And always knowing there was a way out.

"That's what happened with Laura, wasn't it?"

His question confused her. "What do you mean?"

"That night with me was one of our rides. And instead of dealing with the consequences, you had a way out. You went ahead, married Kyle, and when you realized you were pregnant, you just stayed with him. You even convinced yourself that he was Laura's father. That was safer than having to face the truth.''

She turned away once more. "No, that's not right."

But he wouldn't let up. "Why can't you admit the truth?"

She rounded on him with a question of her own. "Why did you tell me to marry Kyle?"

"I knew you would anyway."

"How were you so sure?"

"Because I knew you," he insisted, drawing near. "I knew how frightened you were. You were too afraid to face what had happened between us, what I made you feel."

"You were so cruel. You said horrible things to me."

"I said them before you could." His voice was harsh, but his eyes were full of hurt. He looked young and vulnerable, and he tugged at Marianne's heart with his next words.

"I had to push you away before you pushed me. I didn't mean the things I said to you that morning. But can you tell me you wouldn't have married Kyle if I hadn't been so cruel? Would anything have changed if I had told you how I really felt? Would you have left Kyle at the altar if I had gone down on my knees and begged you to marry me, instead?"

His question hit her hard. All these years, she had told herself Jack's rejection was the reason she had gone through with her marriage to Kyle, that without Jack's cruel dismissal she might have ... might have ... She couldn't complete the second part of the sentence. If Jack hadn't rejected her, what might she have done? She didn't know. She had never known for sure.

Trembling at that admission, she crossed the room to snatch up her purse. "I'm going to leave you to your delusions."

"What's the matter? Still too afraid to face the truth?"

The taunt stopped her at the door, but she didn't turn.

Jack's whisper thrummed across her nerve endings. "Still afraid of what I made you feel back then?"

She closed her eyes, not wanting to admit the truth.

The truth. What had Delilah said today? That it was easier to blame unhappiness or hesitation on something other than the truth. Well, Marianne saw the truth now. Saw what she hadn't been able to see all these years. She had been afraid of Jack, terrified of the powerful passion they had shared. Yes, it had been magical. No, she had never forgotten one moment, one touch, one sigh of pleasure. But it had been consuming, uncontrollable, certainly not safe. She had been frightened, terrified, because, as Jack had put it, when their passion was unleashed there was no net. Jack was a hard, fast ride, full of thrills and danger. He was too real. He made her feel too much.

Hadn't she always known the danger of feelings? Her father blunted his with alcohol. And Delilah...Marianne saw now that Delilah had buried her true self under a lifetime of dedication to job and community. Buried herself. And lived without love. Lived everyday of her life with regrets. Dear God, Marianne didn't want a life like that.

Behind her, Jack said, "Face it, Marianne. Face the truth for once in your life."

Smart, brave Marianne Cole. She had been such a confident little girl, not afraid of strangers, willing to face a crowd. She had always prided herself on being a risk-taker. It was all a lie. All the time she had pretended to be striding along, certain of where she was going, she had really been running. With a suitcase full of fears, she ran away from the painful memories of her childhood. She ran away from Jack. Ran from the power and the accompanying danger of what they could have shared.

"What is it?" he whispered now. "Why are you hesitating? Get out of here. Go chase your neat, tidy little dreams. There's nothing here for you but reality."

She turned then. She faced Jack. For the first time in her whole life, she faced down her fears.

He stood in shadows near the window, just beyond the glow of lamplight. "There's nothing here but me," he said hoarsely. Then he moved into the light. In his face she saw something raw and elemental, stark, unrelenting emotions she might have fled some other night.

Fleeing did occur to her. There was still time to leave. But instead she took a small step forward.

"Ever since you came back," Jack continued, "for all these weeks, we've been circling each other. And you've been afraid. Just as afraid as you ever were."

"You're right." That admission came hard, even though she had accepted the truth. "I'm afraid right now."

"Don't be." He closed the distance remaining between them with three long strides. "Please don't be afraid anymore." There was entreaty in his voice. And a challenge.

She took up the gauntlet by stepping into his arms.

On her lips, Jack tasted her fear. He felt her tremble. He absorbed the doubts still tumbling inside her. But he didn't lessen the pressure of his mouth on hers. He was determined that Marianne would accept at least one truth tonight. Weeks ago, she had acknowledged their desire for one another. But she turned it away with talk of losing his friendship, of controlling impulses. He didn't want her evasions now. He didn't want control.

So he kissed her. Deeply. Until her lips parted beneath his. Until their tongues began a slow, sensual dance. Touching. Teasing. Tempting.

Marianne moaned deep in her throat. Jack heard her handbag hit the floor with a quiet thud and a jangle of keys.

Then her arms twined around his neck. Her body pressed close. So close that it seemed only natural to slip his hands under her bottom, to cup her hard against his growing arousal. He lifted her, turned them toward the couch while her legs wrapped tightly around his hips.

He took one step and they fell together, landing in a sprawl of arms and legs with her beneath him on the soft, upholstered cushions. Jack hadn't intended anything so dramatic. He certainly didn't intend to bang his leg on the furniture's wooden trim. His curse was a definite mood-shatterer.

Marianne giggled up at him. "Couldn't we just have lain down?"

His shin throbbed, but not as much as another part of his anatomy. "Damn it, I was trying to be romantic."

She grasped his loosened tie, pulled him down to her again. His pain was forgotten with her husky, "Try again."

This time he succeeded.

Now there was nothing slow in the twining of tongues and bodies. Nothing teasing in their touches. They kissed and twisted and turned, feverishly shedding clothes as they scrambled to a kneeling position on the couch. Jack's tie sailed through the air. Marianne's blouse and hose. His shirt. Her shoes. His belt. His fingers were at the front clasp of her peachy, lace-cupped bra, his mouth feasting on the satiny skin of her shoulders when she suddenly dived down on the couch again.

"The window," she whispered, as if there was someone who might hear them. "Jack, anyone can see in up here. Hit the lights."

He took her literally, firing one black loafer at the touch-control lamp and then, cursing, another one, which finally found its target.

In the sudden gloom, Marianne giggled again. "Lost your touch with the right-hand curve, haven't you?"

In response, he pulled her up, reveling in her gentle curves as her body slid against his. When they faced one another again, his lips caught hers, and his hand closed over one rounded, peaking breast.

She tore her mouth from his, arching her neck as his thumb and forefinger circled her pebbling nipple. "I guess there are some touches you haven't forgotten."

He parted the bra clasp with a smooth, expert motion, pushing the garment apart, dragging the straps down her arms and tossing it aside. Then he knelt, his mouth and tongue mimicking the action his fingers had abandoned. Her breasts were fuller than he remembered, but still pale against the darker beige of the rest of her body. He leaned back, and in the light that filtered in the window, he could make out the deeper coral of the aureoles surrounding each nipple. Her breasts puckered under his gaze, as if begging for the attention of his mouth again. He complied, bathing each with the firm strokes of his tongue. Her body jerked at this intimacy. But her fingers tangled in his hair, holding him while he suckled first one breast, then the other.

His penis grew turgid, straining against his zipper as he took his mouth from her breast to her lips once. Pressing his hips toward hers, he was frustrated by the clothing that still separated them. But his hands were shaking as he fumbled with the row of buttons that ran down her full, cotton skirt.

"Let me," she whispered.

Again Jack sat back while the skirt disappeared, leaving only peach panties, cut high on the legs, the lace-covered crotch a shadowy, beckoning mystery.

Without thinking, he pressed his mouth against that lace, then drew away. Hooking his thumbs in the fragile strip of material, he tugged her panties down her legs. Marianne skimmed them off with an adroit movement. Then his arms crept around her hips, holding her while he kissed this, her most intimate part. Her breath caught as he dipped his tongue lightly in the moist, rosy cleft. Her hands bore down on his shoulders, her body arched backward. She gasped his name. But he took only that taste before his lips drifted upward, over her belly.

She wasn't as thin as he recalled. But neither was he. And this, after all, was a mature woman's body. There was something infinitely pleasing in the rounded softness of her. He found the reality of her more pleasing than any, more perfect memory. Beneath where his lips now lingered, she had carried his child. The thought was oddly, overwhelmingly erotic.

Groaning, he returned to her mouth once more. Her hands roamed down his back, settling on his rear as she drew him tight against her. This time it was her hands that fumbled with buttons and a zipper. He pushed her fingers away, shed his pants, socks and briefs in one move.

Now there was nothing between them. Nothing to separate their heat. And yet they continued to kneel, facing one another, not touching, not speaking.

Marianne felt the weight of nine years of yearning. Nine years of trying to not to remember, of attempting not to compare this man's touch with her husband's. Would this coupling match the gilt-edged memories she had carried like hidden, treasured valentines? Nine years ago, after a night of unspeakable passion, Jack walked away.

He hurt you then, the old fear in her whispered in reminder.

But this isn't then, her heart retorted.

And for once, her heart won.

Gently, Marianne reached out, touched Jack's face. His beard was rough against her fingers. But the lips he turned against her palm were soft. Her other hand drifted downward, through the thatch of hair on his chest. Across his washboard-flat stomach. Down to the long, velvet length of him. He rose to meet her touch.

He sighed against the hand still pressed to his lips. A shuddering sigh that curled through her, touching her most secret self more surely than any physical foreplay. A moment later, when she straddled Jack's hips, when she took him into her body, she was wet with want, made moist from yearning to hear his sigh of pleasure once more.

He obliged her quickly. Then again. As they bucked and writhed and strained together. As they found their release together.

"I remember," Marianne gasped as they came down from the aching, shuddering heights. "I never forgot, Jack. I never forgot how it felt to have you inside me."

His response was to lay her back on the couch, to cover her perspiration-slick body with his own, to stroke them toward heaven once again.

Quiet darkness greeted Marianne when her senses returned to earth. Jack lay behind her, an arm thrown around her waist, his breathing deep and regular. She stirred, but he clasped her tighter. So she lay motionless, staring across the room. She wanted, oh, how she wanted, to let this moment stand on its own. A beautiful shining hour clipped out of time. By acting on the sexual pull between her and Jack, she had faced one truth, had surmounted one fear. But she wasn't foolish enough to think any problems were solved, any answers had been given.

What was this, anyway? Another night of passion to add to her memory stores? Was it a cure for a nine-year ache? Or was it a beginning?

The first time they had made love, she had awakened without Jack. She had waited for his call, for the sound of his car on the street outside the house. She had been frightened. Afraid of what they had done. Afraid of what would happen next. She hadn't known what she felt for Jack. He was her best friend, and therefore she loved him. But did she love him as a man, the way she thought she had loved Kyle? On that morning, while she lay in her sun-dappled bed, surrounded by the musky scent of sex, she knew she didn't love Kyle. But Jack... Jack and she weren't right for one another.

A few minutes later, Jack had confirmed that opinion.

And because she had been filled with fear, she hadn't fought him. All that day, she had paced through the house, twisting her engagement ring, wondering what she could do. She was twenty-one. Her father had died only weeks before. Her aunt was operating on automatic pilot, too intent on not giving in to her own grief to be of any help. And now, the one person Marianne had always counted on was lost to her, too.

Marianne hadn't known who she loved that morning. She still wasn't sure when she exchanged vows with Kyle.

And now, nine years later, she was still confused over what she felt for the man sleeping beside her. Was it love? Or was it merely pure, powerful sexual desire? She couldn't attempt an answer now while her blood still sang with the memory of his touch.

But one thing she did know. And that was Laura's father. *Kyle*.

Short of a blood test, how was she going to convince Jack?

Doing her best not to wake him, she turned over. There was just enough light now to make out his features. He looked younger. But even in sleep, even after their love-making, there was an unhappy set to his mouth.

She brushed a light touch over his lips. She had sensed a deep unhappiness inside him from the very first day she came home. She thought again of his barren house. She thought of Sally, whom Marianne was certain loved Jack. Sally, with her warm, generous nature, might have made him happy. He said he didn't love Sally. Marianne thought Jack had probably never given love with anyone a chance. But why? Old questions about him tumbled through her. Why was he still in this town? And when would his pretense at happiness became a sham?

He thought Laura was his. He believed it with all his heart. Had believed it for a long time. He thought Marianne had cut him out of Laura's life. She could only imagine how such mistaken knowledge might fester and ferment and poison one's whole life. She knew it was the root of the unhappiness she had sensed within Jack. What would happen when he finally saw the truth?

Marianne's chest tightened, thinking of the tender way Jack had with her daughter. Just after coming home, she had fantasized about what sort of father he would be. Now she knew. He was wonderful with Laura, teasing yet firm, loving her without giving in to all of the child's demands.

He was great. But he wasn't her father.

Marianne couldn't lay by Jack's side any longer. Not with his delusions about Laura between them. She eased up, slipped away. He stirred, but didn't waken. She moved cautiously around the room, finding her outer clothes, pulling them on.

She was down on her knees, looking for her panties and bra when Jack spoke. "What are you doing?"

She snagged her bra from the bookcase beside the sofa. "I have to go home."

"Not yet."

"I know they're probably worried."

Instead of protesting further, he stood, pulled on his slacks. He went around the room, drawing blinds. Then he flipped on the light.

She had to turn away from the emotion that glowed in his eyes. She had resolved not to be seduced by emotion. Until this thing with Laura was straightened out, she couldn't be seduced by Jack.

He had other ideas. When she stuffed her underwear and hose in her purse, he took it away from her.

"Jack, I *have* to go home."

His green eyes were devilish, intent. "It's only midnight. And you're a big girl."

"But I didn't tell them where I'd be. What if Laura needed me?"

"Don't you think they might look here?"

She conceded he was right. But that concession led to a kiss. And then another. Pretty soon, he had her backed up against the desk. Her skirt was to her waist. And he was inside her. Again. Marianne's resolve melted with his first stroke.

The town clock was striking two when she crept in the house.

Marianne was sated, every muscle in her body felt well-loved.

But the issue of Laura's paternity had gone untouched.

Chapter Nine

At six o'clock, after less than four hours of sleep, Jack woke with a start. He sat up, damp with sweat, still caught in a disturbing dream about Marianne.

Blinking, he looked around his bedroom, peered at the clock on the bed stand. Marianne was probably still asleep a few blocks away. But the dream felt real. It had taken him back to nine years ago. The two of them were on Delilah's front porch and Marianne was screaming, accusing Jack of taking advantage of her, of coercing her into making love. The dream had shifted just as Jack denied her accusations. Suddenly, it wasn't nine years ago. It was last night, but Marianne's allegations were the same.

He shook his head, swung out of bed and hustled into the shower. Warm water cleared the last trace of unreality from his brain. But a nagging doubt remained. Had he taken advantage of her?

Nine years ago she said he used her vulnerability and her sadness over her father's death to push her into love-making. Looking back, he wondered if she might have been right. He had never made a conscious decision to seduce her, but he hadn't stayed away, even though he knew his feel-ings were no longer those of friendship. Last night, she had been vulnerable again, feeling unsure about coming home, irritated by the small-town gossip. And then he confronted her about Laura. He went further, pushing her to face the truth of the sexual attraction between them. He challenged her to make love. And she accepted.

How she had accepted.

He stood, water cascading down his body, replaying each sweet, mind-boggling moment of the way Marianne had met his challenge. The memories brought a hardening ache that belied the limits they had reached and stretched last night. The connection between them, the union, went deeper than the chemistry, the pheromones or even the fate he once tried to pin it on. Theirs was a spiritual harmony.

He couldn't bear to think she might have felt forced or manipulated.

Guilt had mounted inside him by the time he reached his office at seven. He made coffee and tried to work with half his attention on the street outside. It was nine-fifteen when he saw Marianne walking from the downtown parking lot toward the newspaper's building. He blew past two clients on his sprint through the office, down the stairs and into the street.

She was all the way across the square, but he called for her anyway, called for her despite their audience. The diner was full again. Frank Harvey was out front of the hardware store, signing for a UPS delivery. A full contingent of the town's retired older men were on the courthouse porch, gearing up for a game of checkers although the temperature already hovered around ninety. But the only person who existed for Jack was Marianne.

In a turquoise dress, a white sash tied at her waist, she whirled around when he called out to her a second time. She stood there on the sidewalk and watched him run across the square toward her. Despite heat and humidity that closed around him like a wet sheet, he ran. He ran because love was bursting inside him like some sudden, unexpected geyser. And his feet gained a mind of their own.

Marianne imagined it was a moment Willow Creek would talk about for years.

When Jack reached her, a fine sheen of perspiration covered his face. And everyone in town was looking at them. "What are you doing?" she demanded.

"We have to talk," he gasped out, then bent forward from the waist, drawing in quick, deep breaths. "Damn, but I'm out of shape."

Thinking of the physical feats they had accomplished last night, Marianne thought of arguing, but now didn't seem the time. In the building, she ignored Francine's obvious interest, shoved him into her office and went to get him a cup of water.

After he gulped it down, she inquired, "Couldn't you have called?"

He looked at her as if she had grown a couple of more heads. "I guess," he admitted. "I just didn't think of the phone."

"So?"

He blinked, still watching her with that dazed expression he'd had when he ran up to her on the street.

She struggled for patience. "Jack? What was it you wanted?"

"I wanted..." He stopped, then got up, shoving his hands deep in the pockets of his navy suit trousers. He paced to the door, then wheeled around. "I was worried. I started thinking about last night..."

Marianne looked down, flexed her fingers on the desk's green blotter. "Me, too." What she thought was that it had been incredibly irresponsible of her to make love with him when he believed what he did about Laura. Not that she would take back those hours with him. Not at all. But at the very least, instead of trying to sneak out and instead of making love with him a third time, she should have made him face the truth. That's what she was determined to do now.

"You regret it, don't you?"

At his question, she lifted her gaze. "Regret it?"

"Us. Last night."

She took her time, studying his inscrutable features before replying, "Do you have regrets?"

"Only that I might have pressured you." He shifted nervously from foot to foot, his gaze skimming away. "I know you think I took advantage of you before you married Kyle, that I used your father's death to force you into... well, into intimacies."

She was surprised. She thought last night's discussion had made it clear they both had said and done things in the past out of fear and confusion. "Taking advantage of me wasn't what you set out to do years ago, was it?"

"Hell, no," he denied hotly. "I know I agreed when you accused me of that on the morning after... after the fact. But I didn't use your vulnerability. Not intentionally, anyway." He raked a hand through his hair, his green eyes wide with what she could only call misery. "But last night... well, I'm afraid you might have felt I took advantage of you again. I mean, you were upset, and I pushed you. So if you felt forced in any way... I'm sorry." His last words were pitifully weak.

Marianne considered slapping him, just the way she slapped him nine years ago. She shook from the amount of control it took to stay behind her desk. Words, angry, eloquent words tried to force their way from her tight, dry throat. But all she managed was, "You're some piece of work, Jack Dylan."

His jaw went slack with surprise.

She attacked before he could do more than gape. "How dare you come over here this way, so worried that you *pushed* me." Rising to her feet, she practically spit the word at him. "Damn right you pushed me."

"Marianne—"

"Wasn't that what it was all about? You pushed me into facing what I felt, facing our... our heat." It was the only word she could think of to describe what they generated together. "You said to face the truth, Jack Dylan, the truth of how we've burned for each other for nine years. I wish to hell you had made me face the truth nine years ago."

"What?"

"Last night you threw my fears and my hesitations and my excuses in my face. And we..." She drew in a deep breath. "We shook the world. Last night, we faced some things we should have faced a long time ago. Are you apologizing for that?"

"No... I mean, yes... I mean..." His distress was palpable. He relieved it with one expressive four-letter word, and still another "I'm sorry."

"Didn't you mean what you said last night about the truth?"

"Yes, of course."

"Then why are you apologizing?"

"Because," he whispered, swallowing. Then his expression hardened, the tentativeness disappeared as he moved toward her. "I'm apologizing because I want it right this time. This morning, I thought you might think I pushed you too hard. And I didn't want that. I want everything perfect this time."

She waited, unmoving as he came around the desk. "Marianne, I'm not about to blow my second chance with you."

Dimly, she was aware of the heads that popped up at the desks and work stations outside the windowed walls of her office. But she didn't care. All that mattered was the look in Jack's eyes. The fierce determination. It was far removed from the look of the young man who had rejected her once. And though she hadn't realized she had been bracing herself for another such rebuff, she felt an incredible relief that it hadn't come.

Jack wanted another chance. A chance she wanted, too. She wanted them to take that chance together.

But only when he understood about the child he thought was his.

"We have to talk about Laura."

He stepped back, expression shuttered. "You said we had faced the truth."

"She's part of the truth." Marianne framed his dear, handsome face with her hands, so that he had to look right at her. "You have to accept that she's not your child. If you don't, there's no chance for us at all."

Jack pulled away. He didn't understand her insistence on maintaining that Kyle was Laura's father. He didn't know what it would cost her to admit that final bit of truth. But one look at the stubborn set of her jaw told him she wasn't about to give in.

So what should he do? Walk out? Sprinting across the square, Jack had realized how much he loved her. He didn't know why that certainty had come to him now, on a hot August morning with half the town looking on. But the knowledge was real. He could call it love now, when he hadn't be able to fathom what love was in the past.

He loved her because she had once encouraged his dreams. Because she had spirit. Because she filled him with fire. He loved her in spite of the lost years with Laura. He could forgive her that youthful mistake. He had regrets from that time, as well. He found, to his surprise, that he could even forgive her for denying Laura to him now. The patience he had used in confronting her about their daughter could also be applied to waiting for her to admit the truth.

For now, he had to prove his love. Win hers in return. It never occurred to him to just ask for that love. Most of Jack's life had been a series of hurdles he had to jump, obstacles to be overcome. Everything he had or was had been earned through grit and work and determination. He would win this, too. He would claim the family he once threw away.

"I want to be Laura's father."

She shook her head, started to protest.

"Hear me out," he said. "I want to be her father. Give me a chance to prove what a father I can be."

"What are you saying?"

He brought their clasped hands up between them. "I'm asking for time. For us. For Laura and you and me. Give me time, Marianne, to prove what I can be to you both."

"You don't have anything to prove, Jack. Not to me. You never did."

He couldn't believe her. Part of Jack would forever remain the country boy who was mystified by Marianne Cole's interest and friendship. Maybe someday he would believe what she said. But not now.

He lifted her hand to his lips, pressed a kiss in the palm. "Come on, Marianne. Proving myself could be so...fun."

He smiled. "Please say you'll give me time to show you how much fun."

Marianne's heart contracted at that smile, at the light that touched his eyes. His expression was the same one that had induced her down to the river on her first day at the paper. It was the same look that had led her on a hundred adventures. Once more, Jack was inviting her on a ride, *the faster the better*, as he had put it last night. And there would be no net. No safety exit. This ride could take them right over the cliff. To happiness. Or to a heartbreak deeper than she had known so far.

There were a hundred and one reasons why Marianne should resist his charming, roguish entreaty. The chief reason was Laura. But she ignored the warning signs flashing in her head. She wanted the ride, wanted the thrill. And someday, when they grew close enough, Jack would accept the truth about her daughter.

So she smiled, and she kissed him. In full sight of God, her employees and whoever else had elected to stroll past on Main Street. She didn't give a damn what they saw or said. Nothing anyone could imagine could top what she and Jack had done last night on his broad, mahogany desk or what she wished they could do right now.

They kissed until Francine rapped on the door and pushed it open. They turned to her, protests on their lips, but her big, bright smile forestalled them. "I hate to interrupt," she said, fairly beaming with approval. "But Jack, your secretary called and you were due in court thirty minutes ago. She says the judge and your client are both about to pop a blood vessel. Is there anything I should tell them?"

With one last, hard kiss, Jack set Marianne away. He did a one-armed vault over the desk, the same move he had executed so neatly at the Dairy Bar weeks ago. And he waved as he ran by the window. Marianne watched him until he disappeared into the door beside the Town and Country Dress Shop.

A sniffle brought her attention back to her secretary. The woman was mopping her eyes.

"Why, Francine, what's wrong?"

"Oh, nothing. Just..." Her sigh was tremulous. "It's just that I remember when you wore braces, Marianne. And here you are..." She drew in a deep breath. "Here you are."

Marianne laughed. Funny how what had seemed irritating yesterday was now so pleasant. "Yes, Francine. Here I am. And we've got a newspaper to put out. So let's get with it, shall we?"

Marianne bought the peach-colored polished cotton Lolly had told her about. She hated to admit the woman was right, but the flared skirt and tight, spaghetti-strapped bodice were the perfect style for her figure and the perfect color for her skin and hair. And the dress was just the right choice for the mid-month dinner dance at Willow Creek Country Club.

She danced in Jack's arms. The weather had taken an unexpected cooling turn, so they danced on a patio strung with Japanese lanterns, a quaint decorating trick Marianne had scoffed at once upon a time. But those lanterns suited the old, plantation-style clubhouse. They added to an ambience set by the three-piece combo tucked discreetly in the trellised corner. And that music provided the precise accompaniment to the laughter of old friends, the tinkle of ice cubes in glasses, the quiet murmur of Southern-flavored voices. The women were all wearing pastels. The men were all drinking Jack Daniel's. It was archaic, Marianne knew, but she was enchanted by it all the same.

Marianne had hated these evenings as a teenager when Delilah made her attend. And no doubt, tomorrow she would summon some justifiable disgust for those people in the group who were nothing but sanctimonious social snobs. But she had grown up. She knew everyone here didn't fit that harsh profile. And for tonight, she was delighted to be here. Delighted to be on Jack's arm.

He looked tall and handsome in his dark blue suit. People could say what they wanted about style, but she didn't believe there was any more fashionable statement than a man in a well-tailored suit, a crisp white shirt and tie. Yesterday, Miss Clara and Miss Louella had told Marianne that Jack was "a real fine catch." Tonight he certainly looked the part.

She liked the admiring glances he drew from women. But she liked knowing she was the one who would drive away with him. Later, they might go back over to the river, make love under the stars that were hanging like scattered gemstones in the Tennessee summer night sky.

Marianne had never dreamed there were so many ways and so many places in which to make love. Jack seemed intent on exploring all of them with her in the shortest amount of time possible. The two of them were good together. She only hoped their sexual harmony would translate into a deeper communion.

The music swung to a close, but she stayed in Jack's arms, pressing a kiss on his chin.

He bent close to her ear. "I can't help wondering what you've got on under that dress, Marianne Cole Wingate. I hope you're going to show me later."

His naughty comment and smile made her pulse pick up its pace. But before she could find a suitable retort, he was drawn away by Jeb and a couple of his political cronies.

Delilah, pretty in a violet chiffon, took hold of Marianne's hand. "You look beautiful tonight, dear. But that's not unusual, of course, since you positively glow these days.''

Marianne gave her aunt a little hug. "I'm happy. Almost as happy as you and Jeb, I think."

Someone tugged Delilah in the opposite direction with a question about the wedding, which would take place in two weeks. Marianne let the other woman go.

Not really in the mood for small talk, she drifted over to the low brick wall that bounded one side of the patio and breathed in the scents of pine trees and newly mown grass. She was happy, just as she had told Delilah. Perhaps it was a fool's paradise, but right now she didn't care.

For two weeks, she and Jack and Laura had been together as much as possible. Dinner most every night. Swimming last weekend here at the club. A quiet evening of Scrabble just last night. They had been spending a lot of time together before she and Jack started this second chance of theirs, but there was a difference now. It was more than Marianne and Jack becoming lovers. The three of them were becoming a unit. Laura seemed to have accepted the subtle shift in the relationship between her mother and Jack with no problem. Marianne had just been honest, told her they were seeing each other, asked her how she felt. It was a testimony to how much Laura had healed that she had not raised any objections in her father's name.

Her father. Marianne sighed, thinking of Kyle. And of Jack's mistaken assumptions.

Her relationship with Jack always came back to this.

Marianne was no idiot. She knew Laura was a dangerous unresolved issue. She and Jack skirted the subject like soldiers in a mine field, as if both of them knew it could explode the bond growing between them. Marianne wanted to put off any confrontations for as long as she could, still hoping time would make Jack believe in her.

He had asked for time to prove himself. She saw now that they all needed time to grow together. Jack was so good for Laura. She adored him and he returned the feeling. Marianne couldn't help but think his love was predicated on something more than a blood tie. Somehow this had to work out.

"It has to," she murmured, sending a fervent little prayer up to the star-studded heavens.

The combo came back from their break and started playing a slow, bluesy tune. Marianne looked around for Jack. However charmed she might be by tonight's soiree, she wasn't going to succumb to the custom of men smoking cigars and talking politics while the women gathered in clumps to discuss fashion and babies. That was too archaic for charm. She had come here to dance.

She found equality had infiltrated this last bastion of the old guard. There were several women with the men who were talking politics in one corner of the patio. Jack was right in the thick of things, so Marianne slipped into the circle next to Uncle Jeb. She listened while one of the older men expounded on his views regarding their current state representative, who wasn't seeking reelection.

"I'm glad he's stepping aside," the man said. "We need some young blood representing the district up in Nashville." He looked right at Jack. "We need someone like you."

Jack didn't seem surprised, giving Marianne the impression that this was a suggestion he had heard before.

She had never imagined Jack in politics. He evidently shared the same view for he shook his head. "I'm content just where I am. If you turn your life over to public service, you never get it back."

While the conversation strayed to other subjects, the man beside Uncle Jeb murmured, "Dylan's the best young legal mind in East Tennessee."

Uncle Jeb's chest fairly swelled with pride. "He reminds me of myself."

The other man chuckled. "I've always admired your modesty, Hampton." He sighed. "I sure wish you could convince him to run for this open seat, though. I'd like to see him in Nashville. He can be a firebrand in court. So he might shake a few of those entrenched bureaucrats out of their complacency if he turned his attention to government."

Uncle Jeb's big, gnarled hand settled on Marianne's shoulder. "This is who you should talk to. This pretty niece of mine probably has more influence on Jack than me these days."

Though flattering, her uncle's description made Marianne feel about sixteen. He meant well, however, so she smiled while he made introductions. The other man was a district court judge. He remembered her father, knew Delilah and asked questions about her plans for the newspaper. Then he returned to the subject of Jack and the possibility of a political career.

"I'm sorry," she replied. "I won't be any help in encouraging him. I've been living in D.C. for years, and I share Jack's jaded view of public life."

The judge expressed his disappointment, but added, "Whatever Jack Dylan does, I know he's going to do it well. Unlimited potential, that's what he has. Why, if he decided to desert Jeb here, he could write his own ticket at any firm in the state. Or the country, probably." The man's eyes twinkled down at her. "And I must add that he has an eye for beautiful and intelligent women."

When Marianne had thanked him and he drifted away, Jack came up behind her, whispering, "Was that old windbag trying to make time with my girl?"

She laughed and drew her arm through his. "Let's dance, shall we?"

But on the dance floor, the judge's comments remained with her.

. . . unlimited potential.

. . . write his own ticket at any firm.

Long ago, Marianne had seen the possibilities in Jack's sharp mind. The years had proven her right.

Inevitably, Marianne was forced to return to the question that had troubled her for weeks. Why was Jack here? If he could go anywhere, why stay in the place he once swore to escape?

She asked him later that night, as they sat at the edge of the river, stargazing.

He groaned at her question. "You don't listen very well, do you? I think I've answered this one."

"Just humor me a minute." She repeated the judge's compliments. "Doesn't it excite you a little that he and others like him think so highly of you?"

He answered carefully. "I'd be lying if I said no. I've worked damn hard. It's nice to know I've earned some people's respect."

"And doesn't that make you want to reach for more than you have?"

He laughed. "I have an extremely busy practice right now. And if Jeb goes through on his promise to retire, I'll be snowed under." He leaned forward, touched her lips with his own. "When will I have time for you and Laura?" He kissed her again, his hand drifting to her breast. "Time for this?"

"But Jack—"

"And this?" His mouth opened over hers while he skimmed peach-polished cotton up over her knees.

She succumbed to his caress, to the lure of moonlight and the passion she knew awaited her. She forgot her questions about his life choices. Marianne had discovered Jack's touch could derail her thoughts quite easily.

But the next morning over breakfast, she thought of the judge's words again. In church, she studied her favorite stained-glass window and wondered if Jack really was content with his practice.

After Sunday dinner with Jeb and Delilah, Marianne begged out of an afternoon of fishing, and sent Jack and Laura off by themselves. As usual, Jeb and Delilah sat in the sunny kitchen with the Sunday papers spread around them.

Pausing just inside the doorway, Marianne said, "I have something I want to talk to you two about."

Jeb lowered the paper and took off his glasses. A smile touched his generous mouth. "Is this an announcement?"

"Of course not."

Delilah sighed in disappointment. "I thought maybe we'd be having a double wedding."

Rolling her eyes, Marianne pulled a chair out from under the table and sat down across from Delilah. "It's nothing like that." She reminded Jeb of the conversation the evening before with the judge, and of the other man who wanted Jack to run for a seat in the state house of representatives. "Jack has every opportunity in the world. Can either of you tell me why he doesn't take advantage of them?"

Jeb and Delilah traded glances.

"Is there some reason I should know about that he's stayed here in Willow Creek?"

Her uncle shifted in his seat, clearing his throat. "I believe he's here because it's where he wants to be."

"You're sure he doesn't feel he owes it to you to stay?"

The older man's surprise was clear. "Has Jack said that to you?"

"Of course he hasn't," Delilah said before Marianne could reply. "I'm certain he doesn't feel that way. I think he loves his work. Loves this town, too."

"But he used to hate it."

Delilah retorted, "So did you, but you're back now."

Marianne dropped her chin to her hand. "Has Jack been tutoring you? You sound just like him."

"Maybe we're all just telling the truth." Jeb fixed her with an unflinching stare. "If you want someone to blame for him staying here, look to yourself, missy."

Delilah sent him a warning glance.

But Jeb, who now had his dander up, said, "You broke that boy's heart."

"Jeb!" Delilah exclaimed.

Marianne sat back in her chair, gaze darting between the two of them. "So you knew about me and Jack, about what—"

"We never knew what happened, exactly," Delilah cut in. "But my goodness, Marianne, I knew it was something. I was in a fog, I admit, trying to pretend Elliot never existed so that I wouldn't have to grieve for him. But I knew Jack was here all the time. That you were close."

"But we'd always been close."

Delilah sighed. "It was different."

"Confound it," Jeb exclaimed. "I'm not afraid to call a spade a spade. Jack was in heat that whole summer, and you walked around pretending not to notice."

"I did not!"

"Oh, yes, you did," he insisted. "Now admittedly, you were upset about your father's death. But that was still no excuse for the way you hung on Jack. You were an engaged woman. If you needed that kind of comfort, you should have gone to Washington and gotten it from your intended."

Delilah touched his arm. "Now, Jeb, you can't blame Marianne too much. She and Jack really were friends."

"Until that summer," Marianne admitted. Uncle Jeb's words had brought a niggling sense of guilt. Had she unwittingly encouraged Jack? After all, she could have pushed him away the first time he kissed her. But she hadn't. She had been startled by his kiss, intrigued by her own response.

Her aunt got up and went to the sink to draw a glass of water. "I sensed something was really wrong between you and Jack the week of the wedding, but I didn't want to meddle. I was certain there had been real trouble when Jack didn't come to the ceremony."

"Didn't come to work, either," Jeb put in. "For nearly a week, he didn't show up. He finally dragged in, looking like a whipped puppy. Said he was going to quit school. I gave him quite a talking to, and he went back, all right."

"Yes, he went back then." Delilah returned to her seat, her soft mouth set in a serious line. "After Christmas, though, he dropped out."

Marianne sat up, shocked. This was the first she had heard of Jack leaving school.

Jeb was shaking his head. "I heard from a friend of mine at the college about what he had done. So I drove out to his parents' place. He was there, working with his brother out somewhere. I had a chance to talk to his mother and father first. They both told me how worried they were about him. The Dylans might not have had the money to educate Jack themselves, but they were proud of him. They wanted him to succeed."

"Did you convince him to go back?" Marianne asked, thinking that was something Jack might believe he owed Jeb for.

Jeb looked down, shuffled his paper and glasses, obviously hesitating.

"He did more than convince him," Delilah said. "He paid for the rest of Jack's schooling."

Again Marianne was caught off guard. "Why didn't either of you tell me this before?"

"Because it was Jack's and my business and not yours," Jeb said with typical bluntness.

"Why should we have told you?" Delilah said, looking almost as irritated as Jeb. "You were gone. Married to Kyle. Expecting a baby. I thought you were happy."

"But Jack had been my friend, and he was in trouble."

Delilah's tone was firm. "I thought it was for the best that you didn't get involved with Jack's problems. I knew there was something painful between the two of you. I knew you called him over and over again that Christmas. And that he never called back. Quite honestly, I thought it was for the best."

"Why didn't you say something?"

The older woman leaned across the table, a pleading look in her eyes. "I wanted you to be happy, Marianne. I wanted all those dreams you had to come true. Goodness knows, your father and I never knew much personal happiness. I wanted you to have a chance. Your mother's death when you were a baby and then Elliot's everlasting turmoil didn't make for much of a childhood, Marianne. I did what I could—"

Marianne reached out, covered the other woman's hand with her own. "You did fine, Delilah. More than fine."

"But Elliot's drinking hurt you. I know you felt responsible for it in some way."

"I just wished he wasn't so miserable. I was a kid. And I took everything personally. I didn't know why just being my father wasn't enough to make him happy. Now I understand." She sighed. "At least I think I do."

Delilah squeezed her hand. "I didn't want any more turmoil for you, Marianne. I thought you were happy with Kyle and that Jack would bring you trouble. Perhaps I was wrong."

"Then you had good company," Marianne murmured. "I thought he would bring me trouble, too. And so did he." She found it strange how everyone had been so intent on saving her from Jack.

"You nearly destroyed him," Jeb said, breaking his silence. "He left town that Christmas, went up to Nashville with a buddy and blew most of his school money in trying to forget something or the other." He looked at Marianne as if she would know what Jack was seeking to forget.

Because she did know, Marianne squirmed under his scrutiny. "What happened when you talked to him about it?"

Arms folded over his middle, Jeb rocked back in his chair. "I wasn't about to let him waste his life. I offered to pay his way through school."

"I'm surprised he took you up on it." Marianne knew more than most how proud Jack could be.

"He insisted on it being a loan, although I would have given it to him."

"So he repaid you?"

"He repaid the money, yes. With interest. But he insisted on doing more. He offered to work three years in the practice. At a good salary, of course. I knew a good bargain when I heard one. So I took him up on it."

Repaying the money and giving up three years of his life sounded like more than enough repayment to Marianne.

Jack didn't owe Jeb anything. But what she still couldn't understand was why he hadn't been champing at the bit to escape after that. She said as much to Jeb and Delilah.

Her uncle exploded again. "What's so all-fired wrong about his being here? I've lived here my whole life, too. That practice was always good enough for me."

Marianne would never denigrate this man or his work. "I'm not faulting your practice, Uncle Jeb, or you. But living here, practicing this kind of law—that's what you wanted. Jack wanted something different. His dreams—"

"Dreams change," Jeb said, leaning toward her. "Haven't yours?"

She could only admit that he was right.

But in her mind Jack had abandoned his dreams.

All because of her.

Delilah touched her arm again, said softly, "After three years, I think Jack realized he liked some of the things he used to think he hated about Willow Creek. You've said the same yourself."

"Yes, but—"

"After three years he was entrenched," Jeb added. "Entrenched in the community and in his clients' affairs."

Entrenched. Marianne hated the word. To her, entrenched meant trapped. She understood that feeling all too well. For too many years, she felt trapped in a loveless marriage. For most of his life, her father had been trapped in this town.

Entrenched didn't mean happy.

Jeb told her to stop worrying about what Jack might have given up. Delilah advised her to look to the future.

But Marianne was caught up in past mistakes.

Late that afternoon, waiting for Jack and Laura to come home, she sat with Laura's kitten in the window seat up in her old room. Though the curtains and bedspread were new and the furniture had traveled with Laura from D.C., the wallpaper was the same as when Marianne slept here. Tiny rosebuds on a sea of paler pink. Marianne could remember staring at the pattern, counting the roses on the night her father died and during that long week before her wedding to Kyle. That week without Jack.

Jeb said she broke his heart. Marianne had always claimed it was the other way around. But whatever the case, what had ignited between them had set off an irreparable course of events. Jack's life had taken a new direction. He said he was happy. But Marianne couldn't be sure. She couldn't help worrying. All she had ever wanted for Jack was for his dreams to come true.

No, she realized. If she were honest, she would admit her real mission had been to save Jack. Just as she had tried to save her father.

Marianne could remember sitting just where she was, trying to plot some way to make her father happy. By the time she was about thirteen, she realized it was useless. Then she and Jack became friends. Arrogant, rough-edged Jack Dylan. She made him her next crusade. What was it about him that made her think of her father? Was it a look in the eyes? Perhaps the never-quite-satisfied curl of his lip? Whatever the case, Marianne had wanted to save Jack from himself.

On the surface, she had succeeded in her mission. He got the education she made him realize he craved. He was a successful man. Only not in the arena of which he dreamed.

Jeb and Delilah said he had made his choices and to let it alone.

Marianne, remembering her father, couldn't. Not yet, anyway.

Chapter Ten

Marianne was restless. And trying hard to hide it.

Watching her from across his living room, Jack saw the telltale signs someone who didn't know her well might miss. The tugging at her hair. The pursing and unpursing of her lips. It had been the same every night this week. Since the dance at the country club, in fact. He wondered what was bugging her.

"Jack?"

He dragged his attention from Marianne and focused on the woman who sat on the couch in front of him. "I'm sorry, Sally. What did you say?"

Sally glanced over at Marianne, too. "Maybe I should go."

"We've just got a few more things to cover."

"But I'm intruding on you guys."

It *had* started out as a rare evening alone for Jack and Marianne. Delilah had taken Laura with her to Knoxville, where they were staying overnight to enjoy the zoo and leave plenty of time for finding Laura a dress for the wedding. Marianne was pleased that her aunt and Laura were growing closer. Jack was happy because it gave him and Marianne an entire night together. They had been leaving to go out to dinner when Sally called with questions about Betsy's custody hearing. Knowing how limited Sally's time was, they told her to come over, and the three of them shared a pizza.

Jack hadn't thought Marianne minded the change of plans, although she had been unusually restless and quiet. But in reply to Sally, she spoke up from her stance near the front window. "You're not intruding on anything. The custody hearing starts Monday, and you and Jack need to prepare. There's nothing more important than that. Besides, it's raining to beat the band. You can't leave in this downpour." As if to underscore her words, thunder cracked, and the table lamps flickered during the flash of lightning that followed.

Tucking a strand of dark hair behind her ear, Sally sighed. "I'm just sorry we couldn't do this at your office, Jack. But I'm having trouble keeping help at the restaurant, and there are only certain people I trust Betsy with these days."

There had been no sign of Sally's sister since she had sued for custody of Betsy. But Jack knew Sally was taking no chances. Betsy had seldom been out of her sight since the night of the July 4th festival. It was only because she wanted to keep Betsy as much in the dark about this hearing as possible that the child wasn't with her now.

Jack flipped through the pad in front of him, trying to remember where they had left off. He needed to keep his mind on business and away from whatever had Marianne so tense.

"Is Betsy going to have to testify?" Marianne asked.

"No," Sally replied at the same time Jack said "Maybe." Sally's mouth thinned.

He spread his hands in a helpless gesture. "The judge may very well want to talk to her. She's not a baby. She'll be nine in January. She's old enough to be asked with whom she wants to live."

Marianne crossed the room to sit down beside Sally on the couch. "Betsy's testimony could work out well, couldn't it? Of course she'll say she wants to stay with you."

Sally shook her head. "I'd rather she weren't put through it. Betsy knows I'm not her biological mother. I was honest about that, and about Renee, from the beginning, and she seems well adjusted about the whole thing. But her counselor at school and the books I've read say adopted children can have some real insecurities. I don't want to bring that on for Betsy by exposing her to this hearing."

"You don't think you should prepare her?" Marianne asked. "Just in case?"

"I'm praying the judge will take one look at Renee and Carl and throw the whole thing out."

Jack had no such delusions. The fact that this matter had already reached a hearing stage spoke volumes. A check of court records had revealed the judge who would hear the case had a history of deciding in favor of the biological mother. True, those cases had dealt mainly with divorces or instances of temporary custody. The fact that Sally had adopted Betsy made this one tougher. But it wasn't a sure thing. Renee was charging that Sally coerced her into the adoption, and she and her lawyers would attempt to prove Betsy would be better off in a traditional household with her husband and his children, rather than with single mother Sally. A private investigator had turned up nothing on any current drug use or trafficking by Renee, or any other wrongdoing on her part, either. Hard as it was to imagine, she seemed to have straightened out her life.

"I wish we could bring up what happened on the 4th," Sally complained.

This was an argument Jack had been having with her for weeks. "We have no proof that Renee had anything to do with that. You'd better hope it *doesn't* come up. They'll try to make you look bad for allowing her to wander away."

Sally sat back, nervously covering her mouth with her hand.

"That's ridiculous," Marianne protested. "Children wander off all the time."

"I'm just warning you." Jack thumped his legal pad to add emphasis to his words. "I'm sure Renee and her counselors will get nasty. I've seen some bad things happen during custody hearings. Emotions run high when a child is involved."

Marianne got up abruptly, crossing back to the window. Jack followed her with his gaze. He had never seen her this edgy before. Maybe he would find out what was wrong when Sally was gone. Frowning, he studied the list of questions he and Sally had planned to discuss. One by one, he checked them off, then tossed the legal pad aside.

He sat forward in his chair, looking Sally straight in the eye. "There's just one last thing. You can still bring in a specialist in family law. I've got a good contact in Knoxville. I could file for a continuance, put the hearing off so she would have time to prepare."

She was shaking her head before he finished the suggestion. "I want you, Jack."

"Come on, Sally. Think about it. This is your last chance to make the switch. It wouldn't hurt me, and it could have a significant effect on the outcome."

She reached out and gripped his hand. "I can't imagine anyone better than you to help me through this. I don' think anyone else could know how frightened and angry am. Or how much I want to win."

Jack squeezed her hand and smiled in reassurance. When he looked up, he saw that Marianne was frowning at him She rearranged her features and quickly turned away. Bu she looked upset.

Perhaps Sally could sense her unease, for she took of then, disappearing into the stormy night despite both Jack': and Marianne's protests. When the front door closed be hind her, the sound of the rain and the thunder seemed louder. Perhaps it was because Marianne was so very quiet

Jack knew what she was thinking. After Sally's state ment about his understanding how much she wanted to wi custody of Betsy, Marianne undoubtedly thought he had told the other woman about Laura. But he hadn't. Sally only meant that he was her friend, and he knew how much her daughter meant to her. He started to explain that to Marianne, but reconsidered. Any mention of his claim on Laura was bound to have her retreating from him.

It had been nearly three weeks since he had asked for time to prove himself as a father. He knew that wasn't long at all. He told himself to be patient. Once, she would have trusted him with her life. But it seemed she didn't trust him with the truth about Laura. It hurt. It stood in their way. The feel ings growing between them were true and strong. If only they could put the question of Laura to rest, he would be the happiest man in the world.

He had to push down his growing frustration as he joined her at the window. He forced a light note in his voice. "You seem down tonight. Anything wrong?"

"It's just the rain."

"You want to go back over to your house?"

"It's so bad out. Let's stay here for the night."

"Okay." He slipped his arms around her. "But come away from the window before lightning finds you."

"Uncle Jeb always says that if lightning's going to strike you, it'll cross a room to do so."

"Well, I'd rather any lightning bolt with your name on it had to work a little harder to find you."

She allowed him to draw her to his sagging, comfortable old couch. He cleared magazines off the upended orange crate he used as a combination coffee table and ottoman and grinned over his shoulder at Marianne. "I may be in the market for some furniture. Do you think it's time?"

She gave him a distracted smile and made a reply completely off the subject. "You're very patient with Sally."

He settled back against the worn cushions, drawing her close against his chest. "This is hard on her."

"I suppose all custody cases are difficult."

"Like I said, I've handled some that got nasty."

"Ever thought of specializing in family litigation?"

"Nope."

"Specializing in anything?"

"I like variety."

Marianne was silent, but Jack could almost hear the wheels turning in her head.

So he cut her off with a question of his own. "Tell me how the paper is."

She pulled away from him. "It's the same. Making the changes I want is slow going."

He tried to draw her out, but she was preoccupied. Finally, she got up, moved restlessly around the room, straightening the single painting on the opposite wall, flipping through his meager collection of CDs.

"Don't you ever feel frustrated with your practice?" she asked finally, turning back to him.

"Frustrated?"

"Maybe limited is the right word."

"I just told you I get lots of variety."

"But are they cases you can really sink your teeth into?"

"I try to think of every case as important."

"But—"

"Marianne, please drop it, okay?" Jack sighed. This was an old discussion, the same one they had been having in one form or another, again and again, since she came home. And now that he thought about it, she had brought it up everyday this week. He was tired of giving Marianne the same old answers. She apparently just wouldn't accept what he told her—that he liked what he did.

"If things had worked out differently between us in the past, you wouldn't be here," she said now.

"Maybe not."

"No." She shook her head for emphasis. "You would be in some top firm, arguing cases that would change the world."

He couldn't resist a little sarcasm. "Like Kyle did?"

"That's not what I meant."

"He put together big deals for big, international companies, didn't he? Is that your idea of changing the world?"

"You know it isn't. That's not what I ever imagined you doing."

"Well, maybe I can't imagine doing anything other than what I do now."

She looked about to protest again when someone knocked on the door. Glad of the interruption, Jack got up to answer it.

The gaunt, ashen-faced man who stood dripping on the porch was an old friend. He was maybe ten years older than Jack, had grown up on a neighboring farm that he still worked.

"Richard," Jack said, surprised. "Come in."

"I should have called," the man said, wiping his shoes on the mat before stepping inside. "I did call your office, but you were gone. I wasn't going to call you at home, but then I was headed downtown when I passed here and saw your car and lights." His Adam's apple bobbed as he swallowed. "I . . . I hate to come to you like this, Jack, but it's Keith again, he—" He broke off when he saw Marianne was in the room.

Jack made the introductions quickly, though he was certain Richard already knew who Marianne was. Few natives of the county didn't know the Cole family. He reminded Richard, "You said something about Keith?"

The man cleared his throat, looked uncertainly at Marianne. Jack took his arm and they stepped out on the porch again.

Richard's son Keith was in trouble. It was nothing new. The boy was half the reason for Richard's hollow eyes and habitually sad expression. Keith was eighteen now, no longer a juvenile, and this time he was being held for armed robbery. If he was guilty, he was in deep, deep trouble. Trouble his family could ill afford—financially or otherwise.

"I hate to ask, Jack, seeing as how I still owe you so much from that trouble last year. But Keith . . . I . . . well, we need your help."

It wasn't the first time a neighbor had come to Jack in the night, seeking his help. He knew it wouldn't be the last. Just as he knew he would always respond.

"You're going out in this?" Marianne asked, gesturing toward the rain-streaked windows when he went back inside to explain.

Jack pulled a Windbreaker from the closet beside the door. "His boy's in trouble. And he needs my help."

"It can't wait till morning?"

"It's bad, Marianne. The boy needs a lawyer now."

"Maybe a night in jail would help."

"That's not my decision." Jack kissed Marianne, drew a hand through her soft hair, whispered a fierce, "Please wait here for me. I'll try not to be too late."

Then he went out in the rain. On the porch, he took the arm of a friend whose shoulders were sloped from life's disappointments, whose heart was probably going to be broken for good by his no-account son. Jack followed the other man's car through the dark, wet streets, just hoping he could do something to help.

In his first year of law school, he had fantasized about fat corporate accounts, fatter salaries and luxurious perks. Marianne had told him she thought he would end up arguing important social issues in front of the Supreme Court, instead. Because she said it, he believed it might happen.

But tonight, while Marianne waited for him, he advised a frightened young man who had toted a gun inside a truck stop and robbed the cash register of a hundred bucks. He helped a despondent father arrange bail. He did his best to put forth some hope. Then he sloughed through the rain again, knowing his best wouldn't be nearly enough to make a real difference for this family.

Jack wasn't sure if Marianne would still be waiting when he got home around eleven-thirty. But she was. Wrapped in a quilt his mother had made, she was curled into a corner on the couch, her blue eyes wide and watchful and questioning. She said nothing, but followed him as he shook the rain off his jacket and headed into the bedroom for some dry clothes.

"So?" she asked, sinking down on the edge of his bed while he threw off his shirt. "What's the story?"

He peeled soaked jeans down his legs. As editor of the newspaper, she would find out the details sooner than most, so he didn't elaborate. "You can read it on the police docket tomorrow."

She didn't push for more. She just carried the jeans into the bathroom and hung them over the shower door while he dried his hair with a towel.

Her eyes met his in the mirror over the sink. "Do you do this kind of thing often?"

He shrugged, reaching for the robe that hung on back of the door. "When someone needs me."

"You just dash right out when anyone calls?"

Perhaps Jack was anticipating sarcasm, or perhaps her voice really did hold a note of derision. Whatever the case, he took exception. "This is what I do, Marianne, what I am. Maybe you don't see—"

"Make me see," she demanded. "Make me understand why this is all so important to you when we both know you could be doing so much more."

"I happen to think what I did tonight was important."

"You helped a friend, yes, but—"

"That's right. I used what I know, and who I am in this town, to help someone. Why are you acting as if that's wrong?"

She put her hands to her temples as if to massage an ache away. "It's not wrong, Jack. That's not what I mean. It's just that I didn't think you struggled through law school to do this sort of thing. I thought your plans and your dreams were bigger." She drew in a deep breath. "I want to know why you've settled for being a small-town lawyer, settled for less than your dreams."

"I don't feel as if I *settled*—"

"Was it me, Jack?" she asked, cutting him off. "Did my marrying Kyle hurt you so much that you turned your back on your other dreams? I know you left school—"

"Jeb shouldn't have told you that."

"You don't owe him anything, you know."

"I know that."

"Then why, Jack? I need to know what happened that changed you so."

He turned on his heel and went to the kitchen, where he poured himself a cup of the coffee left over from their dinner.

Marianne followed him and stood in the doorway, waiting for an answer.

Leaning against the counter, he swirled the coffee around in his mug while he turned her question in his head. What could he possibly say that would make her understand why nights like tonight were important to him?

He started by asking her a question of his own. "What were you going to do when you took that job at the paper in D.C.?"

"I wanted to be an investigative reporter. You know that."

"So how did you get from that to writing a column about everyday people?"

"I just found out what I liked to write. What I was best at. With my column I was able to address issues that were important to me."

"But back here, when you and I made our big life plans together, you never dreamed you'd be writing a column like that, or that you'd come home and write the same sort of material in editorials for your family's newspaper."

"Things change—"

"Why is it you were allowed to change, but I wasn't?"

As he expected, she had no answer for that.

Jack took a long sip on his coffee before he said, "I guess you know I came back here to work three years for Jeb."

"He told me."

Thrusting a hand through his damp hair, he thought back to the summer after graduation when he joined the firm. "I was planning to work out those years. And then I was going. Man, I couldn't wait. That whole first year, I was plotting my escape. Part of those plots were aimed at proving something to you, I think. I don't really understand what all was going through my head then."

"And what happened?"

He had to smile, remembering. "Then this old man came in."

"An old man?"

"Yeah. He wanted a will. He had a good amount of property. Some nice savings. But he wasn't a rich guy, you know. And I..." Jack paused, shook his head. "Well, by this time, Jeb had let me argue a couple of bigger cases. I remember being amazed that there were so many interesting cases right here in Willow Creek. But anyway, I was thinking I was a pretty hotshot lawyer. And here was this guy, so damn serious about this will. I was pissed off because our paralegal wasn't there to get the man's information. I wanted him out of the office. I wanted to go to lunch."

Jack's smile faded as he looked down at his coffee mug. "I guess he could tell I was sort of contemptuous, because about halfway through our meeting, he looked at me and he said, 'Boy, I know this might not seem important to you, but to me it's only my whole life.'"

He looked up again, met Marianne's steady gaze. "*Only his whole life*. Only everything he had spent his life working for. He was putting all of that in my hands, trusting me to make sure everything was done the way he wanted. To some people, to me at first, it wasn't much, *he* wasn't much. But he felt like his whole world depended on what *I* drew up in that will."

Jack turned his head, cocked it to the side, listened to the rain that drummed on the roof. "Everything changed after that day, Marianne. I can't explain it. Maybe it sounds silly to you. But all of sudden, I felt like what I was doing right here in Willow Creek was as important as anything I could do anywhere else. I stopped making plans to leave. It didn't seem important anymore."

Arms crossed, Marianne stared at him. He couldn't tell if he had gotten through to her or not.

Jack drained the coffee and set the mug on the counter. "Do you remember the day I was accepted to law school?"

A smile touched her features. "We got drunk on champagne in the middle of the day and went up on the roof of my dormitory."

"You said we were both going to change the world."

Marianne nodded, thinking of the clear, cloudless blue sky of that day. And the dizzying sense of being invincible. She wondered if she had felt that powerful since.

"Well, I change worlds," Jack whispered, drawing her gaze back to his. "Oh, I know. Most people think of lawyers as slime in a suit. Comedians make jokes about us, some of them deserved, I admit. Other people say we're the reason the system doesn't work. But every once in a while I change somebody's world. It might be in court. It might be in taking a ride on a rainy night with a desperate father. But it matters, Marianne." His voice roughened, became fierce. "What I do *matters*."

His words were eloquent. And Marianne knew Jack believed what he said. He had convictions. And his life had purpose. She thought his intensity and dedication only proved that he should push himself. She still believed he should press his limits, spread his wings, see if what lay over the horizon wasn't just as exciting as what was most familiar.

Her father had refused to try himself. He took the familiar road and ended up hating himself for it. She was still
determined to save Jack from that.

That's what she told him. He argued with her. Again and
again they reached the same impasse. He said he was content. She said it wouldn't last.

Weariness finally drove them to bed. They slipped between the covers in a tense, unyielding silence. But in the
darkness, Marianne went into Jack's arms, surprising him.

Silently, with a sort of desperation, they touched and
tasted, brought each other to the brink of completion with
lips and hands and sweet lovers' words. Jack knew his ca-
resses were an attempt to bridge the distance that lay between them. He thought Marianne's intent was the same.

But their failure was complete.

The moves were right. He slipped inside her with an easy
grace. She moved exquisitely against him, meeting each
thrust of his hips with a gentle, rocking glide of her own.
Her orgasm came with a force that brought her arching off
the bed, twisting around him, forcing his own shattering
completion. Together, they knew earth-splitting pleasure.

But when it was over, when Marianne slept, Jack lay
awake, an awful, aching desperation in his gut.

She didn't understand what he was doing with his life.
Worse, she didn't approve. And God, how he craved her
approval. That was what he had always wanted. From the
very beginning of their friendship, Marianne had told Jack
he could be more. That's what he thought he had become.
But he was wrong. She told him he was wrong.

He remembered that night in his office. She had accused
him of being jealous of her. She said, "You never did half
of what you planned."

She made him question himself. He didn't want these
doubts. He wanted to feel as confident as he had when he

told Marianne about that old man and his will. But he couldn't. He felt almost as lacking and unsure as he had when he watched Marianne drive away after marrying another man. He felt her doubts and her questions pulling at him. He imagined them pulling her away from him. Pulling her *and* Laura away.

And his desperation grew.

He could only think that he had to bind her to him, bind *them* to him for good.

So in the morning, in the sunshine that spread across his bed and turned Marianne's hair to ruddy silk, he woke her with a kiss.

And then he proposed.

Chapter Eleven

When Marianne was a child, Delilah used to tell her that every problem could be solved. All one had to do was make a list of pros and cons, tally them up and act accordingly.

One week after Jack's impetuous, passionate proposal, Marianne sat in her office, staring at just such a list.

Her answer to that proposal had been a flat "no" at first. How could they think of marrying with so many unresolved issues between them?

"We can't," she had said, sitting up in bed, pushing the sleep-tousled hair from her eyes. "We haven't...I mean, it's just too soon."

Jack was insistent. "We've wasted most of our lives being apart."

She took a deep breath and ventured into the most sensitive issue between them. "What about Laura?"

He deliberately misunderstood what she meant. "I think she'll be happy and excited."

"Jack, you know that's not what I meant."

But he wasn't listening. He tumbled her back against the pillows with an agile move. His green eyes were intense, his kiss hungry. "Marry me, Marianne," he whispered against her mouth. "After spending the whole night with you at last, I don't want us to be apart again. Because of Laura, I know we can't do that. So marry me. Please."

"Jack, there's too much we need to consider first."

"We can consider it just as well when we're married."

"But—"

"Marry me," he repeated, his lips roaming down her neck. "I want so much for you and Laura and me to be a family."

She continued to say no.

"But I love you." His voice was a soft rumble against the hollow of her throat. "I love you, Marianne Cole Wingate."

I love you. It was a magic, seductive phrase. Especially when it came from Jack, especially when he kept repeating it over and over, like a sacred litany. He said it as if love solved all their problems. Marianne wanted to believe him. It would be easy to give in to his kisses. To believe the rosy pictures of family togetherness he painted.

"We could make another baby," he murmured as his lips drifted from her throat down to the valley between her breasts. "Laura would love a brother."

Marianne tried to be strong and sensible. It wasn't easy with his words pouring like warm honey over her. *Jack loved her.* That knowledge brought her joy. And somehow, with gentle but insistent ease, he forced a "maybe" from her.

Sanity had returned after they'd made love. She backed away. But all week he had continued to be persistent. Which was why she sat at her desk now, a list of "pros" and "cons" in front of her.

She had come into the office before seven, when the building was quiet and she was alone, in order to set down the situation in black and white. She had a feeling Jack was going to press his case in a big way tomorrow night after Jeb and Delilah's wedding. She had less than forty-eight hours to arm herself, to make a decision.

Marianne studied the paper in front of her. Her lists of pluses and minuses were tallied. But simple arithmetic wasn't working.

The pro column had come to her quickly. At the top there was "passion." She had circled the word in heavy, black ink, thinking to give it more weight. Under it were "friendship, support, understanding, charm, companionship, intelligence," and, even though she considered it shallow, "good looks."

In the con column there were only three entries. One was "love"? The question mark was there because, even though he said he loved her, she still wasn't sure if she was confusing love with lust.

The second entry on the debit side read, "Jack's life choices." Though she had tried to believe he was happy with where he was, Marianne still felt guilty, felt her own choices nine years ago had sent his life spinning off course. She worried about carrying that burden of guilt into marriage. She feared the guilt would somehow take root and grow between her and Jack, choke out their happiness like some poisonous weed. She had started one marriage filled with guilt and didn't want to again. She was also afraid of the awful responsibility she felt for Jack's happiness. Was it realistic? Could she live with it?

And finally, at the end of the cons was one simple word: "Laura." Jack still believed she was his child. So Laura anchored the whole list like a heavy stone.

The neat rows of columns in front of Marianne should have been easy to decipher. The pros far out*numbered* the cons. And yet the cons, especially the third entry, far out*weighed* the pros. Marianne didn't know whether to add, subtract, multiply or divide. In the end, she tore up the list and threw it in the trash.

Thinking she might find the answer to her dilemma elsewhere, she wandered out of her office, through the reception area where Francine was now gearing up for another day. She meandered out into the building as other employees trickled in. She greeted the young reporter she had recently hired. Stopped by the one-man art department to look over a new idea for the paper's layout. She saw the bookkeeper, the advertising manager, the typesetters.

Finally, Marianne stood near the center of the building and just listened. There was a hum in the air as the newspaper came to life around her.

She liked the sound. For the first time since taking over, she realized how much she liked it. Oh, she was still frustrated with slow-to-change clients and employees who still saw her as Delilah's niece and her father's daughter. She was still worried that the bottom line might never improve or that she would be forced into selling. But in the midst of all that, she felt hopeful. And she was excited, too. Succeeding here was a challenge that caused her more excitement than her byline in D.C. had ever generated.

Did Jack feel this way when he walked into his office? When he stood in front of a jury, arguing a case? He said he did. She remembered his face when he told her about the old man who had come to him for a will. She thought of his patience with Sally. She saw him going out in the rain to help a neighbor in need. Maybe he really was happy. She wanted to believe him. All she ever wanted was for Jack to have what he wanted. That's why she had pushed him toward his dreams.

But was it for Jack's sake that she had pushed him?
Or was it for herself?

The questions came at Marianne out of nowhere. The answers were blindingly fast, as well. When they were younger she had pushed Jack, not just for his sake, but to please herself. It made her feel good when he succeeded. And coming home this summer, thinking he might have settled for second best, had felt like a personal failure to her. She had lived so many years with the idea that she had failed her father in some way. Then she carried that guilt forward, applied it to what she perceived as Jack's certain unhappiness.

Marianne's lip curled in disgust with herself. Yes, she was such a little savior. That's why she continued to push Jack, to question his choices. Oh, she couldn't be too hard on herself. She *did* want him to be happy. But perhaps it was time to start listening to him when he said he was content. It was time to realize that she didn't need to save him anymore.

Feeling as if something had been set free inside her, Marianne went back through the building. The clear, blue sky outside beckoned. She pushed through the front doors and stepped into a perfect August morning. Warm, but without oppressive humidity. A day brushed with gold.

Laughing at her poetic weather analysis, she took in the flag snapping in the breeze on the courthouse lawn. She checked her watch as the clock peeled nine times. She nodded at the postman who came whistling by. She waved across the square to Miss Louella. And a familiar flash of red caught her eye. A horn blew as it disappeared around a corner. And in a few minutes, Jack came striding up the sidewalk toward her.

His jacket was off, slung carelessly over his shoulder. His briefcase swung jauntily at his side. He stopped in front of the bank to shake someone's hand. He nodded to two teenage boys who hailed him from a passing car. He paused to slap Frank Harvey on the back. Another man joined them, and full, masculine laughter drifted up the sidewalk toward Marianne.

Something broke open inside her as she watched Jack throw back his head and laugh. He looked so... at home. That was the only description that came to mind. And it fit, she realized. He fit.

The final vestiges of guilt and regret for the past slipped away while Marianne stood waiting for Jack to reach her. Maybe she had pushed him part of the way to his dreams. But in the end, he chose new dreams, and he pushed himself, saved himself. She wasn't accountable for his life choices any more than she had been responsible for her father's unhappiness. Each person had to choose their own path. Jack had chosen his. All she could do was try to grow and change and adapt with him.

All she could do was love him.

Yes, *love*. The realization fell on her like the morning sun, with gentle, warming strokes.

Her first day at the paper, Marianne had looked at Jack and realized he was the reason she had come home. She had been denying that truth ever since. She had pretended to come home for Delilah. For Laura's safety. To rescue the family newspaper. But it was Jack who drew her home. Jack who owned her heart.

On her mental checklist, Marianne took the question mark off of "love," threw it off the con column, along with any lingering doubts about "Jack's life choices." Those were erased.

If important problems were really as simple to solve as Delilah had once told her, the totals on her list would be pretty clear right now.

But Marianne knew nothing had ever been simple between her and Jack. She wanted it too clear-cut. She wanted to believe Jack when he said they should get married now and consider all their problems later. But with the rest of her list in perfect order, Marianne found the question of Laura weighed heavier than ever at the bottom.

Even as she went forward to greet Jack with love buoying her heart, his mistaken assumption about Laura stepped between them. Like a cloud over the sun, it took the gold out of the day.

Marianne accepted Jack's embrace and tried to maintain her smile as she asked, "Are you ready for this morning in court?"

Jack's own grin slipped a notch, too. It was the final day of Betsy's custody hearing. "I make my closing remarks at ten."

After being in court on Monday, Marianne had decided she couldn't bear to return. "Call me," she said now. "Let me know what happens."

Jack took her hand, his gaze imploring. "Please come today. Sally could use the moral support. And so could I."

What Marianne wanted to do was put some distance between them, to think about the realizations she had reached this morning. And to consider how to deal with the problem that still remained.

But the hearing to determine Betsy's fate had been even nastier than Jack had predicted, and Marianne knew he and Sally could benefit by her presence and her support today. Every possible question about Sally's character and her fitness as a mother had been paraded out by the team of lawyers representing Renee and her husband. For every charge, Jack had a rebuttal. He told Marianne nothing had been proven. But the innuendos about Sally had been vile and inflammatory. Jack had repeatedly requested a closed courtroom, but the judge had refused. Openness seemed to be a pet notion of his. His only concession to that rule had been to interview Betsy in private yesterday afternoon.

Marianne hoped the child's happy, bright outlook would cancel out any doubts about Sally. Marianne had to believe Sally would win. But she didn't know how the other woman would ever put her sister's charges out of her mind or how they would leave the minds of the curious onlookers who had filled the courtroom seats. Marianne thought Renee didn't care about Betsy as much as she wanted to punish her sister.

The final decision might well rest on what Jack said in court today. So just before ten, Marianne crossed the square and slipped into the rear door of the courtroom.

Renee's lawyer repeated the same unsavory claims Marianne had heard on Monday. He ended by saying Betsy's best interests lay with her *real* mother.

One by one, Jack knocked the other side's assertions down, as he had done all week. He talked about real motherhood, the kind that came from walking the floor with a crying child or showing up for a school pageant or spending a lazy Sunday afternoon together. *Real* motherhood, he claimed, rose out of love, not mere biology. By that definition, Sally was Betsy's *real* mother.

In her seat near the back of the room, Marianne sat forward, studying the judge's impassive face. Surely he couldn't help but be moved by Jack's impassioned plea, by the images he evoked.

She looked again at Jack, who had paused and now paced away from the podium in front of the judge. He faced the packed courtroom.

"This is a custody suit based on lies," he said, lip curling in derision. "Evasions. Half-truths. *Lies*. And not just lies about Sally Jane Haskins's character. At real issue here is Renee Phelps's reasons for asking for the return of the child she bore, the child she has never been a mother to. She says she's thinking of the child's best interests. I say she's lying. I don't pretend to know her real reasons. But she is lying about her motives in bringing this suit. And to lie when a child's interests are at stake..." He stopped, glanced toward Renee with a look of contempt. "To me, her lies are reprehensible."

Marianne never heard the rest of his summation. She could hear only what he had already said.

. . . lying about the child she bore.

. . . her lies are reprehensible.

Those words clubbed at her heart. Jack believed Marianne was lying about a child, also. His child. So why was she, in his eyes, any better than Renee? It made no sense. He claimed to love her. But he doubted her honesty about something as precious, as important, as her daughter.

How could she marry him? she asked herself. How could she marry a man who thought she would lie about his child? She wanted to. Sweet God in heaven, she wanted to ignore the problem, will it away. She wanted to marry Jack, have the baby he had promised, live happily ever after with him. She wanted to tell herself it didn't matter what he thought about Laura.

But Marianne had learned that she had to face her problems.

Jack had taught her to face the truth.

And that truth made her sick at heart as she fled the courtroom.

Delilah Cole and Jeb Hampton's wedding day dawned as bright and clear as the day before. Some high clouds streaked the sky by midafternoon. But they scooted out of sight before the three o'clock ceremony was over. Temperatures were mild for August, perfect for the backyard reception at Delilah's home that followed the church ceremony.

"To the bride and groom," Jack toasted, lifting a champagne flute over his head. "No one deserves happiness more than they."

A chorus of assents ran through the assembled guests. Across a sea of faces, Jack sought Marianne's eyes and tipped his glass once more toward hers. *To us,* he told her with his glance. *For the happiness we deserve, as well.*

As she raised her glass, he saw her smile was tremulous. He blamed it on the emotion of the day. She had cried during the ceremony. She had stood at Delilah's side at the altar, with her hand on Laura's shoulder and tears slipping down her face. Now she looked as if she were about to cry again. They had been so busy with wedding festivities and preparation last night and this morning that there had been no time to talk privately.

He tried to make it through the crowd to reach her side, but he was stopped every time he took a step forward. For hours, he tried and failed to get away from friends and neighbors, many of whom wanted to discuss his victory in Sally's custody fight. The judge had handed down his ruling only two hours after their summations. The adoption was upheld.

The reception was winding down by the time Jack caught sight of Marianne again. She was headed into the house.

Breaking free of the woman who detained him, he started after her.

But someone else tugged at his sleeve. He looked down and saw Laura. In a sea green dress, with her hair in curls around her face, she looked somehow grownup, somehow more like her mother than ever.

"You said you would dance with me today," she said.

He grinned. "So I did."

"I've been practicing all week with Mommy and Delilah."

"Think you're ready then?"

Her expression was very serious. "I hope so. But I've never danced in public before. And never with a boy."

Sudden, expected emotion clogged Jack's throat. In the not-too-distant future, dozens of boys would vie for the pleasure of dancing with this little enchantress. But her first dance, this dance, would always belong to him. *She belonged to him.* Another man had known her other firsts— first smile, first word, first step. But this was his. His determination stiffened. Somehow, he was going to convince Marianne to marry him. They were going to became a family.

A fierce storm of love shook through him as he took Laura's hand. "Come on," he murmured huskily. "I'd be honored to have this dance."

From the window of Delilah's second-floor bedroom, Marianne watched her daughter dancing with Jack. Laura spun and dipped in the sunlight, moving just as she had practiced all week. Jack was smiling down at her, very carefully guiding those steps, looking enchanted. It was a beautiful picture, and it made Marianne's heart grow heavier than ever.

"Honey?"

She turned to her aunt, who stood in front of a full-length mirror and smoothed a lilac crepe going-away dress over her hips. "Did you say something, Delilah?"

"I said it was silly of me to change. I could have worn my wedding suit to leave in."

"Nonsense," Marianne said, setting aside her sadness to cross the room. "It's a time-honored tradition to change after the ceremony. Besides, it gave you a chance to buy this luscious dress."

The older woman preened a little in front of the mirror, studying the flattering drape of the dress's skirt. "It is beautiful, isn't it?"

Marianne put her hands on Delilah's shoulders, pressed her cheek to hers. "You're beautiful, a beautiful bride."

Suddenly somber, Delilah's gaze met hers in the mirror. "You could be, too. Jack told me that he asked you to marry him."

Turning away to hide her tears, Marianne plucked a small bouquet from the foot of the bed. "Come on, now. Let's get going. There are lots of anxious, unmarried women down there, waiting to catch this. Not to mention an impatient groom, ready for a honeymoon."

Delilah looked ready to say something more, but Marianne didn't allow it. She bustled around the room, shooed her aunt downstairs and supervised the throwing of the bouquet and the showering of birdseed as the two newlyweds walked hand in hand down the front sidewalk to their car.

In no time at all, the crowd began to diminish. A beaming Sally, with Betsy and Laura in tow, caught Marianne on the front porch, where she was saying goodbye to some guests. "These two say they can't be separated," she said. "Can Laura come spend the night?"

Marianne gave her consent, which sent the two girls off in a flurry of petticoats and giggles to fetch the overnight bag they had already packed in anticipation of success. Only when they were gone did Marianne give Sally an impulsive hug. There had been no time to congratulate her before now. "I'm so glad," Marianne whispered. "So glad for you."

The other woman blinked tears away. "It was Jack who did it. He saved her for me."

Another guest called Marianne's name, so there was no time to say more. But later, as Sally walked across the yard with the two excited little girls, Marianne saw the looks that followed the other woman's progress. Some of the glances were sly. Some almost hostile. Marianne sighed. Sally still had some battles to fight.

She was sympathetic. She faced a battle of her own with Jack.

He joined her on the porch when almost all the guests were gone. But there was no time for them to talk. They stood together, sending friends and neighbors off with laughter and good wishes. Many of them lingered until evening shadows began creeping around the edges of the front yard. During the last flurry of departures, Jack disappeared again. And it wasn't until the band and the caterers had packed up and gone that he reappeared on the porch.

He had shed his jacket and tie and rolled his sleeves up to his elbows. He carried a bottle of champagne and two glasses. He had a gleam in his eye, an expectant smile on his lips.

That smile made Marianne realize there was no reason to postpone the inevitable any longer. She took a deep breath and said, "I can't marry you, Jack. I love you, but I just can't marry you."

He stared at her for a moment. Then he very carefully placed the champagne and the glasses on the small table beside the porch glider.

Marianne forestalled his protest. "I can't, Jack. I knew it yesterday in court when you talked about Renee lying about Betsy. You think I'm lying to you about Laura, too. How can you love me when you think such a thing of me? How can we marry when you would put me in the same category with that pathetic woman?"

"It's not the same—"

"Isn't it?"

"The circumstances—"

"There are no circumstances," Marianne cut in, her voice trembling. "Laura isn't yours. That's all there is to it." She clasped her hands together, trying to hold on to her composure. "I want you to go, Jack. I don't want to talk about this ever again. And I don't want there to ever be a possibility that you would say something to Laura that might give her doubts. She and I will move if we have to. But I want you to stay away from her..." Her voice broke. "Stay away from me."

Jack stepped forward, his voice lowered with urgency. "Don't do this, Marianne. We belong together—you and Laura and I. We could be a family."

"No, we couldn't." She shook her head, closed her eyes. "I stood beside Delilah at that altar today, and I listened to the vows she and Jeb took. Those vows of love and honor and respect. I couldn't stand there with you and speak those words, Jack. It wouldn't be right. You couldn't mean them when you think I'm capable of robbing you of your child." She opened her eyes, looked up at him again. "She's not your daughter, Jack. I've said it and said it, and you won't believe me. Now I don't know what else to do except send you away."

Jack's head was reeling. Marianne said she loved him, but she was letting her stubborn insistence that Laura was Kyle's come between them. "Marianne, you can't mean this."

"I suppose a blood test of some sort might finally prove it to you. But that's not the point."

"I don't need proof. She's mine. I've always known she was mine."

Marianne took a step toward him, her eyes wide and tragic and filled with tears. "All this time I've hoped you would see the truth. I thought you had just hung on to this fantasy for so long that you couldn't let it go."

"You're the one who should let go of the fantasy."

Her voice choked. The tears overflowed. "God, Jack, how could you think I would do this?"

"You were young and confused—"

"I could never be that confused. I could never, *ever* have lied to you or Kyle about my daughter."

"Yes, you could," Jack insisted, hearing the desperation in his own voice. "I understand how the lie could have started. I forgive you for how it started."

"Forgive me?" Marianne repeated, wiping tears away with the back of her hand. "I've done nothing to forgive."

The hopelessness of their situation tore at Jack. He could insist and she would deny. And they would go nowhere.

Fresh fury swept through him. He couldn't stop himself from grasping her shoulders. It took all his control to keep from shaking her. "Damn it, Marianne, you say you love me. But that can't be true, either, can it? If you really loved me, you would be able to admit the truth."

"You're wrong." Marianne twisted away from him, eyes now dry and blazing with an anger to match his. "It's all so tangled up inside you that you can't see the real truth."

Jack's hands clenched into fists at his side. "The only thing I don't see is why the lie continues."

She turned her back on him. "Stop it, Jack. Just stop it and leave."

He grasped her arm, pulled her around to face him again. "No, damn you, I won't leave. I'm not walking away this time. I'm not letting you walk away from this." He pulled her into his arms, forced a searing, punishing kiss on her lips.

She pushed him away. "Get out of here, Jack."

He started to pull her to him again, then his hands fell away. He felt as he had nine years ago when he stood on this porch and faced Marianne. Just as before, he had no resources with which to hold her.

"I'm losing you to him again, aren't I, Marianne?"

"What?"

"To Kyle." He forced a bitter laugh from his dry throat. "He's winning again. That's what all this was always about, wasn't it? A contest. Kyle won you. And got Laura by default. Now he keeps her."

"That's ridiculous."

"No, it's not. I'm not good enough to be Laura's father, am I?"

With a muffled exclamation, Marianne stepped toward him again. The anger died in her eyes.

"I was never good enough for you," Jack said. "No matter what you did or how you tried to change me, I never quite made the grade."

"That's not true," Marianne whispered. "Yesterday, I realized—"

"I don't care what you realized." He turned on his heel. "I'm leaving, just like you want."

Though she called his name, he didn't turn around. He crossed the yard's deepening velvet shadows. And a few minutes later, his car's powerful engine roared to life, then thundered away.

In the sudden silence, Marianne sank down on the porch, already realizing what a mistake she had made.

Slumped in the Dairy Bar's corner booth, Jack sat looking out the window. Just outside, a teenaged couple was having an argument. The boy leaned against his car. The girl kept walking away, turning around and then charging back. He wondered what they fought about. Some other girl? Some undesired intimacy in the back seat? Jack wanted to tell them to save their energies for the bigger problems. He felt very old.

"More coffee?"

He looked up at Sally and, nodding, shoved his mug across the table.

She poured the last cupful from the pot she held, then slid into the booth across from him. Her gray eyes were warm, full of sympathy. "Ready to talk about it yet?"

He shook his head.

Sighing, she got back to her feet. "Then I'm going to close up."

"Need any help?" he offered, only halfheartedly.

She grinned over her shoulder at him. "No, thanks. You just sit there and stew for a while longer. The stewing is free around here. But if you drink another pot of coffee, I'm going to have to charge you."

He tried to laugh. But the sound wouldn't come. Good, old Sally. She was a true friend. After driving around the county like a bat out of hell, he had ended up here. She had taken one look at his face, set him down in the booth and forced some coffee into him. She hadn't asked what had happened. She just made herself available to talk. Maybe someday, when he wasn't a raw and bleeding mess inside, he would.

Jack looked out the window again. The teenaged couple were kissing now. They broke apart. The boy slung his arm around the girl's shoulders. They got in the car and drove away just as Sally flipped off the sign in the parking lot. A happy ending, it looked like. Jack tried not to envy them.

"Mom, we're hungry."

Turning, Jack saw Betsy peeking around the door of the staircase that led to the second-floor apartment. He was startled when Laura's head appeared, too. He had forgotten she was here. Hungrily, his eyes drank in the sight of her. She and Betsy hadn't seen him as yet.

"Get back to bed," Sally said, looking up from the counter she was wiping. "It's almost midnight."

"You promised to come up early," Betsy pouted. "You said we'd make popcorn."

"I'm sorry. It was busy down here. I'm still busy. Now both of you go back to bed."

"Oh, Mom." Betsy turned then and saw Jack. And both girls ran giggling over to him even though Sally told them again to go back to bed.

Sally sighed. "Jack, would you run those wild Indians back upstairs. Marianne would skin me alive if she knew Laura was still up."

He started to protest. Just looking at Laura was painful. But then he thought of how Marianne had told him to stay away from her, how she threatened to move away. Jack realized he might never have a moment like this with Laura again.

So he shooed them upstairs, up to Betsy's tiny bedroom, where they scrambled into a bed made up with blue and white checked sheets. Snuggling together, they laughed up at him as he tucked the blankets in. He took one last, lingering look at Laura's face before he reached for the light.

"Wait a minute," she said, sitting up before he could reach the lamp's switch. From underneath her pillow, she pulled a framed snapshot. Jack could see it was a picture of Kyle.

Betsy, whose eyes were already drooping with sleep, explained unnecessarily to Jack, "That's her dad." With the straightforwardness of the very young, she added, "He's dead." She burrowed into her pillow, eyes closed.

"I always kiss him good-night," Laura said. Softly, reverently, she pressed a kiss against that picture.

Jack stared at that picture. Stared at Laura.

Carefully, as if this was a familiar ritual, she placed the photograph back under her pillow. Then she lay down, tucking her hand under her cheek and smiling up at Jack, looking just like her mother, like the sweetest little girl in the world.

And Jack knew. He knew she wasn't his.

The epiphany came to him in a startlingly white flash of light. It made everything clear. It wasn't that Laura looked anything like the man in the photograph beneath her pillow. She was still the very image of her mother. She was just as Marianne had been as a girl. And that's what made Jack see the truth.

Before Jack ever really knew Marianne, he knew what she was—the most genuine, the most forthright little girl in Willow Creek. That little girl could never have grown into a woman who could lie about something as special as this child. If Laura had been Jack's, she would have told him.

"Jack?" Laura said, yawning up at him.

He bent and kissed her cheek. She smiled and closed her eyes, and amazingly enough, he felt the same rush of love he had felt before he realized the truth. He loved her. The child of his dreams belonged to him in a way that was deeper than blood.

This was Marianne's child. And because he had loved her for so many years, because long ago they imprinted themselves indelibly on each other's souls, Laura belonged to him, too.

Quickly, he turned out the light, hurried down the stairs. He had been such a fool. And he had to tell Marianne, had to beg her forgiveness, had to somehow, some way, make it right.

In the restaurant, Sally was filling napkin holders at the booth beside the door. He grabbed her, spun her around, gave her a kiss. She had barely sputtered, "What in the world?" when he was out the door.

Marianne met him in the parking lot.

"I thought you might be here," she said as she slammed her car door.

He had to tell her about Laura. "Marianne—"

She cut him off by stepping into his arms. "I had to find you. I had to make you see that you're wrong." She framed his face with her hands. "You were always good enough for me, Jack Dylan. You're good enough now. Please forgive me for ever making you think you weren't."

He couldn't doubt her words. Her belief in what she said shone in her face. He wondered how he could ever have been foolish enough to doubt anything she said.

Once more he tried to tell her what he had realized about Laura. But she wouldn't let him. "I sat at home after you left, Jack. And I knew it was a mistake to push you away. Even though I don't know how to make you believe me about Laura, I knew it was mistake. I had thought about leaving here, leaving you. That's what I would have done once upon a time. God, that's exactly what I did nine years ago. I ran away. But I have more courage than that now."

She paused to draw in a deep, shuddering breath. "I know how to fight for the things I want. Because of you, Jack, I know how to face what frightens me most. And losing you is the most horrifying thing I can think of."

"You couldn't lose me," he murmured. Softly, slowly, he drew his hand through her hair, brushed his knuckles along the sweet curve of her jaw. He gazed into her face and sent a prayer of thanksgiving toward the heavens. "I'm here, Marianne. I've always been here. Just waiting for you."

Marianne pressed her face tight to his shoulder. "Thank God," she whispered. "Thank God for bringing you back into my life." Tonight, after Jack raced away, she had wondered how she would find the courage to go after him. But then she had thought of her father, who didn't have the courage to go after any of the things he wanted. He had sat back, let the bitterness and disappointment take over his life. She wasn't like him. She knew how to fight for her dreams. She had the courage to fight for Jack, no matter how big the problems they faced.

"I love you," she said, tipping her face back to study his. "I've always loved you."

That's when Jack told her what he had realized about Laura. When she said nothing at first, he pleaded, "You've got to forgive me for being such a fool."

"Of course I forgive you," she answered. "I just wish I could erase all the hurt you've felt about Laura all these years."

He kissed her, feeling like the luckiest man alive. "The feelings I had about Laura were never rational. But nothing that happened that summer felt rational. Somewhere, down deep, I think I always knew the truth. But I had to keep believing she was mine. I held on to that dream as tight as I could. It was the only way I could hold on to my dream of you."

Marianne hugged him close.

This time, when he proposed, she accepted.

While they kissed, the Dairy Bar's neon sign came to life. They turned as Sally's laughter rang out from the doorway.

"You know what I like about you two?" she called. "With you around, this town has something to talk about other than me."

Laughing, Marianne turned to look at the town. From this vantage point, Willow Creek was virtually spread at their feet. She could see the courthouse clock and the front of the newspaper building. It was the town she and Jack had plotted and schemed and dreamed of leaving. She wished they had known their dreams could be found right here, in each other's arms. But it had worked out in the end, she thought as she lifted her face to accept Jack's kiss.

Their dreams, and their hearts, had led them home.

* * * * *

It takes a very
special man to win

That SPECIAL *Woman!*

She's friend, wife, mother—she's you! And beside each Special Woman stands a wonderfully *special* man. It's a celebration of our heroines—and the men who become part of their lives.

Look for these exciting titles from Silhouette Special Edition:

April   FALLING FOR RACHEL by Nora Roberts
Heroine: Rachel Stanislaski—a woman dedicated to her career discovers romance adds spice to life.

May   THE FOREVER NIGHT by Myrna Temte
Heroine: Ginny Bradford—a woman who thought she'd never love again finds the man of her dreams.

June   A WINTER'S ROSE by Erica Spindler
Heroine: Bently Cunningham—a woman with a blue-blooded background falls for one red-hot man.

July   KATE'S VOW by Sherryl Woods
Heroine: Kate Newton—a woman who viewed love as a mere fairy tale meets her own Prince Charming.

Don't miss THAT SPECIAL WOMAN! each month—from some of your special authors! Only from Silhouette Special Edition! And for the most special woman of all—you, our loyal reader—we have a wonderful gift: a beautiful journal to record all of your special moments. Look for details in this month's THAT SPECIAL WOMAN! title, available at your favorite retail outlet.

TSW2

Take 4 bestselling love stories FREE

Plus get a FREE surprise gift!

Special Limited-time Offer

Mail to Silhouette Reader Service™

3010 Walden Avenue
P.O. Box 1867
Buffalo, N.Y. 14269-1867

YES! Please send me 4 free Silhouette Special Edition® novels and my free surprise gift. Then send me 6 brand-new novels every month, which I will receive months before they appear in bookstores. Bill me at the low price of $2.71 each plus 25¢ delivery and applicable sales tax, if any.* That's the complete price and—compared to the cover prices of $3.50 each—quite a bargain! I understand that accepting the books and gift places me under no obligation ever to buy any books. I can always return a shipment and cancel at any time. Even if I never buy another book from Silhouette, the 4 free books and the surprise gift are mine to keep forever.

235 BPA AJH7

Name	(PLEASE PRINT)	
Address		Apt. No.
City	State	Zip

This offer is limited to one order per household and not valid to present Silhouette Special Edition® subscribers. *Terms and prices are subject to change without notice. Sales tax applicable in N.Y.

USPED-93R

©1990 Harlequin Enterprises Limited

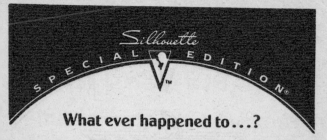

Silhouette
SPECIAL EDITION™®

What ever happened to...?

Have you been wondering when a much-loved character will finally get their own story? Well, have we got a lineup for you! Silhouette Special Edition is proud to present a *Spin-off Spectacular!* Be sure to catch these exciting titles from some of your favorite authors.

TRUE BLUE HEARTS (SE #805 April) *Curtiss Ann Matlock* will have you falling in love with another Breen man. Watch out for Rory!

FALLING FOR RACHEL (SE #810 April) *Those Wild Ukrainians* are back as *Nora Roberts* continues the story of the Stanislaski siblings.

LIVE, LAUGH, LOVE (SE #808 April) *Ada Steward* brings you the lovely story of Jessica, Rebecca's twin from *Hot Wind in Eden* (SE #759).

GRADY'S WEDDING (SE #813 May) In this spin-off to her *Wedding Duet*, *Patricia McLinn* has bachelor Grady Roberts waiting at the altar.

THE FOREVER NIGHT (SE #816 May) *Myrna Temte*'s popular *Cowboy Country* series is back, and Sheriff Andy Johnson has his own romance!

WHEN SOMEBODY WANTS YOU (SE #822 June) *Trisha Alexander* returns to Louisiana with another tale of love set in the bayou.

KATE'S VOW (SE #823 July) Kate Newton finds her own man to love, honor and cherish in this spin-off of *Sherryl Woods*'s *Vows* series.

WORTH WAITING FOR (SE #825 July) *Bay Matthews* is back and so are some wonderful characters from *Laughter on the Wind* (SE #613).

Don't miss these wonderful titles, only for our readers—only from Silhouette Special Edition!

by
Lindsay McKenna

Morgan Trayhern has returned and he's set up a company full of best pals in adventure. Three men who've been to hell and back are about to fight the toughest battle of all...love!

You loved Wolf Harding in HEART OF THE WOLF (SE#818), so be sure to catch the other two stories in this exciting trilogy.
Sean Killian a.k.a. THE ROGUE (SE#824) is coming your way in July.
And in August it's COMMANDO (SE#830) with hero Jake Randolph.

These are men you'll love and stories you'll treasure...only from Silhouette Special Edition!

by Laurie Paige

Come meet the wild McPherson men and see how these three
sexy bachelors are tamed!

HOME FOR A WILD HEART, July 1993—
Kerrigan McPherson learns a lesson he'll never forget.

A PLACE FOR EAGLES, September 1993—
Keegan McPherson gets the surprise of his life.

THE WAY OF A MAN, November 1993—
Paul McPherson finally meets his match.

Don't miss any of these exciting titles—only for our readers and
only from Silhouette Special Edition!

Silhouette

SPECIAL EDITION®

From this day forward

**Coming in August,
the first book in an exciting new trilogy from
Debbie Macomber
GROOM WANTED**

To save the family business, Julia Conrad becomes a "green card" bride to brilliant chemist Aleksandr Berinski. But what more would it take to keep her prized employee—and new husband—happy?

FROM THIS DAY FORWARD—Three couples marry first and find love later in this heartwarming trilogy.

Look for
Bride Wanted (SE #836) in September
Marriage Wanted (SE #842) in October

Only from Silhouette Special Edition

SETD-1

MEN · MADE IN AMERICA

Fifty red-blooded, white-hot, true-blue hunks from every State in the Union!

Beginning in May, look for MEN MADE IN AMERICA! Written by some of our most popular authors, these stories feature fifty of the strongest, sexiest men, each from a different state in the union!

Two titles available every other month at your favorite retail outlet.

In July, look for:

CALL IT DESTINY by Jayne Ann Krentz (Arizona)
ANOTHER KIND OF LOVE by Mary Lynn Baxter (Arkansas)

In September, look for:

DECEPTIONS by Annette Broadrick (California)
STORMWALKER by Dallas Schulze (Colorado)

You won't be able to resist MEN MADE IN AMERICA!

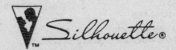